John E. Eardley-Wilmot

Reminiscences of the Late Thomas Assheton Smith, esq.

The pursuits of an English Country Gentleman

John E. Eardley-Wilmot

Reminiscences of the Late Thomas Assheton Smith, esq.
The pursuits of an English Country Gentleman

ISBN/EAN: 9783337227326

Printed in Europe, USA, Canada, Australia, Japan

Cover: Foto ©Andreas Hilbeck / pixelio.de

More available books at **www.hansebooks.com**

REMINISCENCES

OF THE LATE

THOMAS ASSHETON SMITH, ESQ.

Oh! ye who knew his healthful day,
And saw him make triumphant way
O'er frowning fence, o'er hill and dale,—
Saw him the swollen brook assail,
And with what ease he could efface
The various obstacles of Chase,
Say—Who could beat him in its race?

ANON. from the Sporting Magazine.

Venatu invigilant pueri, silvasque fatigant;
Flectere ludus equos, et spicula tendere cornu :
At patiens operum parvoque assueta juventus,
Aut rastris terram domat, aut quatit oppida bello :
Canitiem galeâ premimus ; nec tarda senectus
Debilitat vires animi, mutatque vigorem.

VIRG. Æn. ix.

LONDON : PRINTED BY SPOTTISWOODE & CO. NEW-STREET SQUARE.

PREFACE.

AFTER the death of Mr. Assheton Smith, his widow
entertained a strong desire to rescue his character
from the reflections which had been cast upon it by
one of the leading journals. Feeling that justice
had not been done him, she requested the author,
who may rather be called the compiler, of the following narrative, to draw up a Memoir of him. For
this purpose, she authorised him to ask permission
of the Editor of the Field, to make use of the able
and interesting articles which from time to time
appeared in that publication, descriptive of the life
and pursuits of Mr. Assheton Smith, and which she
considered gave the best and most accurate represen-
tation of the character and qualities of her husband.

This being willingly accorded, the author promised his assistance, and had many conversations with her on the subject of the Memoir, in which she evinced the deepest interest. In fact, it appeared almost wholly to occupy her thoughts during the few months she lived after the death of Mr. Smith. Only a short time before she died, but when as yet her illness had not assumed an alarming aspect, the author went expressly to Torquay by her desire, to receive her instructions respecting it, but on his arrival she was too ill to see him, and he never afterwards saw her again. Some letters and memoranda in her own writing, showing how anxious she was for the realisation of her wishes, have been delivered to him since her death, by one of her nearest relatives, who was with her during her last illness. He has therefore undertaken the task as a solemn duty committed to him, to be discharged as zealously as if her life had been spared, but with sincere regret that she has not been allowed to witness its performance. In endeavouring faithfully to record what materials he has been able to collect, respecting the life and character of one of the greatest, if not the greatest, of British sportsmen, he has had much gratification in being able, from his personal knowledge of him, to pay this humble tribute to his nobler qualities as a man and as a Christian.

The text of the articles in the Field has been incorporated into the following pages, not always word for word, or in the order in which the anecdotes appeared, but as they blended best with the current of the narrative. The author returns his grateful acknowledgments to several friends of the late Mr. Assheton Smith for authentic particulars respecting him; and for their kind assistance in a labour rendered somewhat arduous, in consequence of the very long period of time which has elapsed since Mr. Smith was in the zenith of his reputation as a rider and Master of hounds. His thanks are especially due to the Rev. Henry Fowle, of Chute Lodge near Andover, who lived with Mr. and Mrs. Smith for many years on the most intimate terms of friendship, and heard many of the raciest and most characteristic anecdotes from the mouth of the gallant sportsman himself.

The genealogical account of the ancestors of the Tedworth family has been derived from Mr. William Craven of Clifton, to whom the author also expresses his obligations.

Bath, December 1859.

FOXES' HEADS ON KENNEL DOOR AT TEDWORTH.

CONTENTS.

CHAPTER I.

Preliminary Observations.—Birth and Parentage of Mr. Assheton Smith.— Some account of his Ancestors. — Anecdotes of his Childhood. — He is sent to Eton.— His Fight with John Musters.— He is entered at Christ Church, Oxford.—Becomes famous as a Cricketer.—Begins to hunt in Leicestershire with Hugo Meynell.— Billesden Coplow, 1800 .   . . Page 1

CHAP. II.

He succeeds Lord Foley at Quorn, in 1806, and hunts Leicestershire until 1816, when he succeeds Mr. Osbaldeston in Lincolnshire, and keeps the Burton Country until 1824.—Ceases to be Master of Hounds for two years, during which he hunts with the Duke of Rutland, and in the neighbouring Countries.— Takes up his residence in 1826 at Penton Lodge, Andover, and creates a new Country for himself between Andover and Salisbury Plain.—His Marriage.—Death of his Father . . 28

CHAP. III.

He rebuilds Tedworth, and goes to reside there in 1830. — Description of his Kennels and Stables. — Favourite Hounds. — The Great Annual Meet at Tedworth. — He represents Andover and Carnarvonshire in Parliament. — Some Account of Vaenol and his Estates in North Wales.— Slate Quarries of Llanberris   71

CHAP. IV.

His Love for Science and Ship-building. — He builds several Sailing and Steam Yachts. — His Claim to be the Practical Originator of the " Wave Line " considered. — Claims of Mr. Scott Russell . . . . Page 101

CHAP. V.

Great Meet at Rolleston · in 1840. — Health of Mrs. Assheton Smith. — He builds the Great Conservatory. — Tries Hydropathy.—Anecdote of the Fox-hunter who tried it.—Worcester and Porthdynllaen Railway.—He is fined for an Assault.—He hunts the Tedworth Hounds himself until a short period before his Death 123

CHAP. VI.

His severe Illness at Vaenol in 1856, and partial Recovery. — Relapse and Death in 1858 145

CHAP. VII.

His Character.—Personal Appearance and Habits.— Impetuosity of Temper.— Generosity of Disposition.— Skill in Games and Sports 157

CHAP. VIII.

His Character as a Master of Hounds, Huntsman, and Rider. — Testimony of contemporary Sportsmen. — Anecdotes of his Horsemanship. — His vast Estates are left entirely to the Disposal of his Widow, who survives him only a few Months 176

APPENDIX.

	PAGE
Orator Hunt	231
Song on Melton Mowbray, 1813	232
Cricket Matches	237
Gentlemen and Players (First Match)	242
Public-School Matches	253
Billesden Coplow Poem	255
Mr. Meynell	263
The Craven Country : Ben Foot	264
Tom Edge	265
Mr. Osbaldeston	266
The Burton Country — Sir William Miles	266
Jack Shirley	267
Tom Wingfield and Joseph Harrison	268
Mr. Lindow	268
Sir James Musgrave	268
Sir H. Goodricke	269
Mr. Valentine Maher	269
Ayston	270
Bitch Pack	270
Mr. Assheton Smith's Falls	271
Jack O'Lantern	272
Fire-King	272
The Kennels at Tedworth	274
Hunting Morning	275
Hollow Water Lines (additional letter from Mr. Napier)	275
Mr. Holyoake, now Sir Francis Goodricke	276
Sir Bellingham Graham	277
Dick Burton	277
Visit to Belvoir, 1840	277
Manager	278
Shankton Holt	278
Dick Christian's Hero-Worship of Mr. Assheton Smith	279
The Duke of Wellington's opinion of Fox-hunters	279
Fox-hunters	280
Nimrod	280
Pluck	280

PAGE

Good Huntsman 281
Riding over Hounds 281
Size of Hounds 282
British Hounds described by Somerville 282
Music of Hounds 283
Boldness 283
Huntsman, First Qualification of a 283
Cicero 284
Bullfincher and Ox-Fence 284
Second Wind 284
Speed 284
Stratagem in distress 285
The right Scent 286
Field Lectures 286
Runaway Horse 287
Grafton Hounds 287
Price of Hounds 287
Old Jack O'Lantern.— Leap near the Coplow . . 288
Favourite Hounds 289
George Carter 289
Chorister 290
Lord Plymouth's Quorn Picture 290
Sir R. Sutton 291
Tedworth Hunt 291
Tedworth Hunt after Mr. Smith's Death . . . 297
Mr. Horlock 299
Objection to Fox-hunting 299
Joys of Hunting 299
Opinions of Addison and Cervantes on Hunting . . 300
Want of Enthusiasm 301
Vaenol 301

Αἰὲν ἀριστεύειν. Hom. *Il.*

REMINISCENCES

THOMAS ASSHETON SMITH.

CHAPTER I.

PRELIMINARY OBSERVATIONS. — BIRTH AND PARENTAGE OF MR.
ASSHETON SMITH. — SOME ACCOUNT OF HIS ANCESTORS. — ANEC-
DOTES OF HIS CHILDHOOD. — HE IS SENT TO ETON. — HIS FIGHT
WITH JOHN MUSTERS. — HE IS ENTERED AT CHRIST CHURCH,
OXFORD.—BECOMES FAMOUS AS A CRICKETER.—BEGINS TO HUNT
IN LEICESTERSHIRE WITH HUGO MEYNELL.— BILLESDEN COPLOW,
1800.

"Nunc Athletarum studiis, nunc arsit equorum." HORAT.

MOST of the ingredients in national character are
universal in their characteristics, and belong to no
particular time or place. The statesman, the orator,
the poet, the warrior, standing out in relief on the
records of every country, give to those who come
after them, throughout the universe, high aspirations
for noble thoughts and noble deeds. On the other
hand, all nations have some pursuits and some features peculiarly their own, strongly marking out and

distinguishing their inhabitants by an unmistakable individuality, and influencing them either for good or evil. It would be curious to examine how far the occupations of men tend to elevate or degrade their tone of thought or action. This was a science reduced to practice by the Spartans, among whom moral education was always closely blended with physical exercise. Their history proves that athletic sports may strongly influence the character of a nation. While the lovers of the chase require no social nor philosophical motives to bespeak their attention, this consideration may induce even those who are only familiar with fox hunting by description to look with favour on the following memoir. The manly amusement of fox hunting is entirely, and in its perfection exclusively, British. Its pursuit gives hardihood, and nerve, and intrepidity to our youth, while it confirms and prolongs the strength and vigour of our manhood; it is the best corrective to those habits of luxury and those concomitants of wealth which would otherwise render our aristocracy effeminate .and degenerate; it serves to retain the moral influence of the higher over the lower classes of society, and is one of the strongest preservatives of that national spirit by which we are led to cherish, above all things, a life of active energy, independence, and freedom. It might be added that, in a political point of view, its beneficial effects are not small as regards the employment of labour, the market of home-grown produce, and the maintenance of our superior breed of horses, most valuable for the purposes either of war or peace. The gentleman of whom we propose to give some anecdotes was a model of the British fox hunter. He was for exactly half a century a master and owner of hounds. Of iron nerve and constitution, he was, by universal acknowledgment, the best, as he was the foremost, rider of his day.

We shall see, in the course of the following pages, that fox hunting however was not his only pursuit. As a most useful country gentleman, a good classical scholar, an excellent man of business, warmly devoted to science, and a generous distributor of his wealth, he turned to a good and useful account those mental, physical, and worldly advantages wherewith Providence had liberally endowed him.

Thomas Assheton Smith was born in Queen Anne Street, Cavendish Square, London, on the 2nd of August 1776. His grandfather, Thomas Assheton, Esq., of Ashley Hall, near Bowden in Cheshire, had assumed the name of Smith on the death of an uncle, Captain William Smith, who died without issue. Captain Smith was a son of the Right Hon. John Smith, Speaker of the House of Commons in the first two parliaments of Queen Anne, and who had been in the preceding reign Chancellor of the Exchequer.

The Ashley Hall estate had come into the family by
the marriage of Katharine, daughter and heiress of
William Brereton, Esq., with Ralph Assheton, Esq.,
of Kirkby near Leeds, second son of Sir Richard
Assheton of Middleton in Lancashire. The estate
was sold in 1846 by the subject of the present
memoir to Mr. (now Lord) Egerton, of Tatton Park.
Mr. Assheton Smith was also a descendant of the
feudal lords of Assheton-under-Lyne in Lancashire,
described by Dr. Ormerod, of Sedbury Park, the
historian of Cheshire, as " the knightly family of Assheton-under-Lyne," whose ancestor, Ormus Magnus,
the Saxon Lord of Heletune, and founder of the Church
of Ormskirk, married Aliz, daughter of Herveus, a
Norman nobleman, grandfather of Theobald Walter,
Lord of Amounderness, and Chief Butler of Ireland.

Mr. Assheton Smith's mother was Elizabeth,
daughter of Watkin Wynn, Esq., of Voelas, North
Wales. His father died at Tedworth on the 12th of
May 1828, aged 76. The family consisted of eight
children, three sons and five daughters. The eldest son
died in early infancy. The third, William, a gallant
and distinguished officer in the Royal Navy, met a
premature death by drowning, in 1806, in the heroic
attempt to rescue some fellow-creatures from a similar
fate. Mr. Smith never alluded to his brother without
evincing deep emotion. On his epitaph, in the church
at Tedworth, we find this record of his act and life:

To the Memory

OF

WILLIAM ASSHETON SMITH,

SECOND (*surviving*) SON OF

THOMAS ASSHETON SMITH, ESQ.

OF TEDWORTH.

HE WAS BRED TO THE SEA,
AND WAS LIEUTENANT OF THE TÉMÉRAIRE *
IN THE BATTLE OF TRAFALGAR;
IN WHICH BY HIS BRAVERY AND CONDUCT
HE CONTRIBUTED TO THAT GLORIOUS VICTORY.

ON HIS RETURN TO ENGLAND
HE WAS APPOINTED TO THE NAMUR:
WHEN BEING AT ANCHOR NEAR ST. HELEN'S
A BOAT WITH FOUR MEN IN IT,
BELONGING TO A SHIP,
GOT ADRIFT IN A VIOLENT GALE.
HIS HUMANITY, EQUAL TO HIS BRAVERY,
URGED HIM TO LEAP INTO ANOTHER BOAT
FOR THE PURPOSE OF SAVING THEM.
BUT IN THE GENEROUS ATTEMPT
HE WITH SEVEN MEN LOST THEIR LIVES,
ON THE 16TH OF JANUARY 1806
IN THE 24TH YEAR OF HIS AGE.

TO RECORD THE VIRTUES OF A BELOVED AND GALLANT SON
THIS MARBLE IS SET UP
BY HIS AFFLICTED FATHER.

Thus the subject of our memoir, who was virtually the second son, alone survived to inherit the family estates. Of his five sisters three were married, viz. Jane, who became Mrs. Satterley; Elizabeth, who married Major William Buckler Astley; and Emma, who became Mrs. Illingworth, and subsequently Mrs. Jervis. Two died unmarried, viz. Fanny and Harriet. An only daughter of Major Astley married

* The Téméraire was in the hottest part of the action, and engaged with two French ships at the same time.

Captain Duff, whose son, George William, inherits, by the will of the late Mrs. Assheton Smith, the landed property and slate quarries in Caernarvonshire.

Of the boyhood of Mr. Smith, in consequence of the great age to which he lived, there exist but scanty records. An anecdote, however, which he related of himself, at a late period of his life, shows that when quite a child he evinced that inflexible and stubborn resolution which was throughout his life a ruling principle of his character. While walking in the shrubbery at Tedworth, with the friend who has kindly contributed many anecdotes to the present memoir, the more valuable because committed to memory and carefully cherished during a long and uninterrupted intimacy, he pointed out an old yew-tree which had witnessed the infliction of corporal chastisement by his father for some fault of which the son persisted in declaring he was innocent. "It was under that tree," he said, "that I then made a solemn vow never to do anything from violence or compulsion, and on that principle I have always acted in after life." I have reason to believe, adds his friend, that he observed this vow as religiously as did the youthful Hannibal the famous oath imposed on him when only nine years old by his father Hamilcar. Acts of parental severity were, in conformity with the lesson he learnt on this memorable occasion, condemned by Mr.

Smith, and his maxim was that kindness and reason will always effect more with children than the use of the birch. He occasionally adverted to the above anecdote of his father's correction of him in another way. There was a picture of him over the ante-room at Tedworth, done when he was a boy about four years old. His white felt wide-awake is in one hand, the other resting on the back of a large greyhound, the only dog of that description Mr. Smith said he ever had. The countenance of the youngster rather shows that something has gone wrong with him. Mr. Smith's friends used jokingly to remark this to him, and he said that, just before this picture was taken, his father met his nurse and himself near the yew-tree before mentioned, when the nurse said : "I can do nothing with Master Smith, sir ; he will do nothing he is told." His father without another word laid the child across his knee, and gave him a severe whipping. This, Mr. Smith remarked, appeared to him so extremely unjust, namely, to inflict punishment before his parent heard what he had to say, that he from that hour determined never again to do what he was told. The first accident which ever befel him was some time before the above flagellation, and almost in his earliest childhood. His mother found him lying on his nurse's lap, and looking like a tench just taken out of the water, in a gasping state. "What is the matter with the

child?" she inquired. "*Nothing;* he is doing *nicely*,"
replied the nurse. Upon examination, however,
Mrs. Smith found that he had succeeded in dis-
gorging a large pin which he had swallowed, and
which he was *munching* as boys do lollypops. In
1783, when only seven years old, he was sent to
Eton, at that time, as it is now, the best school in
England for making a man at once a scholar and a
gentleman. He was the youngest boy in the school
when he went, and he continued there until 1794,
a period of eleven years. It was here that he first
acquired that ardent love for athletic exercises, for
his skill and proficiency in which he was afterwards
so eminently distinguished. He excelled especially
in cricket, and his fondness for this noble game he
long retained in after life, as these pages will fully
testify hereafter. Boating was also one of his favourite diversions. His Eton career is, however,
rendered most memorable by his famous battle with
Jack Musters, still spoken of by Etonians as one of
the most hard fought and severe contests ever recorded in the annals of youthful pugilism. So
equally were these young champions matched, that
their protracted struggle ended in a drawn battle.
They shook hands, and to the credit of both be it
recorded, the most perfect harmony and high feeling
towards each other existed between them ever
afterwards. Both were masters of hounds, and both

were celebrated as first-rate horsemen as well as sportsmen.*

Mr. Smith's skill in pugilistic encounters, and his determined courage in standing up, even against superior strength, often served him in good stead afterwards, when, as master of hounds, he came in contact with "roughs," who imagined they might bully him with impunity. Two anecdotes relating to this subject may well find a place here. During the early part of his hunting in Leicestershire, he was solicited to stand for the borough of Nottingham. This undertaking at that time was just as hazardous as for a Tory to stand for Westminster against such an idol as Sir F. Burdett then was. The very peril, however, was an inducement for Tom Smith to come forward ; and a reception such as was to be expected awaited him. The town was placarded with " No Foxhunting M. P.," and the electors

---

* Mr. Musters is well known to every reader of Lord Byron as the successful rival of the poet for the hand of the beautiful Mary Chaworth, while his fame as a fox-hunter has been immortalised by Lowth as being one of the foremost at the brook in the celebrated Billesden Coplow run :

> " After him plung'd Joe Miller, with Musters so slim,
> Who twice sank, and nearly paid dear for his whim."

It was said of him that he could ride, fence, fight, play at tennis, swim, shoot, and play at cricket with any man in Europe. In almost, if not all of these accomplishments, he would have found his match in the subject of our memoir. He died at Annesley Park, Notts, on September the 8th, 1839.

carried their virulence so far as to dress up a guy with a red coat and a fox's brush appended to it, which they burnt in effigy before the hustings. Mr. Smith's appearance there was the signal for a most tremendous row; and not a word of his speech, when he came forward to address them, would they hear. There, however, he remained, in defiance of their yells and hooting, till at last with a stentorian voice, heard above the uproar, he cried out, "Gentlemen, as you refuse to hear the exposition of my political principles, at least be so kind as to listen to these few words. I will fight any man, little or big, directly I leave the hustings, and will have a round with him now for love." The effect of this "argumentum ad homines" was electric. It had touched a sympathetic cord. Instead of yells and groans, there were rounds of cheers ; and from that hour to the end of the contest, in which, after a hard struggle, he was beaten, not a single interruption nor act of molestation was offered to him.

On another occasion, when about to enter one of the banking houses at Leicester, he hitched his horse's bridle over the iron rails in front of the bank. While his master was inside, the horse stood across the street. A coalheaver coming by with his cart gave the nag a flanker with his whip, which nearly sent him into the bank window. This brought out

the squire. " Why did you strike my horse ? " was
the inquiry. " Because he was in my way," was the
reply. " Defend yourself," was the rejoinder ; and
the coalheaver doffed his smock frock while the
squire buttoned up his coat and turned up his cuffs.
At it they went with a hearty good will. For the
first time in his life Tom Smith found he had got
his match and something more to contend with ; for
the fellow stood six feet and weighed fourteen stone.
There was no flinching on either side, and they
followed one another up and down the street as
closely as a loving couple in a country dance. The
noise, however, soon brought the constables, and the
combatants were separated amidst the cheering of
the crowd. " You will hear of me again," said
the squire to his resolute antagonist, as he mounted
his horse and rode quietly away. So they parted,
each having had apparently pretty well enough.
Mr. Smith went out to dine with his friend Edge, to
whom, although much punished, and it is reported
with a beefsteak over his eye, he told the story with
great relish. On the following morning the squire's
groom was seen inquiring where the coalheaver lived.
His residence having been pointed out, the man
knocked at the door for some time. At last it was
opened by his wife. " Does the man live here who
fought the gentleman by the bank ? " inquired the
servant. " He *did* live here, if he is still alive," re-

plied the poor woman, " after the terrible beating he
got yesterday." Groans were heard from a bed on
which the man was lying, having the fear of an
arrest for striking a gentleman before his eyes.
" Mr. Smith has sent me to give you this five pound
note, and to tell you that you are the best man that
ever stood before him." " God bless his honour,"
exclaimed the fellow, jumping up from the bed, for
he was more frightened than hurt, and being greatly
relieved by this unexpected and fortunate turn of
events. " Thank him a thousand times. I dearly
arned the money, for his blows are like the kick of a
horse ; but tell him for all that, to show my gratitude, I will fight him again any day for love."
This anecdote speaks well for both. It turned out
on inquiry that this man was the champion of the
surrounding country and the terror of the neighbourhood. Therefore we may hope that the bruising he
met with from a gentleman, whom, doubtless, before
the " mill," he held very cheap, did him good.
Many years afterwards, when Mr. Smith was upwards
of seventy years of age, he evinced the same daring
spirit. A rough country fellow threw a stone at
one of his hounds, for which the squire struck at
him with his hunting whip. " You dared not strike
me if you were off your horse," said the clodhopper.
In a moment the squire had dismounted and had
raised his hands in artistic attitude, upon which

the cowardly rascal fairly took to his heels and fled, amidst the jeers and ridicule of his companions. This graphic scene occurred at Chapmansford, before a large field of sportsmen, who will well recollect the circumstance.

To return to his early boyhood. He was fond of adding to the statement of his having been eleven years at Eton, the remark, " and while there I learnt nothing." Here, however, the squire did not do justice to Etona Mater. No sharpwitted lad can pass through the wholesome discipline of a public school and pick up nothing. Even allowing that such a character as that of Mr. Smith would have distinguished itself under the application of any species of scholastic discipline, yet in his case the emulation, and high tone, and chivalrous feeling to be found in a public school, must have been eminently to his advantage.

Mr. Smith was always strongly in favour of the fagging system, as teaching boys to do many things useful to them in their future career, and giving them an independence of thought and action of the greatest service to them afterwards in their professional struggles. His maxim was, that if a boy were not well thrashed when he was young, he would need it when he became a man; and he ridiculed the idea, that because a youth had brushed clothes, or cooked a mutton chop for his master at Eton, or Winchester,

his feelings or demeanour as a gentleman would be
injuriously influenced when he grew up. It is notorious that those who most cheerfully endured the
hardships in the Crimea, and roughed it best, were
public schoolmen. Even as regards scholarship, Mr.
Smith could not have quitted Eton without benefit.
Where otherwise did he acquire that taste for classical
literature which characterised him through life?
Where did he get his love for Horace, so as to be
able to quote long passages with enthusiasm? Horace
and Pope were his favourite authors, and he knew
the whole of the Epistle of Eloisa to Abelard by
heart. He was also an enthusiastic admirer of
Shakspeare, and frequently cited parts of his plays
with great emphasis and feeling. The magnificent
lines in Hamlet, where Polonius gives his parting
advice to Laertes, beginning, " These few precepts in
thy memory, look thou character," he often repeated
with much force and vehemence of delivery, " suiting
the action to the word," and said they were the finest
that ever were written. He laid particular stress on
that passage :—

> " This above all, to thine own self be true;
> And it must follow, as the night the day,
> Thou canst not then be false to any man."

In the sentiment here so nobly conveyed may be
traced the mainspring of his conduct in after life.
There was, however, one part of Polonius' advice

which the squire did not strictly follow out in his
own person, nor exactly put faith in, namely, on the
subject of dress :

> "Costly thy habit as thy purse can buy,
>   But not express'd in fancy ; rich, not gaudy,
>   For the apparel oft proclaims the man."

He was never very studious of his personal appearance, except as to neatness in his youthful days,
although he looked thoroughly the gentleman. Until
quite late in life he hardly ever wore a great coat.
One of these lasted twelve years ; no small proof that
its services had not very often been required.   His
friends persuaded him at length to exchange this for
one made of the fashionable material of the present
day, warm and woolly, but light ; which, however,
he said did not suit a sportsman of the olden time ;
and he seldom donned it except in the most inclement
weather.   He always maintained that the tempe-
rature of the body and an equal flow of animal
spirits are better raised and kept up by active movement than by additional clothing ; and as for physic,
he " would not even throw it to the dogs ; " remembering the lines of Dryden : —

> "Better to hunt in fields for health unbought,
>   Than fee the doctor for a nauseous draught."

What, however, Mr. Smith did *not* learn at Eton
was *arithmetic*. This most useful science he acquired

to great perfection during the time he was laid up at
Melton Mowbray, in consequence of a severe fall
while hunting, when he broke his ankle. While
limping about the town, and bewailing the hard fate
which kept him from the hounds, he happened to
enter the post office, and seeing the young woman
who assisted in it, and who was very good-looking,
casting up a bill rapidly, he said : " I wish you
would teach me arithmetic." The bargain was soon
struck, and with the help of his pretty instructress,
by whose side he was as gentle as a lamb, added to
Joyce's arithmetic, he completed his education in this
branch of science in six weeks, and was ever after remarkable for his skill in figures and calculations. Not
only was this knowledge rendered available by him in
his practical knowledge of shipbuilding, but it served
him also in the management of his estates, the accounts of which he always minutely inspected himself.
During his annual visit to Vaenol, during the autumn,
he scarcely ever missed for a single day going down to
his port and looking over the books in which were
entered the transactions of his slate quarries. He
always used to say that no gentleman could be
much imposed upon who superintended and looked
into his affairs as closely and regularly as he did.

In 1794 young Smith quitted his favourite haunts
at Eton to become a gentleman commoner at Christ
Church, Oxford. Long before this period, however,

he had served his youthful apprenticeship in the
hunting field.

> "Puer Ascanius mediis in vallibus acri
> Gaudet equo; jamque hos cursu, jam præterit illos." VIRG.

His first rudiments in this noble sport had been
acquired, when he was quite a child, with some
rabbit beagles at Sedbury Hill; and he soon afterwards accompanied his father's pack of fox-hounds
on a pony. These hounds for many years hunted
alternately hares and bag foxes, and showed some
famous sport in both capacities. Even at this period
his father was justly proud of his son's superior
horsemanship, though the old gentleman confessed
to a friend, from whom the following anecdote is
derived, that he was not a little jealous of it. The
father of Mr. Assheton Smith, relates the same individual, told me that once at his club a party of
sportsmen were speaking of the riding of Sir Henry
Peyton and his son, and some one present remarked
that no father and son could beat them; upon which
the old gentleman observed: "I will back a father
and son against them for 500*l.*" When requested to
name his couple, he replied: "*I* am one, and Tom
Smith (as he invariably called his son) the other."
Whereupon the bet was declined, with this handsome
compliment, that "*the Tom Smith* had long since been
an exception in every match, his superior horsemanship being so generally acknowledged."

C

And yet the late Sir Henry Peyton and his son [*], the present baronet, were incontestably first-rate riders as well as sportsmen. Nimrod places the father in the front rank, and after describing his good qualities, remarks that nothing more is wanting to complete the portrait of a perfect horseman; while of the son he says : " I scarcely know in what terms to speak of him. Were I to declare that from all I have seen and all I have read of him he is the boldest and best horseman England ever produced, I should be afraid of looking upon the wall and seeing Assheton Smith, John White, and half a score more crack names staring me in the face, and ' Hold hard, Nimrod,' in big letters. But, really, taking him over the country and over the course, he must be as near excellence as human ability and physical energies can place any one." [†]

On another occasion, although of course long subsequently to his having left Oxford, Mr. Smith's father said that he went on a visit to his son, then residing at Quorndon Hall and keeping the hounds. He was mounted on a splendid horse belonging to Tom Smith, and they had a splendid burst over the cream of the country, with a whoop at the end.

[*] A writer in the Sporting Magazine, October 1834, signing himself "A Rambler in Green," calls Mr. Peyton "the best horseman in England."

[†] Hunting Reminiscences, p. 267.

While Tom Smith was holding up the fox to throw into the hounds, Lord Alvanley observed, " How I wish your father had seen this finish." " Depend upon it he has," replied Tom Smith, without looking up; " and I advanced," related the old squire, who told the anecdote himself, " and made his lordship a low bow."

" Was your father a good rider ? " asked a neighbour once of the son. " He was what was *then* considered such," was the reply; " but on a very different principle to what I have adopted, and simply this,—he clung on by his *hands*, and *I* by my *legs*." *

The old man always spoke with gratitude and admiration of the extraordinary alacrity evinced by his son on one occasion, when news was brought to him in the hunting field that his father was dangerously ill. There were no railroads nor telegrams in those days, but simply by *horse power*, without changing his dress, and only stopping on the road to get a fresh hack, taking the first that presented itself, he arrived at Tedworth almost as soon as they thought the intelligence had reached him, and at a most critical time. Doctors were differing as to the expediency of bleeding the invalid, which Dr. Cline † recommended. Tom Smith at once

---

* This is what he always termed his "*gripe* on a horse."

† He went round by London, whence his own chariot with four post-horses brought Dr. Cline down.

decided with Cline; and thus in all human proba-
bility saved his father's life, for he rallied immediately
after this course of treatment had been adopted;
the coma from which he was suffering being the
result, as Cline had suspected, of his having been
upset in his phaeton at Vaenol some time previously.*

We have no very minute details of young Smith's
career at the University, where he remained four
years. He hunted regularly while at Christ Church;
and mostly with old John Warde's hounds in Oxfordshire and Northamptonshire. He also excelled as a
batsman in the cricket-field on Cowley Marsh and
Bullingdon, was a fearless swimmer, and could pull
a sturdy oar upon the Isis. During the long va-
cation his father used to make up cricket-matches
for him on Perriam Down, celebrated as the most
agreeable meetings in Hants, for the hospitality
of Tedworth was open to the players and their
friends; and the fair sex had their share of the
day's amusement by the festivities being closed
with a dance. For the purposes of social enjoyment
nothing can exceed a good cricket match in the
grounds of an English country gentleman, if only
the skies be auspicious. The sport has far more
variety and excitement, and far less formality, than

---

* Before Cline arrived, the doctors who attended him, supposing
he was suffering from debility, had ordered him nutritious food and
stimulants, but as there proved to be slight concussion of the brain,
he was getting rapidly worse.

archery ; and if the ladies cannot have a share in the actual game, they have their interest in the contending sides, and there is always, or ought to be, an abundance of spectators to make the time pass agreeably away.   Another great advantage of cricket is, that the game can be participated in by all ranks of society ; by which means a healthy and kind feeling is kept up between the higher classes and those beneath them; the peer and the peasant, by mixing together, learn to value and respect each other, without any inconvenience arising from familiarity on either side.   This remark is applicable to fox-hunting, but in a minor degree, in consequence of the more expensive and therefore more exclusive character of the latter pursuit.   On leaving Oxford, Tom Smith became a member of the Marylebone Club, and a regular attendant at Lord's.*

* The Marylebone cricket ground was opened in 1787, and called Lord's, after Mr. Thomas Lord, the lessee.   The first match played on the "new ground," as it was termed, took place on the 21st, 22nd, and 23rd June in that year, between five of the White Conduit Club, with six picked men, and eleven of All England. The game was won by the latter.   The club had originally met in White Conduit fields, but afterwards the cricket ground was on the present site of Dorset square, where the above match took place.   It was transferred to its present site in St. John's Wood, about the year 1810.   The late Duke of Dorset was one of the oldest supporters of the game, but had nothing to do with Dorset square.   His grace was a Duke when a boy at Harrow, and always had a double thrashing when punishment was awarded to him by his schoolfellows,—one for his offence and the other because he was a Duke.

In the appendix to this Memoir will be found a collection of the most celebrated cricket matches in which he was engaged from 1802 to 1820. It will be seen that he played on the side of the gentlemen in the first match they ever undertook against the players of England. It is remarkable that the side on which he played was almost invariably successful; and he may be said to have been one of the best, if not the best, batsman of his day.

Mr. Smith's devotion to cricket, however, only served him for diversion during the summer months, while the hounds were idle. At the fall of the leaf he was quickly in the saddle again. He used to say many years afterwards, that on the first of November his Hampshire woodlands "stripped for business." He always loved to begin early, for he remarked that when foxes have been once rattled they are not so easily found by fox takers or keepers. Before he devoted himself to fox-hunting he was a first-rate shot; but in the latter part of his life he seldom handled a gun, though the extensive turnip fields about Tedworth afforded excellent partridge shooting to his friends, and his keepers always turned out capital dogs. Mr. Smith used, while a youth, always to shoot the first week of the season at Sutton, a large farm belonging to his father near Winchester race-course, which the old gentleman subsequently sold, as was said at the time, to pay for the Quorn establishment. A circumstance that tells

well for the seller ought not to be omitted.   His
man of business told him that a Mr. Meyler (whose
property joined his, and who was afterwards killed
by a fall from his horse in the New Forest) would
give him a *fancy price*, considerably more than the
estate was worth.   To his honour Mr. Smith
senior, desired the attorney to offer it to this person
first, and at its market value.   He, however, declined it, and it was bought by Mr. Wickham.
" His son was riding, the first time I ever saw him,"
relates a friend who met him out with Mr. Warde's
hounds at South Grove, about this period, " in a
green coat on Black Marquis, a famous and favourite
horse of his father's, and as usual alongside of the
hounds.   Coming to a formidable ditch, the old horse,
to his rider's great surprise, stopped short, when,
without turning him, he made him take the fence
standing, observing : ' You and I will be soon better
acquainted.'   And so it proved, for Marquis refused
nothing else in the run."

As early as the year 1800, when the subject of our
memoir was only twenty-four years old, we find him
signalised in song, as a most successful and daring
rider.   In the celebrated run from Billesden Coplow,
on the 24th February, in that year, when Mr.
Meynell hunted the Quorn country, four gentlemen
only, with Jack Raven the huntsman, were up at the
finish (when they changed foxes at Enderby), al-

though the best horsemen of the day were out. There were several copies of verses written on the occasion, which quizzed many, and commended few. Those who love hunting, and can enjoy it, will not be displeased with a quotation from one of the songs.

> " Two hours and a quarter, I think, was the time;
> It was beautiful—great—indeed 'twas sublime:
> Not Meynell himself, the king of all men,
> Ere saw such a chase, or will ere see again.
> Tom Smith in the contest maintained a good place;
> Tho' not *first* up at last, made a famous good race.
> I'm sure he's no reason his horse to abuse,
> Yet I wish he'd persuade him to keep on his shoes:
> You must judge by the nags that were in at the end,
> What riders to quiz, and what to commend." *

The hand of our hero, so long afterwards renowned for its handling of the slack rein like a skein of silk, must have served him well even at this period, in so tremendous a flight, and before a whole host of the best riders in Europe. A few years later, in a song on a chase run by the Duke of Rutland's hounds, written by Lord Forester, Tom Smith is recorded as having been the only man who could stop the hounds when they were running head " over Belvoir's sweet vale." Well, indeed, might it be remarked of him, " that amidst the multitude of Smiths, there was

* These verses are an extract from Mr. Bethel Cox's poem. The one best known and most celebrated was by the Rev. Robert Lowth, son of Dr. Lowth, bishop of London. As it has become very scarce, it has been thought worthy of insertion at full length in the Appendix.

only *one* Assheton Smith," and well did he support the credit and character of this truly English name.

Until Mr. Smith made his début as a master of fox hounds in Leicestershire, he continued to hunt in Oxfordshire and Northamptonshire. John Warde, the "father of fox-hunting," as he is styled by Nimrod, and "glorious John," by his brother sportsmen, hunted the Craven country at that time, and used to come up in March every year for two or three weeks to Weyhill, where the hounds had a temporary kennel. Until Mr. Smith, however, cleared the country in 1828, after he came into possession of the Tedworth property, at the death of his father, much sport was impossible. The riding of Dick Knight, huntsman to the Pytchley at the time Mr. Smith had the Quorn, was of a character very similar to that of our squire. An annual visitor to Northamptonshire was in the habit of riding as close to Dick as he could, but was invariably beaten in a run. At the commencement of one season, the gentleman was on a new horse, a clipper. He said to Knight, "You won't beat me to-day, Dick!" "Won't I, sir," was the reply. "If you do, I'll give you the horse," said the gentleman. The one rode for the horse, the other for his honour. At last they came to an unjumpable place, which could only be crossed by going between the twin stems of a tree, barely wide enough to admit a horse. At it went Dick, throwing his legs across his horse's withers, and 'got *through*. The horse was sent to him next morning.

While Mr. Warde hunted the Craven country, Mr. Smith once went during a hard frost to see his celebrated pack. The ground was covered with snow and as hard as cast iron, but at the pressing solicitation of Mr. Smith, the old Squire of Squerries* permitted Neverd, who then hunted his hounds, to take them to Winding Wood, a covert of Mr. Dundas's, just to *find a fox*, but with positive orders not to let them leave covert. Tom Smith was riding " Blue Ruin," a favourite hunter of Mr. Warde's (who also rode out), and as soon as they found their fox, he slipped a couple of sovereigns into the huntsman's hands and told him to hand over his horn. No sooner was this done, than the fox broke covert, and away went Smith sailing by the side of the hounds. The scent, as is often the case in a frost, was breast high, and regardless of the state of the ground, the young squire, as usual, took every fence that presented itself. After a very sharp run, the hounds swung back into the wood where they had found. Here the horsemen found old Warde in a towering passion, swearing his hounds would be cut to pieces, and his favourite horse spoilt. " Only give me five minutes more and I will kill your fox," said Mr. Smith; which being assented, or rather submitted to, for denial was useless, was soon accomplished. Tom

* The family seat in Kent.

Smith brought out the brush, and presented it with this flattering speech: " Your hounds, sir, are the best I ever rode by the side of, and I will give you three hundred guineas for Blue Ruin." This pacified the placable old master, who often afterwards related the anecdote with no little zest. He, however, refused to sell his favourite hunter. Mr. Warde was a master of hounds for fifty-two years; he was twenty-two years in Oxfordshire and Warwickshire, thirteen in Northamptonshire, six in the New Forest, and eleven in Berkshire. The famous Bob Forfeit was his huntsman in Oxfordshire. Mr. Smith had the highest opinion of his breed of hounds, and took some of them with him into Lincolnshire. Mr. Warde's mastership of hounds exceeded in length of time that of Mr. Smith by the interval the latter hunted at Belvoir, after he left the Burton country.* There was an excellent song written in 1823, when Mr. Warde hunted the Craven country, of which the following is one of the stanzas:—

" Here is health to John Warde, and success to his hounds:
  Your Quornites may swish at the rasper so clever,
And skim ridge and furrow, and charge an ox fence;
  But will riding alone make a sportsman? No, never!
So I think we'd just send them some tutors from hence.
  In the van place Charles Warde, Fulwar Fowle, you'll accord,
With Villebois and Wroughton, might teach them the ground;
  And if they'd be ruled, or deign to be schooled,
They might yet take some hints from John Warde and his hounds."

---

* Two years, viz. from 1824 to 1826; Mr. Smith was a Master of Hounds from 1806 to 1858, barring these two years.

CHAP. II.

HE SUCCEEDS LORD FOLEY AT QUORN IN 1806, AND HUNTS
LEICESTERSHIRE UNTIL 1816, WHEN HE SUCCEEDS MR. OSBAL-
DESTON IN LINCOLNSHIRE, AND KEEPS THE BURTON COUNTRY
UNTIL 1824. — CEASES TO BE MASTER OF HOUNDS FOR TWO
YEARS, DURING WHICH HE HUNTS WITH THE DUKE OF RUTLAND,
AND IN THE NEIGHBOURING COUNTRIES. — TAKES UP HIS RESI-
DENCE IN 1826 AT PENTON LODGE, ANDOVER, AND CREATES A
NEW COUNTRY FOR HIMSELF BETWEEN ANDOVER AND SALISBURY
PLAIN.—HIS MARRIAGE.—DEATH OF HIS FATHER.

" Gaudet equis, canibusque, et aprici gramine campi." HORAT.

" Never did I hear
Such gallant chiding ; for besides the groves,
The skies, the fountains, every region near
Seems all one mutual cry. I never heard
So musical a discord, such sweet thunder."
Midsummer Night's Dream.

IN 1806 Mr. Smith left Northamptonshire, and
collecting a first-rate pack from different kennels,
the best portion having been purchased for 1000
guineas of Mr. Musters, of Colwick Hall, on that
gentleman's giving up the Nottinghamshire country,
he succeeded Lord Foley at Quorn. Here, with a
fine stud and with splendid hounds, he kept the
game alive for ten years, during which time the
sport he showed was unrivalled. His feats of horsemanship, his excellent management of the hounds,

and the fields he drew together, will live in Leicestershire as long as fox-hunting is dear to the Englishman as a national sport. It may be almost said, that even at this remote distance of time, the woodlands and open of that unrivalled country still echo with the music of his gallant pack. During his stay in Leicestershire, Mr. Smith resided at Quorndon Hall, a no less celebrated sportsman, Mr. Thomas Edge, of Strelley Hall, Nottinghamshire, being his messmate for some time. It was said of Edge, although he weighed twenty stone in the saddle, that no man could beat him for twenty minutes. His brother John was no less fast after hounds. Tom Edge had three splendid horses, Banker, Gayman, and Remus. For the first and third of these conjointly, Lord Middleton offered him two thousand two hundred guineas, which offer was refused, while Mr. Compton offered him fifty pounds for one day's hunting on Gayman. Gayman carried his owner every Monday for nine seasons in succession.

After giving up Leicestershire, where he was succeeded by Mr. Osbaldeston, Mr. Smith took his stud to Lincoln to work the Burton Hunt. He held this capital country for eight years, until 1824, when he was succeeded by Sir Richard Sutton, and after an interval of two years, went into Hants.

The celebrated Nimrod *, who was an eye-witness,

* Charles Apperley, Esq., author of "The Northern" and "German Tours" in the Sporting Magazine.

thus testifies to Mr. Smith's management of the
Quorn :—

"Lord Foley was succeeded in the possession of
the Quorn hounds by that most conspicuous sportsman of modern times, Thomas Assheton Smith, who
kept them eight or nine seasons. As combining the
character of a skilful sportsman with that of a desperate horseman, perhaps his parallel is not to be
found; and his name will be handed down to poste-
rity as a specimen of enthusiastic zeal in one individual pursuit, very rarely equalled. Mr. Smith did
not become a master of fox-hounds because it was the
fashion to be a master of fox-hounds, neither did he
go a hunting because others went a hunting, neither
did he ride well up to his hounds one day and loiter
a mile behind them the next. No; from the first
day of the season to the last he was always the same
man, the same desperate fellow over a country, and
unquestionably possessing, *on every occasion and at
every hour of the day*, the most bulldog-like nerve
ever exhibited in the saddle. His motto was, 'I'll
be with my hounds;' and all those who have seen
him in the field must acknowledge he made no vain
boast of his prowess. His falls were countless; and
no wonder, for he rode at places which *he knew* no
horse could leap over; but his object was to get, one
way or the other, into the field with his hounds. As
a horseman, however, he has ever been superexcellent.

He sits in his saddle as if he were part of his horse,
and his seat displays vast power over his frame.   In
addition to his power his hand is equal to Chifney's,
and the advantage he experiences from it may be
gleaned from the following expression. Being seen
one day hunting his hounds on Radical, always a
difficult, but at that time a more than commonly difficult, horse to ride, he was asked by a friend why he
did not put a martingale on him, to give him more
power over his mouth. His answer was cool and
laconic: 'Thank ye, but my left hand shall be *my*
martingale.' Mr. Smith was the first gentleman who
fulfilled the character of huntsman to his hounds in
this far-famed country. In this occupation his desperate style of riding was of very material service to
him, as he never had his eye off his hounds, unless
when left behind by a fall, though he was quickly in
his place again after that. The best of horses, Jack
O'Lantern, Tom Thumb, his Big Grey horse*, and
Gift, good as they were, would however sometimes
stand still with him in a burst, and then he would be
obliged to wait for a whipper-in to come up and take
possession of his horse to proceed with; but this, of
course, was not an every day occurrence. As a
huntsman, then, he may be said to be eminent in
chase; decidedly so, because nothing stopped him in

* The Big Grey was his name.   Dick Burton stands by his side
in Ferneley's well-known picture.

his casts; and we know how many foxes are lost by
an ugly fence being in the way at this critical time.
Leicestershire is a country of all others in which wide
and bold casts are successful." *

Mr. Smith had the assistance, either as kennel
huntsmen or whippers-in, of some of the most skilful
of their craft. Jack Shirley, who had been huntsman
to Lord Sefton, Dick Burton, Joe Harrison, and Tom
Wingfield, all in turn were worthy of their new master.

Tom Day came to him afterwards from Sir George
Sitwell, who hunted Derbyshire and Yorkshire.
"What a capital hand over the country," exclaims
Nimrod, " was Jack Shirley in those days, and what
a capital anecdote did Mr. John Moore tell me of
him from his own experience. He was riding Gadsby,
a celebrated hunter of Mr. Smith's, but then a good
deal the worse for wear, over one of the worst fields
in all Leicestershire for a blown horse, between
Tilton and Somerby, abounding with large ant-hills
and deep holding furrows. The old horse, said
my informant, was going along at a slapping pace,
with his head quite loose, down hill at the time,
whilst Jack was in the act of putting a point of whipcord to his thong, having *a large open clasp knife
between his teeth at* the time." †

* Hunting Reminiscences, p. 42.
† Ibid. p. 297. Jack Shirley accompanied his master into
Lincolnshire. Mr. Smith used frequently to amuse his field, when

The following quotation from the same high authority respecting another feature in Mr. Smith's mastership of the Quorn will not be unacceptable. "Every person who has been in Leicestershire knows the necessity of having good command over the field, a very serious and often hazardous duty devolving on the master of the pack. Here Mr. Smith was also successful. He set out by declaring that he was not the best-tempered man in the world; and he hoped, if at any time he said what might be deemed harsh to his brother-sportsmen, they would attribute it to his zeal to show sport, and not to an intention to give offence. We have the pleasure of stating then, that, with one or two trifling exceptions, producing no serious results, he passed through his fiery ordeal, continued for the number of seasons I have mentioned, and quitted his proud station as master and huntsman of the Quorn hounds in 1819*, esteemed as a sportsman and valued as a man. There may be some who may tell me his language was sometimes coarser than occasion could justify, and it is not for me to decide the point. All I will say is, his language was never that of a bully, for a braver man never stepped on the earth, nor one who displayed in

the hounds were running "slow," by calling up Jack, who was a great favourite, to *bore a hole* in an impenetrable bullfinch. Many a pint of blood did he lose in this service.

* This is an error. He left the Quorn in 1816.

clearer colours the thorough courage of a true-bred
Briton.   Indeed, I may ask with the poet —

> 'Is there the man into the lion's den
> Who dares intrude to snatch his young away?'

and answer, ' Thomas Assheton Smith is he!'"

Nor was the renown thus acquired by this eminent
fox-hunter obtained in an age of few first-rate riders,
or among a scanty crop of illustrious sportsmen.
These were the days of Meynell, Warde, Osbaldeston,
the two Rawlinsons, one of whom afterwards took the
name of Lindow, John Moore, Captain Baird, Maxse,
Colonel Wyndham, Sir James Musgrave, the two
Edges, Lord Kintore, Davy, Sir Henry Peyton, Sir
Harry Goodricke, John White, and last, though not
least, the splendid rider, Valentine Maher.   With more
than one of these names the record of some famous
run is associated.   White, of whom the old song says,

> " White on the right, Sir, midst the first flight, Sir,
> Is quite out of sight, Sir, of those in the rear."

was the only man who stuck close to Mr. Smith on
the Belvoir Day with the Duke of Rutland's hounds,
when the fox led them nineteen miles point blank,
and every other rider was beaten off.   Lindow was
the owner of the celebrated Clipper, considered " the
best hunter in England;" and it was on his back that
he and Mr. Smith, who was mounted on Garry Owen,
after a tremendous run with the Quorn, found them-

selves alone with the pack, while Tom Wingfield, the whipper-in, was visible at some distance alongside of them, flying down the wind to stop some earths which he knew of. Both horses at length fairly stopped, but the Clipper held out the longer of the two.

Mr. Smith used to say that the two best runs he had in Leicestershire were—one of forty-seven minutes, from Coplow to Hallaton, and the other one hour and twenty-seven minutes, from Cream Gorse to Stockerston, the fox being killed both times.

His fame and success in Lincolnshire were in no wise inferior to what had attended him at Quorn. Many of the Melton men followed him, knowing that he was sure of good sport wherever he went; but scarcely one of them was prepared for the formidable drains or dykes in the Burton Hunt, and their horses were unfit for the country. Shortly after their arrival there, they found a fox near the kennels, and he crossed a dyke called the Tilla. Tom Smith rode at it, and got in, but over, and was the only one who did. Fourteen of the Meltonians were floundering in the water at the same time, which so cooled their ardour, that they soon returned to Melton, dropping off one or two at a time, always excepting Sir H. Goodricke, Captain Baird, and one or two others. Mr. Smith once took a most extraordinary leap in Lincolnshire. The hounds came to a cut or navigable canal, called

the Fosdyke, over which were two bridges, one a
bridle bridge, the other used for carts*, running
parallel to each other at several yards' distance.   At
one end of these bridges there is usually a high gate
leading into the field adjoining the canal, and along
each side of them is a low rail, to protect persons
going over.   Smith rode along one of these bridges,
and found the gate at the end locked, whereas he
saw the gate open at the end of the parallel bridge.
He immediately put his horse at the rails, and
jumped across and over the opposite rails, on to the
other bridge, to the immense surprise and gratification of all who witnessed the feat.

It was after his first season in Lincolnshire, that
Mr. Smith brought the late Lord Raglan from Ostend
to England in his yacht, after the battle of Waterloo,
where the gallant officer had lost his arm.

It has been stated that, at an earlier period of the
same year, he took the Duke of Wellington over to
Calais, and that he afterwards brought the first intelligence of the victory to England, but these facts
he invariably disclaimed.   The Duke was always a
warm personal friend of Mr. Smith ; he admired his
manly straightforward bearing and good sense, and,
as regarded his horsemanship, always said of him that
he would have made one of the best cavalry officers

---

* They cross the canal into the lands of different land-owners,
which accounts for their being so near each other.

in Europe. He was a frequent visitor at Tedworth, as Mr. Smith was at Strathfieldsaye, and his Grace was one of the most constant attendants at the meet of the Tedworth Hunt. The above remark by the Duke calls to mind another saying respecting Mr. Smith, which was, that many of the most distinguished riders in the Peninsular war owed their horsemanship to him.

From 1826 till 1828, Mr. Smith established his quarters at Penton Lodge, near Andover; having ceased to be a master of hounds after he gave up the Burton country in 1824, but having hunted regularly with the Duke of Rutland's, and other packs in the surrounding countries. At Penton he commenced operations with a scratch pack, which he soon got into good order; but, until the death of his father, no very active steps were taken to bring the country into the condition in which it is now. On 29th of October 1827, his marriage took place with Maria, second daughter of William Webber, Esq., of Binfield Lodge, Berks. He was then fifty-one years of age. In the following year, upon the death of his father, he removed his hunting establishment to Tedworth, and soon afterwards set about making very extensive alterations. The old house was pulled down and rebuilt, Mr. Smith being in a great measure his own architect. While the plans were being prepared by the surveyor whom he employed to carry

out his designs, the man of science said it was not
possible to retain the old dining-room as it stood.
Mr. Smith was firm, and said that it must be done;
he drew a plan of his own, and accordingly it remains
to commemorate the genius of its late owner.   But
the chief improvement, which it is our business to
narrate, was the metamorphosis of that formerly in-
tractable woodland country about Tedworth into a
fine fox-hunting district.   The quick eye of Tom
Smith had long perceived the vacancy between the
New Forest and the Craven country*, and he now
began to put his long-cherished designs into execution.   Before his time, except during Warde's
solitary month, no hound had ever opened in those
big chases, from year's end to year's end.   During
his residence at Penton, the country had not been
preserved long enough always to insure a find, and
the patience of the master had been often severely
tried in drawing during a whole morning.   Occasionally a two-o'clock fox would give them a ride
home by the light of the moon; for, when he was
found, he was very likely to be

"A traveller, a stranger, stout, gallant, and shy,
   With his earths ten miles off, and those earths in his eye."

---

* Mr. Warde being asked what were the boundaries of the
Craven country, replied, "It is a simple triangle, bounded by
London, Oxford, and Bath." The organ of acquisitiveness must
have been largely developed in this gentleman's cranium.

A tale is still told with glee by the veterans of that sporting district, and listened to with instinctive dread by the cock-tails.   It goes, that a straight-necked wild'un, found at Doyly, ran to the other side of Newbury; that he was lost at dusk in some old buildings; that they left off twenty-two miles from home; that the horses were all knocked up; and that the squire borrowed a pony at the George Inn, at Hurstbourne Tarrant (where he left his beaten nag), the owner of the animal at the same time giving him an admonition to take care that it did not kick him off.   It was not much bigger than a Newfoundland dog.   The transition from two splendid horses and a capital hack in the morning, to the back of this diminutive sheltie in the afternoon, was some-what ridiculous, but did not affect the squire's mode of riding, for his masterly hand persuaded the little animal to carry him to his own door within the hour, the distance being a dozen miles, good measure.

Nimrod thus describes a great meet at Weyhill, in December 1827, the year after Mr. Smith came to Penton.   Speaking of the country, he observes, " there is nothing but beds of flints;" and as for the Hampshire woodlands, " they are the worst country in the known world."   George Gardener was at that time Mr. Smith's head whipper-in. There were 300 horsemen in the field.   "Not only was the appearance of the hounds, as hounds, splendid indeed, but their performance was equally good.* The scent was wretchedly bad, but they stooped to it like rabbit beagles; and unfortunate as our day's sport in other respects was, any one would have had a treat in seeing this highly bred pack pick their way, as it were, inch by inch, over one stubble field. I must own I was delighted, and I wish some huntsmen I could name had been present to take a lesson from their huntsman, Mr. Smith, whose patience and judgment were conspicuous on this trying occasion. I may say *trying*, because his fox was but just before him, and he had the eyes of a very large field upon him. But he never lifted his hounds a yard, though the line of country was *apparently* before him; and thus did he hit off his fox, for he did not take that line." †

Nimrod adds, respecting what he terms the foundation of an " independent dynasty " by Mr. Smith in Hants:—" When I first heard of his hunting the Andover country, I set it down as a mere frolic of the day, never dreaming that he intended persevering in doing so. It now appears that he is in real earnest, and the gentlemen of his neighbourhood must be highly pleased with the compliment he has paid them, in selecting so magnificent a pack of hounds to hunt their country."

* Mr. Smith had Sir R. Sutton's pack this year.
† Sporting Magazine, December 1827, p. 150.

Mr. Smith once at Tedworth, a wondrous change came over the spirit of that country. No one but a man of the most iron will and undeviating purpose would ever have dreamed of converting the immense tracts of woodland, dense and ungovernable, which thirty years ago covered the face of what is now called the Tedworth country, into rideable fox coverts. When Mr. Smith first proposed to the landed proprietors of the neighbourhood to hunt the country, he received permission with a smile, accompanied with the remark, that he would find it utterly impossible on account of the enormous size of the woods (several of them containing on an average more than a thousand acres each), and also on account of the badness of the scent,—two of the fox-hunter's greatest drawbacks. The gentry, however, and farmers, soon finding the man they had to deal with, rendered him every assistance; the former letting him their coverts at a reasonable rent, the latter preserving foxes, of which up to this time there had been a great scarcity, as if they were prize pigs. Under such good auspices, and with means and appliances to boot, Collingbourne, Doyly, Doles, Wherwell, and Faccombe, which had hitherto been without any straight rides, and consequently of little use comparatively for hunting, were rendered "negotiable" in the hands of the squire, some at his own expense, the others by his influence with the proprietors. The extent of wood levelled to the ground by his orders was something miraculous, and the green rides opened, as if by magic, in those hitherto impermeable fastnesses will remain a lasting memorial of the good to be achieved by spending money for any purpose among the labouring classes. Andover at that time assumed the appearance of a manufacturing town in miniature, or rather of a great timber mart. Numbers were employed in felling the magnificent sticks of oak and elm. Here might be seen knots of sturdy labourers grubbing up the stumps of trees which had stood in those forests for ages ; there a busy crowd piled up or carried away the underwood : the thick glades, which had till then never seen the light of day, now resounded with the axes of the woodmen and with the crash of the falling timber; while the aged and decrepit might be seen bending under the loads of faggots, freely given to them, to cheer hearths which had till the time of Mr. Smith but scantily felt the genial warmth of fire. Even in renting the rides the squire proved himself a first-rate tenant, for both these and the adjoining fences were always kept in order, while the admission of air through the thick plantations tended greatly to promote the growth of the timber. By these means, woods which had hitherto been seldom approached by hounds, except to whip off, heard with joy the horn of the hunter.

The only hounds Mr. Smith had of his original

pack, at the time of his coming into Hants, were Bounty and Solyman; and the pack he collected was formed of drafts from at least a dozen different kennels. In the first season, owing to the scarcity of foxes, and the wildness of the pack, he killed only four and a half brace of foxes. In the following year he purchased Sir Richard Sutton's famous pack, and at the same time was presented by him with a capital hunter, Rob Roy, which Sir Richard paid him the compliment of saying, "perhaps he might ride, but no one down there could." In the squire's hands he was as quiet as a lamb, and soon verified the remark which old Jack Shirley (who rode him up) had made, "that he would be found a bad 'un to beat." An intimate friend of Mr. Smith relates that it was his good fortune to witness a verification of the above remark, at Burderop Park, in 1827. Lord Kintore at that time hunted that country known to sportsmen as the Vale of White Horse, and on the day in question was mounted on his celebrated Apollo mare, with Provincial reserved as his second horse. The hounds went away at a racing pace towards Broad Hinton, and Tom Smith on Rob Roy, though quite a stranger to the country, took his usual place, and cut out the work. His Lordship in vain tried to catch him, until a check occurred in a lane; into this the peer jumped over a gate, and out of it over another. "When his Lordship wishes to hit off his

fox, he must return into this lane," said Mr. Smith to
the relator of the anecdote.   Lord Kintore and Mr.
Smith spoke highly of each other's riding more than
once after this memorable day.   Every one recollects
the famous story of Lord Kintore coming once to
a "stopper" in the Vale of White Horse, which defied the whole field.   Seeing a countryman on the
other side, "Catch my horse," exclaimed his Lordship, and drove at it.   Both were thrown; but the
rustic did as he was told, and having picked up both
the steed and his rider, Lord Kintore galloped away,
leaving his friends in mute astonishment on the wrong
side of the fence.   It must be recollected that Lord
Kintore, on the above occasion at Burderop Park, had
out his two best horses (Provincial was bought in at
Tattersall's not long before for four hundred guineas),
whereas Mr. Smith was riding Sir Richard Sutton's
gift horse, which no one else could ride.

The horses he brought into Hants from Lincolnshire were, Lovinski, Beiram, The Grey, Screwdriver, Young Jack-o'Lantern*, and last, though
not least, Ayston.   Screwdriver was a fine dark
chestnut, seventeen hands high: Mr. Smith got him
a bargain, in consequence of his having come into
Stamford six times without his rider.   Screwdriver

---

* There were three members of the Lantern family all celebrated, Old Jack-o'Lantern, Young Jack-o'Lantern, and Charlotte
Lantern. Mr. Smith always said that Young Jack was the best
horse of the three.

was not his original name, but the first time
the squire mounted him, as he showed signs of
being unruly, one of his friends asked him what
"*screw*" he had there. The end of the run, however,
showed the "screw" almost the only nag up, and
from that day he went by the name of Screwdriver.
Jack-o'Lantern was a blood-looking bay with crooked
fore legs, the son of a chestnut of that name, but a
far better horse than his sire, in his owner's opinion.
He was an old horse when he came into Hants, and
as perfect a hunter as man ever rode.   "I remember,"
relates an eye-witness, " a tremendous day, early in
the season, the weather hot and the ground deep, when,
after two hours in South Grove, the fox went away
to Milton Hill. Here for the first time in his life
Old, for he could no longer be called Young, Jack
stood still, and the squire said he would never ride
him again, and he never did."

The most extraordinary horse of all was Ayston, a
yellow bay horse, all over a hunter, and with excellent
shoulders, but "*pigeon*-toed," and so bad a back that he
had to be led to covert; doubtless thoroughbred, as the
squire used to say, " inasmuch as I bought him war-
ranted not so."   But even with the above disqualifi-
cations, in a hard run with plenty of fences, and
through dirt, the horse was never foaled that could
beat him.   His master would at no time have taken
a thousand guineas for him.   Ferneley has faithfully

represented him in the fine sporting picture that still
adorns the billiard-room at Tedworth*, and in which
the squire's seat on horseback is true to the life.   He is
surrounded by some of his favourite hounds—Watchman, Commodore, Romulus, Dimity, and others.   " On
two occasions (out of many)," says a contemporary,
" I can instance the superiority of this gallant horse.
The squire had been riding him with a hanging fox
around the deep rides at South Grove all the morning,
while all the field were standing still; at last they got
away through the heavy clays and perpetual ploughs
towards Grafton.   One of the sportsmen, Mr. Hawkins,
viewed our fox emerging from the Vale on to the grass
downs towards Collingbourne Woods, some way ahead.
Some of them cut across, and got on to these downs,
and had a steady pull at their horses.   Meanwhile
the squire, as usual, was riding as honest as a school-
boy in the Vale with his hounds.   Presently they
came up with the horsemen on the turf, and old
Ayston cut down every nag among them in fair
galloping across the downs, notwithstanding his
previous episode in South Grove and the Vale."   At
another time this same gallant animal cleared the
deer hurdles in Conholt Park, nearly six feet high,
and pounded the whole field.   Mr. F——, who had
ample opportunities of forming a judgment, says, " he

* See illustration.

was, in my humble opinion, the very best hunter I
ever saw;" and an old sportsman observed in his hearing, "that the man did not live who could make a fence
sufficiently strong to stop Ayston, with the squire on
his back, and with a fox sinking before his hounds."
It was with Ayston, that the squire astonished the na-
tives on his visit to Lord Moreton, when he took with
him his capital huntsman and whipper-in, Dick Burton and Tom Day.

Mr. Smith used to relate the following anecdote
of the purchase of one of his best horses, but
its name is not recorded. "When I had the
hounds in Leicestershire, an Irishman rode up one
morning to meet them on a splendid horse. I saw
directly he could not ride; and as one of my whips
was on a slow one, but a capital fencer, I offered him
to ride the whip's horse for the run, and that I would
get on his: I soon found I was on a first-rate one.
He jumped the park wall where we found the fox,
and carried me in splendid style. After a capital
run no one was left with the hounds but Lord Jersey
and myself. At last his horse declined, and I took
the fox from the hounds about five hundred yards
further on. On joining me his Lordship said, ' You
are on the best horse in the country.' I said, ' Keep it
to yourself for a few minutes.' The field came up,
and with them the Irishman, who had been going in
comfort on the good fencer. ' Do you like my horse

well enough,' he said, ' to give the price you talked of in the morning?' (The sum was not openly named.) 'I do,' I replied in a careless tone. Lord Jersey pulled off his hat *coram omnibus*, and said, ' Tom, I congratulate you; you have the best animal in Leicestershire.'"

Even the success which Mr. Smith experienced at Tedworth before his father's death, limited as it was when compared with the sport he created afterwards by the clearing of the woods, completely took the old gentleman by surprise. He had entertained a firm idea, that to drive a fox out of the vast woods adjoining Tedworth was a feat beyond the power of man to accomplish; and he was accordingly at *first* strongly opposed to his son's leaving the grass countries to establish a pack of hounds for the purpose of hunting the bleak downs and interminable copses of Wilts and Hants. For this reason, extraordinary as it may appear, he was the only landowner, when Tom Smith came in 1826 to reside at Penton, who refused his son permission to draw his pet home covert, Ashdown Copse. "Where does Tom Smith meet next week?" said he, one evening, to a neighbour, when dining with him at Tedworth. " I think," was his guest's reply, " that he will bring his hounds to Ashdown Copse on Monday." " Then, if he does," said the wrathful old squire, " I will bring an action against him, by Jove. And pray, sir, what makes you

smile, may I ask?" he added, observing his friend
slightly amused at the threat. "It is no joke, I promise you." "Excuse me, sir," replied his guest,
"but I was thinking, if Tom Smith were cast for
damages, who would have to pay the bill." Shortly
after this the prohibition was withdrawn.

Mr. Assheton Smith's father was remarkable, like
his son, for inflexibility of purpose, but in him it
bordered too closely upon its neighbouring vice, obs-
tinacy. He always entertained a great objection to
Mr. Telford's proposal to cross the Menai Straits by
means of a suspension bridge, which he affirmed must
necessarily interfere with the navigation; and when
serving on a committee of the House of Commons, as
member for Andover, he found the feeling of his
colleagues favourable to the project, he threw his hat
upon the floor, and vowed most solemnly, that even
if the bridge were completed he would never cross it
as long as he lived. This vow he kept, always making use of a boat in order to reach the opposite shore.
When George IV. returned from his visit to Ireland, he
stayed at Plas Newydd as the guest of the Marquess of
Anglesea. On that occasion Mr. Smith, sen., took the
chair at a public meeting at Carnarvon, when it was
determined to present an address to the king, and a
committee of twelve of the leading gentlemen of the
district was appointed to convey it to Plas Newydd.
In the course of the proceedings, a discussion took

E

place as to the proper dress in which the committee
should appear before royalty. While some proposed
court dresses, and others uniforms, the chairman,
who had on a cutaway coat with breeches and leather
gaiters, said, that whatever others might do, he, at
all events, should go before his Majesty in the dress
he had on. No notice was then taken of what he said,
but when the deputation met at Vaenol for the purpose of crossing to Plas Newydd, which they did in
his boat, the bridge being at that time in process of
building, to the surprise of all, they found their chairman in exactly the same dress which he had worn at
Carnarvon. When they were introduced to the king,
Mr. Smith, as chairman, advanced first, when his
Majesty, taking both his hands in his own, and without appearing even to notice his uncourtly appearance, accosted him with the greatest kindness, saying,
"Your son Tom accompanied me in his yacht to
and from Holyhead." Mr. Smith afterwards acknowledged that the superior breeding and kind manner of
the king made him thoroughly ashamed of himself,
and fully sensible that he had been wrong.

"The Christmas Foxhunter," writing in the Sporting Magazine for March 1835, gives an excellent
description of a famous run which had taken place in
the December previous, from the osier beds at Amesbury to Salisbury Plain, a distance of sixteen miles,
and had lasted an hour and fifteen minutes. The

hounds had found their first fox among the osier beds, and he had given them a clipping run, and escaped by "speed and bottom." A second fox being found not far from the same spot, he crossed the Avon at Amesbury, taking the river like an otter, and shaking his brush to the wind, made for Salisbury Plain. The horsemen were obliged to go half a mile back to a bridge, as the river was nowhere practicable, while the fox was visible before them two miles ahead. Thus many were altogether thrown out. The ground was very dry, and the hill from Amesbury, with the killing pace the hounds were going, tried those who got away severely. Mr. Smith rode Golden Pippin, and was first in sight of "the Plain;" as he passed Stonehenge, the animal was half inclined to stop and contemplate the "architectural beauties" of that wondrous pile, but his "accomplished rider" persuaded him otherwise. Many horses declined here, and it was at this place that one of the sportsmen met with a severe fall. Having passed Stonehenge, the hounds being in full cry, heads up and sterns down, Gay Lass leading, and Bar-maid and Dairy-maid close to her haunches ("the ladies" were out that day, said by Dorset in another number of the Sporting Magazine to be really magnificent, of great power and symmetry unquestionable), the fox passed through the village of Barwick to Wishford, took the river Willy, and ran up the hill to Grovelly Copse, where they killed him. The run was over the lightest and most picturesque part of the country.*

Stonehenge witnessed at another time a very severe run, in which a misadventure befell a heavy parson, whose horse came down across some cart ruts, in a manner which Dick Burton would describe as a *buster*. His reverence was much shaken, and did not come to himself for a few seconds. When he did, he seated himself upon the greensward, and mildly observed, "I wish those confounded Romans had pecked in the ruts before they left this part of the country!"

Mr. Smith's stud at Tedworth was in general far superior to what it had been at any previous time. While in Leicestershire and Lincolnshire he had never been in the habit of giving high prices, and used to say that, till he came into Hants, he never gave above 50*l.* for a horse. Nevertheless, he contrived to find or make first-rate hunters, even at this low rate. It is not often that racers make hunters, but Mr. Smith bought Shacabac out of Mr. Lechmere Charlton's stables, and made a very good one of him. At an early period in his life he hunted regularly with Lord Sefton, who succeeded the famous Meynell in Leicestershire. Lord Sefton's huntsman was Stephen Goodall, who, though an excellent sportsman, was incapacitated by his weight from living

* Sporting Magazine, vol. x., 2nd series, p. 347.

with his hounds when running hard. "I always like, Mr. Tom Smith," said Goodall to him, "to see you out on a *grey horse*, for then I know where the hounds are, and the shortest way to get to them; and am satisfied, when *you* are there, *I* shall not be missed." Stephen had a great objection to being weighed, but Mr. Harrison got him once into a patent weighing-chair, without his being aware of it, and saw the finger pointing over nineteen on the dial.* In the famous Billesden Coplow run, above-mentioned, Mr. Smith was allowed to have the best of it down to the brook at Enderby, where his horse fell in. He told a friend that he bought the horse he that day rode, called Furze-cutter, for 26*l*., and sold him after the run to Lord Clonbrock for 400*l*.; "a pretty good comment," he remarked, "on the place I maintained on that day."

It may not be inappropriate here to record the following anecdote, related by a Mr. Davy, whose prowess has been recorded by Nimrod, and of whom Mr. Smith said, "he was the only man of whose riding I was ever jealous."† A large field were assembled at Ashby Pastures, and a fox went away with the pack close at his brush.

* Stephen was well known for his performances on Curricle, afterwards bought for the Prince of Wales.

† "Mr. Davy's hand on a horse was proverbial," says old Harkaway in the Sporting Magazine for August 1834. "Like Paganini, he could play on four strings or one."

A long green drove ran parallel with the fields, down which all the horsemen rode save *one*. A high blackthorn hedge screened the hounds from their view, and they were riding for hard life. All at once some horse was heard on the same side as the hounds, rattling over the gates, and crashing through the bullfinchers at such a pace, that Davy and another remarked, " Some fellow's horse has purled him and run away." The illusion, however, was soon dispelled by the hounds swinging across the drove, and Tom Smith, on Jack-o'Lantern, sailing by their side ; having beaten every man among them, though they had only to gallop over plain grass, and he had to encounter both gates and fences, and of the stiffest character. This, Davy confessed, was one of the greatest triumphs in horsemanship he had ever witnessed. He also mentioned, that on another occasion, after a very sharp run late in the season, the hounds were running into their fox in an orchard on the top of a hill at Rolleston (Mr. Greene's). Up the hill, in his usual place, rode the squire, when some very formidable posts and rails met him, which Jack-o'Lantern got over without a fall by breaking the top rail. " You may guess what sort of fence it was," said Davy, " when I tell you not a man would face it *even then*."

Besides Jack-o'Lantern, the squire had at that

time some other capital horses, and among them Filch, Gadsby, and Gift. The last-named was a present from Long Wellesley, who said that no man could see a run on him. "He only wants a rider," said Tom Smith. "Will you ride him then at Glen Gorse?" rejoined Long Wellesley. "Willingly," exclaimed the squire; and, as usual, picked up the fox, after getting eight falls over gates, when Long Wellesley begged his acceptance of him.

The history of the education of Jack-o'Lantern was thus related by Tom Edge, an intimate friend of the squire, and for many years, as has been already mentioned, his messmate at Quorn. "We were riding," said Tom Edge, "to covert through a line of bridle gates, when we came to a new double oaken post and rail fence. 'This is just the place to make my colt a good timber jumper,' said the squire, 'so you shut the gate, and ride away fast from the fence.' This was accordingly done, when the squire rode at the rails, which Jack taking with his breast, gave both himself and his rider such a fall, that their respective heads were looking towards the fence they had ridden at. Up rose both at the same time, as if nothing very particular had happened. 'Now,' said Tom Smith, 'this will be the making of the horse; just do as you did before, and ride away.' Edge did so, and Jack flew the rails without touching, and was a first-rate timber fencer from that day. What made this feat the more remarkable was, that it did not come off in a run, but in what is called 'cold blood.'"

Screwdriver, whose acts have been already mentioned, once fairly dislodged the squire into the middle of a gorse cover. He was finding his fox in some very high gorse, near Conholt Park, and was sitting loosely on Screwdriver—who, by the way, even after Mr. Smith took to him, always retained his untamable temper—when the wilful animal started aside, and kicked him over his head. Nothing, owing to the height of the gorse, could be seen of the squire, but Screwdriver kept kicking and plunging in a circle round him. "Let go the bridle, or he will be the death of you," said a nervous well-meaning farmer. " He shall kick my brains out first," was the reply of the still prostrate sportsman, who was soon up and righted in the saddle.* Although his falls were numerous, owing to his never allowing his hounds to get away from him, yet he was very seldom seriously hurt. Only on two occasions had he a bone broken: once at Melton, when he consoled himself by learning arithmetic from the pretty damsel at the post-office; and afterwards

---

* "Nothing is so low," said Mr. Smith, "as moving about after a fall, saying, 'Catch my horse; pray catch my horse!'" His own plan was never to let go of the bridle under any circumstances.

when one of his ribs was fractured, owing, as he said, to his having his knife in a breast-pocket.

His presence of mind, when falling, never deserted him ; he always contrived to fall clear of his horse, and *never to let him go*. The bridle-rein, which fell as lightly as breeze of zephyr on his horse's neck, was then held as in a vice. In some instances, with horses whom he knew well, he would ride for a fall, where he knew it was not possible for him to clear a fence. With Jack-o'Lantern he was often known to venture on this experiment, and he frequently said there was not a field in Leicestershire in which he had not had a fall. "I never see you in the Harborough country," he observed to a gentleman who occasionally hunted with the Quorn. "I don't much like your Harborough country," replied the other, "the fences are so large." "Oh !" observed Mr. Smith, "there is no place you cannot get over with a fall."* To a young supporter of his pack, who was constantly falling and *hurting* himself, he said, "All who profess to ride should know *how* to *fall*."

"No man," writes Nimrod in 1841, "knows so well as Mr. Smith does *how to fall*, which accounts for the trifling injuries he has sustained; and I once saw an instance of his skill in this act of self-preservation. He stuck fast in a bullfinch, on his tall

---

* Mr. Stanhope, who hunted with Sir Bellingham Graham in Leicestershire in 1833, rivalled Mr. Smith in the number of his falls.

grey horse, his hinder legs being entangled in the
growers, and there was every appearance of the
horse falling on his head into a deep ditch below
him.   A less cool man than Mr. Smith might have
thrown himself from the saddle, in which case, had
the growers given way at the moment, for the
animal appeared suspended by them, his horse might
have fallen upon him ere he could have gotten out
of his way.   Mr. Smith, however, sat quiet, and by
that means the well-practised hunter got his legs
free, and landed himself in the field without further
difficulty.   At one time it appeared to me as if
nothing could prevent both falling headlong into
the ditch." *

In his later years, as his income increased, price
was no object to him in the purchase of his horses.
Among those for which he gave large sums were
Election, Netheravon, Fire King, Black Diamond,
Ham Ashley, and King Dan, who will live long in the
memory of those who witnessed their symmetry and
prowess. He gave Lord Rosslyn 400 guineas for Rory
O'More, one of the best animals he ever possessed.
Fire King also well repaid his price, whom the members of the Tedworth Hunt will long remember as
willing to run away with everybody, and able to do
so even with the squire.

Nor was Mr. Smith in any way sparing of

* Hunting Reminiscences, p. 297.

expense in securing the very best blood for his
pack. In addition to Sir R. Sutton's hounds, he
bought those belonging to Sir Thomas Boughey,
and, later, the pack of the Duke of Grafton. In
particular he prized most highly the stock of Mr.
Warde, and, as a proof of this, on one occasion he
deputed Mr. F—— to offer Mr. Horlock, who had purchased Mr. Warde's pack for 2000*l*., one thousand
guineas for twenty couples, which Mr. Smith was to
pick out from the kennel, without any reference to
guide him but his own well-practised eye in the
selection.

One of the most surprising, and at the same
time interesting, scenes to witness was the "fas-
cination" he seemed to possess over hounds, and the
strong attachment they always evinced towards their
master. "I recollect," relates one of his friends, "his
once having out five couples of drafts whom he had
never seen before. Sharp, his kennel huntsman at
that time, gave him names written down; he then
called each hound separately, and gave him a piece
of bread, then returned the list to the huntsman, saying, '*I know them now;*' and so they did him." On
other occasions when the fixture was "Oare Hill,"
and the hounds were awaiting his arrival, Dick Burton used to say, "Master is coming I perceive by the
hounds;" and this long before he made his appearance.
When he came within three hundred yards, no hunts-

man or whip in the world could have stopped the pack from bounding to meet him. In the morning when let loose from the kennel, they would rush to his study window or to the hall door, and stand there till he came out.

His especial favourites in the kennel at different periods were the following : Solyman, a very fine and large grey hound. Nimrod says he was the largest ever bred in England, standing twenty-seven inches high, and with bone equal to many ponies. Mr. Smith was fond of remarking that he would as soon take this hound's word about a fox as any man's in England. This saying is like what Mr. Osbaldeston said of his horse Vaulter, that he never told a lie in his life. Solyman had, however, his peculiar days (like other dogs), and sometimes would do very little. Another great favourite was Vanquisher, from Sir R. Sutton's kennel, a beautiful hound who always kept close to his master's horse, never drawing before the fox was found, and then close to the fox till he was killed. Next comes Trimmer, a grey fine-shaped hound, also from Sir Richard Sutton. This hound, he used to say, was the most perfect and complete in all his good qualities, such as finding, hunting, and chasing, of any hound he ever rode after. Trimbush was another especial favourite; and Nigel, not unlike in size and colour (black-pied) to Trimbush, was equally valued. . .

Nigel always showed the greatest animation, even when very old, directly a fox was afoot. He seemed to undergo a metamorphosis at once from age to youth, and became full of life and spirit. Rifleman was also the double favourite both of the master and mistress, and had almost the privileges of a parlour boarder.

Towards the end of the squire's hunting career, Commoner, Conqueror, Flamer, and Lexicon invariably went out whenever he joined the field. He said it cheered him to see their old honest faces, although their day for affording sport was over. There is always, he said, a gravity and importance of demeanour in the countenance of a good hound, as if he knew his superiority over the rest of the canine species. He was very careful in not speaking to them when they were at fault, so as to draw their attention off their work, for, like Beckford, he could see an expression of rebuke in their faces, as much as to say, " What do you want ? let me alone." One of the old hounds still remains, the patriarch of the pack, and as finely shaped a foxhound and as good a one as ever man rode after. This is old Nelson, well worthy of the name he bears. On the first day he came, he singled out Mr. Smith, attached himself to him, and always afterwards was the first to salute him whenever he entered the field. He came from the Duke of Rutland, and is of the same size as many of the best hounds in the pack ; in fact, a perfect model for a foxhound, answering in every way to Mr. Meynell's well-known description—" short back, open bosom, straight legs, and compact feet ;" and to that by Beckford, equally familiar to sportsmen, " Let his legs be straight as arrows, his feet round and not too large, his chest deep and back broad, his head small, his neck thin, his tail thick and bushy; if he carries it well, so much the better."—*On Hunting*, p. 29. Yet notwithstanding Beckford, than whom there cannot be better authority, for his work may be said to be the fox-hunter's text-book, speaks of a thin neck as recommending a hound, Mr. Smith used to like " throaty hounds," for he said " that by getting rid of the throat, the nose goes along with it, for a throaty hound has invariably a good nose."

It may not be out of place here to describe the animated and interesting scene which invariably occurred when the squire joined his hounds at the meet. Directly he appeared, every hound rushed towards him, and if ever there was a *hearty welcome* given to man by " dumb animals," that was the welcome. It could not be said, however, to be given by " dumb animals," for each hound had a peculiar winning note of its own to express its joy, and no one could for a moment doubt the reciprocal delight both of master and hounds. This was the more singular as Mr. Smith never fed his hounds in the kennel, but, directly the hunting was over for the day, he mounted his hack and galloped home, and the hounds returned quietly with the whippers-in.

It did not add little to the character of this sylvan scene, to see the well-mounted field, and the cordial greeting which the knot of scarlets gave to the master of the hounds. No time, however, was lost in salutations, for business was to be done. So alongside of his hack the squire's hunter was brought, and without dismounting, he vaulted from one to the other, almost without rising from the saddle of the steed he quitted. This was always looked upon as an extraordinary feat of agility, and it could not have been performed without great muscular strength.* Mr. Smith continued this practice almost up to the time of his death; and only two years before that event took place, he was stopping on horseback at the door of one of the clubs in St. James's Street, when a horse was brought up which his owner complained of as being most difficult to manage. The squire had him led up alongside of him, and jumped on his back in the usual style, although quite strange to him, when, to the astonishment of every one, after a turn or two with him up

---

* "In June 1858, a few months before his death, Mr. Smith was in Rotten Row, and at Tattersall's, as usual, on Blemish; and when he rode into the ring one morning, and saw Rarey driving his zebra round it, he made his servant bring his horse alongside, and quite gloried in showing the celebrated American how he could still change horses in a run without dismounting."—*Silk and Scarlet*, p. 284.

and down the street, he brought him back as quiet as a lamb. In fact, he seemed to possess the same fascinating power over horses, which he has been already shown to have had over hounds. Much of this power is doubtless to be attributed to his wonderful delicacy of touch in handling a horse.

The above instance is not the only one where animals, violent and irritable in other hands, have been known to be comparatively quiet in his. There was, however, one exception, and this was in a beautiful brown thoroughbred horse called "Cracker," who took an unaccountable dislike to the squire's red coat, although on all other occasions he was perfectly tractable. It is related by one of his friends, that he saw this hunter, on his master's attempting to mount him, kick him down in the most savage manner. Tom Smith was not the man to give in even after such opposition as this, but at length, after many entreaties on the part of his wife, he consented, with great reluctance, to part with him, although for many good qualities as a hunter he was a great favourite. He became afterwards the property of a celebrated vendor of pale ale.

The influence which Mr. Smith appeared to wield over horses, materially contributed to his excellent management of them. He used to say that as soon as he mounted a strange horse, the animal would turn his head round, and seemed to smell at his left boot, and after that they were acquainted. It must have been an interesting sight to have seen him witness a private rehearsal between Rarey and Cruiser, which he did in the last summer of his life, when he expressed himself much pleased with Rarey's extraordinary power in taming vicious animals.

When Lord Kennedy made a match for 500*l.*, for Captain Douglas to ride a steeple chase against Captain Ross's Clinker, over five miles of the severest hunting-ground in Leicestershire,—namely, from Barkby Holt to the Coplow,—his Lordship purchased "Radical" of Mr. Assheton Smith for 500 guineas for the purposes of the match. This noble animal was a most difficult horse to ride, and Mr. Smith's remark was, "whoever rides him must be as strong as an elephant, as bold as a lion, and as quiet as a mouse." He himself rode Radical in a double snaffle, or rather, a snaffle and a gag rein, his favourite bit at that time, as he said it was the lightest or severest, as the case might require. He afterwards adopted a double bridle, known as the Bentinck bit, being an invention of the late lamented Lord George Bentinck. This was a very severe instrument, and only suited for such light hands as those of Mr. Smith. In those of others it often caused accidents, as, owing to its unusual severity, few horses would go against it. To return to the match, Radical was beaten by Clinker, when Lord Kennedy offered to double the stakes on condition that Mr. Smith would ride Radical. On this being mentioned to him, his reply was, " Much as I esteem the implied compliment, I will not turn *rough-rider* to please any man living." The truth was, he always held steeple chases in aversion, and said they were an unfair and cruel tax on the powers of a horse, and, moreover, patronised by such as preferred seeing others break their necks to the risk of breaking their own. Clinker was afterwards beaten by Clasher, who was ridden by Mr. Osbaldeston, Dick Christian riding Clinker. The ground selected was that from Great Dalby to Tilton, a distance of five miles. Mr. Osbaldeston afterwards crowned the victory he had already obtained, by defeating Captain Ross himself, the squire being mounted on Pilot, and the captain on Polecat.

Mr. Smith was once riding Radical, soon after he had made him handy, in the Market Harborough country, when he observed, even while the hounds were drawing, a fellow, dressed like a horse jockey at a fair, following close after him over every leap he took. On inquiry he ascertained that the said fellow was a horse doctor, and had made a bet that his horse would jump anything that should be cleared by Radical. Matters went on pretty smoothly until they found, when the squire's rival for some time followed close, until they arrived at a hog-backed foot style with a tremendous drop, and with steps into a

road. This Radical cleared, but his unfortunate follower's horse, striking the top bar with his knees,
came headlong into the road with his rider, who was
carried home senseless. The next day, as the squire
was riding through the village, he was mobbed and
hooted by the old women, as being the man who had
nearly killed their hard-riding farrier. This anecdote
is not unlike that told of Burton, the Nuneaton tanner,
who always made a dead set at Mr. Smith in a similar
way. The tanner was habitually attired in a light-
coloured green coat, from which he received the name
of the Paroquet, and he rode remarkably well. The
squire at last being determined to shake him off, sent
Jack o'Lantern at an almost impracticable flight of
stiff rails, the top bar of which he broke, and, to his
dismay, made the passage easy for the tough man of
hides, who was soon once more at his side, and was
not destined to receive *his tanning* at all events that
time.

There was another strong reason why horses and
hounds became so docile and tractable with Mr.
Smith, and that was his just treatment of them,
which brutes are sensible enough to comprehend and
appreciate. It is a fact well recorded, that he was
never known to strike a horse or hound unfairly or
lose his temper with them. " How is it," asked a
friend, " that horses and hounds never seem to pro-
voke you?" " They are brutes and know no better,

but men do," was the pithy reply.   He used to say
that horses had far more sense than dogs.   There is
another fact which Mr. Smith himself used to mention
with no common pride.   Notwithstanding the gallant
manner in which he always rode, and never turned
from any fence that interfered between him and his
hounds, he never had a horse drop dead under him, or
die from the effects of a severe day's riding.   This was
a boast which no other master of hounds could make,
who had ever hunted half as long, or ridden half as
hard, as the squire of Tedworth.   Nevertheless, the
boast must be qualified by the circumstance, that it is
not every fox-hunter or master of hounds who could
afford a fresh horse as frequently as Mr. Smith.

We are reminded, by the mention of the name of
the late Lord George Bentinck, that this respected
nobleman lived on terms of intimate friendship with
the squire, by whom he was much admired for his
high character, his manly bearing, and his unswerving rectitude in matters connected with the turf.
By his influence Mr. Smith was persuaded to have
some brood mares at Tedworth, and for a short time
to be a member of the Jockey Club.   The squire,
however, soon declined this new pursuit ; he loved
the straightforward honesty of a fox-hunt, but observed that the chicanery of racing was ungenial to
him.   Nevertheless he once actually rode and won a
race.   This was on the Winchester course.   He had

put a hard-pulling raking horse, called "Spartacus," into the Hunters' Stakes there, who so overpowered his rider ("I think," said Mr. Smith, himself relating the anecdote, "it was young Buckle") that he bolted, and was consequently distanced. The squire challenged the winner for 50*l.*, owners to ride (Bob Lowth was the adverse jockey), and he won easily each heat. During the time he was a member of the Jockey Club, Lord George Bentinck wrote and asked him to come to Newmarket to support his Lordship on some intricate question relating to the turf. This Mr. Smith declined to do, alleging, as an excuse, his having been a member so short a time, and not wishing to identify himself with any discussions relative to racing, in which he did not profess himself an adept. Not long afterwards Mr. Smith invited his Lordship to hunt at Tedworth, and, as Lord George had then sold all his hunters, offered to mount him on Election, about A 1 of his whole stud. The reply was, "Dear Mr. Smith,—I have always been accustomed to drink out of a large cup, and cannot stoop to a little one. I decline hunting on another man's horse when I have no longer hunters of my own. Your letter reminds me that *you* are the *only* one of my father's old friends who, when solicited, would not support his son in his endeavour to reform the Augean stable." Mr. Smith had forgotten the incident, but it had remained "*altâ mente repostum*" in

the breast of his Lordship.   The anecdote is characteristic of both.   Lord George was a frequent visitor
at Tedworth, was a gallant rider, and could view a
fox (so said the squire) farther than any man living.
He once, during a fast run, charged Wilbury Park
pales on Wintonian, a racer who had never faced
timber before.   Fortunately they broke, and the
horse made a gap large enough for a flock of sheep
to pass through; but his rider escaped a fall.

CHAP. III.

HE REBUILDS TEDWORTH, AND GOES TO RESIDE THERE IN 1830. — DESCRIPTION OF HIS KENNELS AND STABLES. — MORE FAVOURITE HOUNDS. — THE GREAT ANNUAL MEET AT TEDWORTH. — HE REPRESENTS ANDOVER AND CARNARVONSHIRE IN PARLIAMENT. — SOME ACCOUNT OF VAENOL AND HIS ESTATES IN NORTH WALES. — SLATE QUARRIES OF LLANBERRIS.

> " Nec tibi cura canum fuerit postrema."   VIRG.
> " Quique sui memores alios fecere merendo."   VIRG.

DURING the period occupied in the rebuilding of Tedworth, viz. two years (from 1828 to 1830), Mr. Smith continued to reside at Penton. In the latter year he moved his establishment to the new mansion. During the previous season he had commenced his stables and kennels, which were built entirely after his own plan. They were spacious, airy, and every way well suited to the purpose for which they were designed. Every hunter had his loose box; he was never tied up, and thus had plenty of room to move about in. There was also a spacious covered ride, a furlong in circumference, for the horses to take their exercise in. The writer, on a visit to Tedworth in the autumn of 1845, saw fifty horses in the stables, including hunters, carriage-horses, and hacks, all in first-rate condition, and each apparently as familiar with the squire as a pet dog would be.* Among these he recollects that Nether-avon and Black Diamond excited his highest admiration.

The kennels are situated about ten minutes' walk from the house, and close to the Home Farm They were originally built by Mr. Smith on rising ground above the stables; but owing to the hounds constantly suffering from kennel lameness, although every precaution of draining, ventilation, and paving was resorted to, the situation or subsoil (chalk upon strong clay) was deemed unhealthy and condemned. Mr. Smith, with his usual discernment, had remarked that the lame hounds, when removed below the hill to his Home Farm, and turned into the calf-pens there, soon recovered. This induced him at once to fix on that spot, well sheltered by trees and buildings from the north and north-east, for the site of the present excellent kennels. He drew the design for them on half a sheet of paper, which was afterwards put to a scale, and carried out exactly according to the plan by his own carpenter and bricklayer. Passing up the shrubbery and skirting the edge of the farm-yard, you come at once upon a slope of undulating greensward, and here, under the eye of one of the whippers-in, scores of loose hounds might be seen taking their exercise. On the top of the hill, open towards the

* The name of each horse was in printed letters over his box.

south-west, ranged the kennels, four in number, and as snug in their accommodation as the greatest lover of hounds could desire. Here flourished Tomboy, Tarquin, Trimbush (of whom we have already spoken), Tigress, and Traffic, of Burton blood. Tomboy was notorious for always bringing home the fox's head, no matter how distant the kill. Those who were out that day will well recollect Traffic and the hunted fox rolling off the thatch of a house together, at the close of a quick run from Collingbourne Wood to Fosbury, and back to Dean Farm; while others will not forget the courage of Trimmer in lugging a marten cat out of a hurdle pile in Doyly Wood single-handed. A sporting farmer once seeing these, and numerous other hounds as good, running in a cluster and close behind their fox, exclaimed joyously, " They goes at 'un like my wether sheep into a tie of turnips, *all first.*" Mr. Smith at first had the flooring of his kennels paved with flint stones; but on one occasion, when his hounds were suffering from shoulder lameness, he found it necessary to move them so quickly that a roomy cart-shed was provided for them. The flooring of this shed was of chalk well rammed down, on the principle of the old Roman barn-floors mentioned in Virgil's Georgics, "*cretâ solidanda tenaci.*" Here the hounds soon recovered, and, upon the flint stones in the kennel being removed, a great deal of moisture was found collected underneath, although there was no land-spring near. This convinced the squire that Virgil was right, and from that time the yards of the kennels were laid with hard clay or chalk. The hounds were strangers to shoulder lameness ever afterwards. Their sleeping-apartments were raised four feet from the ground, each hound, like his master, going upstairs to bed. They were thatched with reeds, for the sake of warmth in winter and coolness in summer, each lodging-house being made to hold twenty couples of hounds. The yards annexed to the respective kennels are raised in the centre, with gutter bricks all around them, converging to the sides, so that the water, which is laid on by pipes with taps to them, is instantaneously carried off, and there is no underground drain near to catch and detain the moisture. Close by is the huntsman's house, so that all riot and disturbance are quelled immediately on any outbreak. The old cart-shed is still retained for young hounds, and as a place of litter for puppies. Adjoining the kennels is a spacious paddock enclosed all round with a lofty wall, in which the hounds can run at large when inspected by the huntsman or by strangers. Built into the wall about the centre of it is a pavilion, with a raised platform, and having a door of admission only on the outside, for the accommodation of ladies who come to see the hounds.

Let us cross from the kennels to the beautifully

smooth lawn in front of the dining-room at Tedworth.
The spectator, standing at one of the windows, looks
into an open part of the park, studded here and there
with noble timber. It is the first morning in November, somewhat dark and lowering, but the clouds,
sailing through the sky steadily from the south-west,
give indications of a good hunting-day. The leaf
has not yet wholly fallen, but the gust is sweeping
it in eddies from each group of trees over the stately
hall. The woods which fringe the distant hills are
clothed with their richest mantle of russet and gold.
The best pack in the kennel are already rolling themselves and disporting upon the grass; the huntsman
and whippers-in are not far off, splendidly mounted,
and, with their equipments, a sight to look at. In
every direction are pouring in horsemen of every age
and calling, coats of every colour, but the " pink "
far predominating, and a sprinkling of the loveliest
women in the world, either on horseback or in carriages. It is the opening meet of the season, and
Tedworth's hospitable mansion is thrown open to
every comer. In the midst is the squire on one
of his well-known steeds, to all cordial and affable,
for all a hearty welcome, for some a sporting
joke, for others a jovial laugh. Here may be seen
a throng of eager sportsmen, discussing with enthusiasm the prospects and pleasures of the season
now about to commence; there a group encircling

a lovely horsewoman, to be the subject of many a
toast by and by, when the claret circulates freely
after the toils and perils of the chase.   In the meanwhile what capital cheer within the hall, what barons
of beef, what interminable venison pasties!   Breakfast ended—and no superfluous time is wasted in
despatching it—away go the field to a wood not very
far off, near to which is the residence of one of the
keepers, whose pretty little daughter Mr. Smith is
accused of presenting not unfrequently with a new
dress, only because Reynard is always to be found
at home there.   Scenes like these gladden the heart,—
truly they deserve a better hand than ours to paint;
nevertheless it may be that more than one sportsman
will look at the copy, not without some " pleasures
of memory," for the sake of the original.

But although Mr. Smith was, at the period of his
life we are endeavouring to sketch, warmly devoted to
fox-hunting, and indeed made it his science, he was not
neglectful of the duties which, as a landed proprietor
and English country gentleman, he had to discharge.
He sat in Parliament for Andover for several years,
and up to the passing of the Reform Bill in 1832.
His politics were of the old Tory school, and, in consequence of his strenuous opposition to that measure,
he lost his seat.   While in the House of Commons,
he regularly attended the debates, and never lost an
opportunity of recording his vote for his party. · He

subsequently represented Carnarvonshire in more
than one Parliament, but his name is seldom found
in the debates. He was always more a man of action
than a man of speech, and his example might well be
followed by many of the legislators of the present
day, who discuss measures over and over again, long
after the nation has made up its mind about them,
and at the same time show no disposition to deduce
from their arguments any tangible and useful results.
Before railroads almost annihilated time and space,
Mr. Smith used frequently to hunt his hounds at Tedworth in the morning, and then post in his light
chariot with four horses to Westminster in the
evening, announcing to the field that he must be
allowed to meet at "twelve" next day. Having
voted in the division, he did not fail to be at the
covert side at the hour appointed.

It was at the time when he lost his seat for
Andover, viz. 1832, that, in consequence of the
riots which took place in that year, he raised a
corps of Yeomanry Cavalry at his own expense.
He was Captain, and the troopers were chiefly his
own tenants or farmers of the neighbourhood. They
were reviewed on one occasion in Tedworth Park
by the late Duke of Wellington, who spoke in
high terms of their efficiency and soldierlike
appearance. After the inspection and review, the
troops were entertained at Tedworth House. These

volunteers, who could well have helped to defend Old England against invasion, if necessary, were most of them good men over a country, and as such much more likely to do service in the time of emergency than a body of cavalry who are obliged to go round by the road, because they can neither skim ridge and furrow, nor clear a dark fence at the end of it. It is well known that the Duke himself, in choosing his aides-de-camp, always preferred fox-hunters, because he said they knew how to ride straight to a given point, generally had good horses, and were equally willing to charge a big place or an enemy.

We have spoken already of his Grace's fondness for fox-hunting. He was no less liberal in supporting it. On one occasion, when the subscription to a good pack fell off, and some lukewarmness showed itself among the contributors, being asked to give his assistance, he said laconically, " Get what you can and put my name down for the difference." That difference was 600*l.* a year! Yet, because the great Duke was a fox-hunter, no man doubted his master mind, as a general and a statesman. Mr. Smith's character has found its detractors because of his devotion to the sport. But, as has been well remarked, the very manner in which he was able to follow the pursuit, by his position, his wealth, his influence, and his superior talent as a master of hounds, served to raise the science of fox-hunting to that degree of perfection which places it beyond the reach of imitation in other countries, and serves to retain for it all its national characteristics.

Nevertheless, we shall see, in the course of this memoir, if we have not already made the discovery, that the squire was not a fox-hunter and nothing else. It was the man who did credit to the pursuit, rather than the pursuit which did credit to the man. In the management of his fine estates, both in Hants and Carnarvonshire, he found full occupation for the discharge of his duties as a country gentleman. His tenants vied with each other in eliciting commendation from their landlord, by the good order and husbandry with which their lands were farmed. They well knew that the acute and observing eye of the squire would quickly discover any signs of carelessness and bad management; while, at the same time, they took care that when the hounds came their way, there should not be any complaint of the want of foxes. During the panic created by free trade, at its commencement, a worthy farmer remarked to Mr. Smith, that the cultivation of corn would soon cease. "So much the better," observed the squire, smiling at his tenant's apprehension; "for then I shall hunt over a grass country." On another occasion, Lord Southampton said to a farmer who was too fond of over-riding his hounds, "I think, sir, that Sir Robert Peel's Bill will stop you, though *I* cannot."

The cottages in the village of Tedworth were models of neatness and comfort. These Mrs. Smith used herself to overlook, and the healthful and cheerful faces of the inmates well testified the care taken of them. No one could notice the tidy garden around each homestead, with the honeysuckle or rose festooning around its porch*, and the scarlet Pyracantha climbing its walls, without feeling that here that truly English picture was fully realised, of a country gentleman living in the midst of his people, spending his money, where it ought to be spent, upon his own estate, and winding himself closely into the attachment and hearts of his dependants.

At the time we speak of, the schools did not exist in the condition they are in now. These were added to the village in 1857. Not many hundred yards from the Hall is the old church, lying under the Downs, and with scarcely a habitation near it, except the house of the minister. From the churchyard, the eye, passing over the mansion, and the trees surrounding it in the valley, takes in a range of hills, stretching themselves one above another in the direction of Marlborough, and which the horseman may traverse for many miles without ever leaving the

* There is scarcely a cottage without its porch and double seat within.

turf. On this extensive domain there was scarcely
a man, woman, or child, who could not receive employment if they wanted it, and there was always a
fair day's wage for a fair day's labour. The summer
months were generally passed by Mr. Smith on his
property in Carnarvonshire, and he returned to Tedworth for cub-hunting in the early autumn. Let us
follow the squire and his establishment into North
Wales. He was for some time a member of the Royal
Yacht Club, and from the earliest period of life fond
of sailing. With nautical science he was quite as
familiar as he was with fox-hunting.

In the Straits of Menai, on the banks of which
stood Vaenol, his residence in Wales, he had ample
scope for indulging his sea-going propensities. Vaenol had originally belonged to the Williams family of
Fryars, Anglesea; but Griffith Williams, in the reign
of Queen Anne, having no issue, bequeathed the
estates to the crown. Her Majesty granted them to
the speaker of her House of Commons, and they thus
became the property of the Smith family, who had
had previously no connexion with the Principality.
The grounds slope down to the water's edge, and
Mr. Smith could step immediately on board his yacht,
which lay at anchor at no great distance from the
shore. Opposite Vaenol, on the other side of the
Straits, is Plas Newydd, in English, "the New
Palace," the property of the Marquess of Anglesea,

formerly graced by the presence of her Majesty when
Princess Victoria, and of her august mother.   Mr.
Smith himself lived there for some time, while
Vaenol was undergoing alterations.   The mansion is
now tenanted by the Dowager Lady Willougby de
Broke.   During the period of our gracious Queen's
residence at Plas Newydd, she condescended to visit
the squire of Tedworth at Vaenol, and presented him
with a portrait of herself and of the Duchess of Kent,
one of the few engraved only for private circulation.
This souvenir of the royal visit was highly prized by
Mr. Smith, and it filled a most conspicuous place on
the walls of the mansion to the time of his death.
His loyalty to his Queen had in fact something of the
romantic in it.   Her name is to be found at all points
of his immense property.   The handsome hotel at
Llanberris, from which the tourist commences his
toilsome ascent to the cloudy summit of Snowdon,
was built by him, and named Victoria ; that quarry
whence comes the green slate, now so much in fashion
for ornamental buildings, was for its superior quality
called Victoria ; three of the best steam-yachts of the
many he built, and of which we shall presently speak
more in detail, were named "Fire-Queen." Her Majesty
is said to have asked Mr. Smith why he called the
first of these the " Fire-Queen." The reply of the
veteran was characteristic. " An' it please your
Majesty, I had a yacht called the ' Fire-King,' which

was superior to any I had before: this is superior to
that, and I call her 'Fire-Queen.'"

At no great distance from Vaenol stands the port
of Dinorwic, formed by nature for security, but
considerably enlarged by Mr. Smith in 1828, and
now affording shelter in tempestuous weather to as
many vessels as are to be found passing up and
down the Menai Straits.   Here is safe anchorage for
sixty or seventy craft of two hundred tons burthen,
awaiting their cargoes of some of the best slate in
the world.   The mountain where this useful and
valuable material is to be found is owned on the one
side by Col. Douglas Pennant, and on the other by
Mr. Smith; they are quarrying away as fast as
they can to meet each other, though it will take a
century to do it.   It has the appearance of a colossal
plum cake, out of which two boys are each trying
to take the largest slice he can.   The harbour of
Port Dinorwic is beautifully situated in the very
centre of the straits, equidistant from the open sea
at Carnarvon Bay and from Puffin Island.   From
an eminence above the port are seen the magnificent
structure of Stephenson and Telford's more elegant
and graceful work.   Opposite is the pillar erected
to commemorate the gallantry of one of the bravest
of the house of Paget.   To the left, as the traveller
gazes up the straits in the direction of Orme's Head,
is the pretty town of Beaumaris, and immediately

above it the extensive woods encircling the noble mansion of Baron Hill. Nature has indeed been bountiful to the inhabitants of this picturesque locality. Here at every turn is abundant scope for the imagination of the painter and the poet in the dark overhanging masses of every shade and colour; while the man of business and commerce, as he stands at the door of the Victoria Hotel at Llanberris, hears with interest and admiration the incessant echo of the hammers, and watches the busy movements of the workmen, clinging apparently to the almost perpendicular sides of the cliffs. At the port the excellent arrangements for transporting and shipping the slates do not escape his notice; although he must be rather surprised to see " Duchesses " and " Countesses " so roughly handled.* The following accurate and graphic description of Mr. Smith's quarries has been furnished for this memoir by Mr. Millington, son of the gentleman who has for many years most ably and zealously superintended the works.

" The Dinorwic slate quarries are situated on a mountain called the 'Elidir' (one of the Snowdonian range, and contiguous to Snowdon), which rises about 2000 feet above the level of the sea : they derive their name of Dinorwic, or Dinorwig, from an ancient manor in which they are situated, and

---

* Slates known and honoured by these titles.

lie partly in the parish of Llanberris, and partly in that of Llandemilen, in the county of Carnarvon. The period at which slate was first found in these quarries is unknown, but the regular and systematic working commenced about sixty years ago, and they have been gradually increasing in extent. The great increase, however, has taken place since 1828, when the late Mr. Assheton Smith succeeded to the property at the death of his father. On entering into possession, he carried on the works in a most vigorous and enterprising manner, opened many fresh quarries, and extended those already in work, so that in the space of thirty years they have quadrupled in extent. There are now employed about 2400 men and boys; and the amount expended monthly in wages and materials exceeds 9000*l.*

" There are various descriptions of slates produced, varying in quality, as best or fine slate, seconds or strong slate; and also in colour, as grey or light blue, dark blue or purple, red, and also green; the last named, however, being found in but small quantities. The body of slate rock is of very considerable extent. The present workings (May 1859) cover a space of not less than one square mile; the highest elevation of the quarries now open is about 1500 feet above the level of the Llanberris lakes, and about 1800 feet above the level of the sea. The depth of the slate rock has never been ascertained, but it is supposed to be between 1500 and 2000 feet. The rock in these quarries has been worked to the depth of 300 perpendicular feet. The roofing slates are split and dressed in numerous sheds, situated on the rubbish banks adjoining the quarries. The slabs are manufactured at powerful steam and water-mills in the immediate neighbourhood. Convenient tramways, about twenty-three miles in extent, are laid along the various workings and quarry banks; upon these small waggons are run, into which the slates and slabs are loaded and taken to the inclines, whence they are let down by wire ropes to the railway terminus. The inclines are laid up the precipitous side of the mountain, and are eighteen in number, averaging six hundred feet in length. At the railway terminus adjoining the quarries, the small loaded waggons are placed upon large trucks (each holding four), and are then formed into trains, and drawn by locomotives to the shipping port. From the quarries to the port, the railway, called 'the Padarn Railway,' is rather more than seven miles in length, and was constructed by the late Mr. Assheton Smith at a very considerable outlay about the year 1843, solely for the purposes of the works. The place of shipment is a commodious harbour called 'Port Dinorwic,' a private port, used only for the shipment of slates from the Dinorwic quarries, and is situated in the

Menai Straits, half-way between Bangor and Carnarvon. It was commenced on a small scale by
the late Mr. Smith's father, but was enlarged and
extended to its present size by Mr. Smith himself,
who also added to it two commodious and convenient docks. About 120 vessels can lie alongside
the quays and in the docks, securely sheltered from
all winds. Slates are shipped largely from hence
to most of the sea-ports of England, Ireland, and
Scotland, to the Baltic and German ports, and exten-
sively to the United States of America. A branch
of the Carnarvon and Bangor railway connects this
port with the Chester, and Holyhead, and London
and North-western lines, by which means slates are
conveyed in large quantities to the manufacturing
and midland districts of England."

The genius that could invent and organise the
vast improvements recorded in the above narrative
must have been of no mean order; while we admire
the spirit and enterprise that thus furnished constant employment all the year round to so many
thousands. The tourist is permitted to ride up the
inclines, and thus to visit the quarries. This is
an adventure requiring no little nerve, for although
every precaution is taken to prevent danger, and
such is the strength of the machinery, that an accident has scarcely been ever known to occur; yet
the stoutest heart may well throb, as the traveller,

in making the ascent, looks down from midway up into the dark watery gulf of Llanberris, many hundred feet beneath him. This feeling will not be diminished in his descent, although made with the utmost care, and with no greater velocity than the ascent. The cable which serves to raise and let down the carriages is of many folds of twisted copper wire, and the weight of those coming down serves to raise those going up. This cable is no less than a thousand yards in length. There can be imagined no grander scene than is beheld from the railway leading to these inclines. Immediately in front is the majestic range of Snowdon, and a few miles distant to the right of the traveller, as he makes his pilgrimage upwards, is Bethgelert, famous for its being the centre of many a lovely valley, and for its romantic legend of the death of Gelert, most faithful of hounds:

> "And till great Snowdon's rocks grow old,
> And cease the storm to brave,
> The consecrated spot shall hold
> The name of Gelert's grave."

Quitting the harbour of Dinorwic, where thousands of slates are stacked in every direction ready for embarkation, we either mount immediately the first incline, at the top of which is the railway terminus, or taking the route across the open country, we pass through the centre of the slate district into the bowels of the black rock (Allt Dû), overhanging the Upper Lake of Llanberris.

On our arrival at the quarries we make the best use of our time, in acquiring information as to the mode in which the works are carried on. The slate is cut by piecework, the " bargainers," as they are called, taking each a certain number of feet in width, and to such a nicety can they blast the sides of the quarry, that they have been known to continue "on their lines" for twenty-five years without encroaching an inch on the adjoining bargainer's tenure. The steam-engine (by David Brothers, Sheffield) has been at work ten years, and not unfrequently both day and night, and yet it was never known to be out of order. The quarrymen have such faith in it that they affirm it would work just as well on slates as on coal or coke. The machine for dressing the slates, styled the guillotine, the invention of Morin, from the same country as came its formidable namesake, is almost as dangerous to handle; this instrument, after cutting away clean the four sides of the slate, pushes the latter from the block into the basket. Not far from the guillotine is the large graving tool for planing billiard tables. Every now and then the bugle sounds from the door of a small white hut, conspicuous about the centre of the mountain, not as at Tedworth, to cheer gallant steed and hound, but to warn the workmen and spectators that the blasting coil is about to be set fire to. Scarcely have they time to get behind the rocks, when splinters of slate are falling in all directions, and huge fragments of mountain are hurled into the lake below. The office of Mr. Ellis, the manager, has been made bomb-proof to prevent accidents. In July 1857, 220,000 tons were levelled at one blast from the Wellington quarry, and at a cost of only sixteen shillings. The blasting takes place once an hour, when grace, as it is called, is given to the men for ten minutes, during which each labourer is allowed to take out and light his pipe. Smoking is not permitted except at these intervals. A number of boys begin their education as future quarrymen in collecting the odds and ends of broken slate, picking out those pieces which may be useful, and wheeling them in their tiny carriages along a tramway to the huts, where they are clipped and turned to account. Occasionally a shout of glee is a sign that they have lit upon a piece of quartz, which they offer to visitors in exchange for copper. The number of tons annually carried away by the railway averages 1,200,000. The quarries abound with a vast number of workshops, where almost everything is manufactured " on the premises," from the first loaf the quarryman eats, to the slab which forms his gravestone, and tells in rude Welsh poetry his past good qualities and his future hope.

A large proportion of the young men now employed

upon the mountain were born almost in the quarries; some from the condition of daily labourers have risen to a considerable degree of affluence; others have emigrated to the gold fields of Australia ; where their skill in quarrying, and their hardy and temperate habits, have stood them in good service: while there are to be found those still at work among the slabs, who have returned with nuggets enough to buy mountain homesteads, and are industriously increasing their means by following their old employment. Like the inhabitants of all mountainous districts, the Welsh are ardent lovers of their own unconquered country, and whether accident, duty, or ambition casts their temporary lot in other lands, a home in their own locality is a vision they never lose sight of.

Mr. Smith had an excellent plan of encouraging integrity and good conduct among his workmen. About thirty years ago, he began the system of allotting portions of mountain to the most deserving. The selection according to merit was entrusted to the quarry manager already mentioned, who was born among them, and has held his office of trust for forty-five years. From eight to fifteen acres were meted out to each at a nominal rent, with the understanding that he should build a cottage for himself. In this way nearly two thousand acres of land are now under continuous cultivation, which formerly were covered with furze and heather. The occupiers are allowed to sell their estates to their fellow labourers: some few have availed themselves of this permission, but for the most part they remain on their little farms after ceasing to work, and enjoy in their old age a comfortable retirement. Mr. Smith was influenced by another motive in scattering the houses over the district, instead of collecting them into a large town. He thought that his men would incur less temptation to resort to the public houses after their day's work, especially in the dark winter evenings, if they had a long distance to go from their homes for the purpose of obtaining drink. This dispersion of his labourers has proved very successful. As we pass through the village of Llandinorwig. and onward through a locality dotted far and wide with the cottages of a rapidly increasing population, like sentinels encamped around the new church, we observe with pleasure the healthful and ruddy countenances of the children, and the neat appearance they everywhere present, even on working days. Each happy troop bears about it ample evidence that the parents are stayers at home.

When the present steward first began his duties, the number of workmen in the quarries amounted only to 300: at the present time they exceed 2000, and during the lifetime of Mr. Smith, not one of them was taken before the magistrates for dishonesty. Such a fact speaks volumes: it is a signal contradiction of the reproach often uttered, that kindness to

the poor meets with no return: it redounds to the
honour of the employer who rewarded in the manner
above mentioned the industry of his workmen, and to
that of the men, who thus profited by the advantages
held out to them.   It is a pleasing sight to behold
the groups of labourers on the mountain side at dinner time; scarcely a man of them all but has in his
brawny hand a newspaper or periodical wherewith
he whiles away his time until his hour of rest has
elapsed.   Intelligence has made ample strides in
these remote regions.   Mr. Smith's principle of education always was, to prepare a youth for the position
in society he was to fill when grown up to manhood.
He had the child of his labourer taught his duty to
God and man, and gave him sufficient learning to
enable him to discharge both duties efficiently; but he
always held, that the great mass of superfluous knowledge with which children are crammed in the present
day, only tends to fill their minds with ideas unsuited
to their station in society, and to render them discon-
tented with their condition.   This theory he reduced
to practice.   The elements of a Christian education
he furnished to his little colony in schools, built
upon his estate, and provided with teachers at his own
expense.   Not satisfied with this, he built a church
with free sittings for 600 souls, and considered one of
the handsomest in North Wales; also a parsonage
house, to which he annexed twelve acres of glebe land,

two more being given for a churchyard, and he moreover endowed the incumbent with a comfortable income. A fund is chargeable on the Welsh farms for necessary repairs. The consecration of the church took place on the 24th of September 1857, when a collation was given to upwards of five hundred people: the door of hospitality was open to all who chose to enter. The value of these donations amounts at the lowest estimate to 16,000*l*., the church and parsonage alone costing 8000*l*.

Mr. Smith was never known to refuse a site for church or chapel upon his land, if the request was made in a proper manner. An elder of the Calvinistic body has related that they never applied to him for a site for chapel or schools but it was at once and cheerfully granted. This was the more liberal as he was himself a staunch member of the Church of England. Both he and Mrs. Smith invariably went to church on foot, and made it a rule, except in case of illness, never to have either carriage or horse out on a Sunday. On one occasion, the squire was known to refuse a gift of land for church purposes; but in that case the over-officious citizens had plans drawn out, the site determined on, and estimates prepared before the lord of the soil was consulted, so that his refusal under such circumstances cannot be much wondered at. Dr. Cotton, the Dean of Bangor, who was much beloved and respected by Mr. and Mrs.

Smith, seldom resorted to him in vain for aid in works of charity.   On one occasion, being fond of a joke, as most Welshmen are, he asked him for an old pair of boilers.   Mr. Smith told him he had not got such a thing by him; and so the matter ended for the time. In a few weeks the dean went again, saying, " You have so many steamers, you must have an old pair of boilers you can give me," whereupon the squire said, " Come, Dean, tell me what you really want? what is it?"— and on the dean owning that he did not want the boilers, but the boilers' worth, a cheque for the required sum was immediately handed to him.

Mr. Smith was fond of taking parties from Vaenol to see the quarries, and always had his joke with the young ladies who inquired if it was not dangerous to ascend the inclines, by asking his agent, who frequently accompanied him, how long it was since the last accident.   His favourite spot on such occasions was the Braich quarry (Anglicè, arm of the mountain), which commanded a magnificent prospect of Llanberris Pass.   A signal was hoisted on the house, when he intended going from the port by the train. This was responded to from the top of the first incline, and a comfortable omnibus, with as much glass about it as could enable those within to see the most of the view, there awaited the arrival of his guests, and conveyed them along the edge of the lake, until they were obliged to dismount for the purpose of commencing the steeper part of the ascent. Close to the inclines, and nearly opposite Dolbadarn Tower, stands a pretty cottage, built by Mrs. Smith for the reception of their friends after the fatigues of their visit; here they found abundance of good cheer, as well as a most lovely prospect.

In the vicinity of the Llanberris quarries are the lakes of Llyn Peris and Llyn Padarn, only separated from each other by a narrow neck of land over which runs the road to the village; a small gurgling stream connects the two sheets of water; the railway, emerging from the mountains at the lower end of Llyn Padarn, takes its name from it. These lakes abound in that beautiful fish the char, to take which by rod and line has baffled the most talented disciples of Izaak Walton. The trout, which are also very numerous, do not here grow to any size, and, curiously enough, they are generally to be found of the same weight, and as level as a pack of fox-hounds. About four years ago twenty of these fish were caught at one haul in the engine-house reservoir, their combined weight being 22 lbs., and they were so exactly alike, that it was impossible to pick out the largest or the smallest; we were told they were as red and as good as salmon. These trout were taken more than 2000 feet above the level of the two large lakes, and the net in which they were caught is still to be seen hanging in one of the workshops. Dragging, however, or casting, is not the only sport which the quarrymen enjoy. Occasionally they come upon the drag of an otter, and then a most motley pack of otter hounds, followed by a field of eager hunters, all on foot, and armed with poles, expel the enemy of the finny tribe from his haunts, and the chase is ended in the lake, which, if the otter once gains, further pursuit is useless.

The entire region round about might very appropriately be called slate country; everything is slate, from the lofty chimney of the engine-house and the kitchen table of the cottage to the fences and gateposts of the fields, and the footpath itself, which marks out the traveller's track towards Snowdon. The sleepers used on the railway are blocks of slate, rough hewn for this purpose by quarrymen of advanced age, who can prepare the sleepers when they are no longer fit for any other work. Slate is uppermost in the mind of almost every man you meet. A stranger dining at the hotel at Bangor, and sitting next to a " native," who descanted on the merits of his district, was requested by him to pass the " slate " instead of the salt.

We cross over the road between the two lakes with Dolbadarn Tower, once the residence of Llewellyn, the last Prince of Wales of British line, close above us to the left, and pause for a few minutes to look up

the inky waters of Llyn Peris, one mile in length, to
the Pass of Llanberris, above which the frowning
mountains seem to stretch their shadowy arms across
to arrest the traveller in his course. At this moment
a large quantity of broken slates are thrown over the
rubbish heap, which projects far into the lake, and
the sound is as if all the crockery in the world has
been broken at once. The embankment from the
Wellington quarry threatens in time to reach the
opposite shore, and is terribly destructive of the
picturesque. In some parts this lake is forty fathoms
in depth. We are presently in the splendid saloon,
or coffee-room, of the Victoria Hotel, which neither
Mr. nor Mrs. Smith lived to see completed, mea-
suring fifty feet long by thirty-six wide, and lofty in
proportion. From hence to the top of Snowdon is
a distance of five miles, entirely over the Vaenol
estate — one half of the mountain belonged to Mr.
Smith, the other half is owned by Sir R. Williams
Bulkeley. The ascent is made with less labour to
the traveller from Llanberris than by way of Capel
Cerig or Beth Gelert. The windows of the hotel
command a fine view of the slate quarries; and as it
is now evening, and the works above have all at once
become silent, it is curious to watch the quarrymen
who live along the line of railway returning home.
This they accomplish by the aid of thirty velocipedes,

which are placed on the railway and worked by the
men themselves, by means of a windlass.   Each velocipede contains eight persons, and proceeding along
the line, in the direction of the Port, it deposits the
labourer at the nearest point to his respective dwell-
ling.   The last man remaining returns back towards
the quarry, to take up a fresh load, or leaves his
velocipede on the line until the next morning.
Formerly there were twenty-six boats upon the lower
lake to do the same duty, but since the railroad has
been made they have fallen into disuse.   The workmen
are classified in a threefold division, of quarrymen,
rockmen, and labourers; all are employed at piecework, and are paid their wages once a month,
though money is frequently advanced to them for fuel,
provisions, or blasting powder, which last they always
find for themselves.   Coals are delivered to them
along the line of railway, or at the foot of the quarries,
for those who reside in the higher district, free of
carriage, and at the lowest price.

This lengthened account of Mr. Smith's Welsh
property will, perhaps, be less interesting to the
sporting reader than what has been related of him
as a rider and a master of hounds.   But as the
object of this memoir is to describe him, not only
as a sportsman, but as fulfilling the duties of a
landed proprietor, a man of wealth and influence,

and a country gentleman, in an exemplary manner, it is hoped that that portion of it, which endeavours faithfully to delineate him in these capacities, will not be regarded as generally the least worthy of perusal. In the following chapter we shall examine his claims to be considered a man of practical science.

CHAP. IV.

HIS LOVE FOR SCIENCE AND SHIP-BUILDING. — HE BUILDS SEVERAL
SAILING AND STEAM YACHTS.— HIS CLAIM TO BE THE PRACTICAL
ORIGINATOR OF THE " WAVE LINE " CONSIDERED. — CLAIMS OF
MR. SCOTT RUSSELL.

> " Tu regere imperio populos, Romane, memento,
> Hœ tibi erunt artes."   VIRG.
> " Certare ingenio, contendere nobilitate."   LUCRET.

IN a letter from Mr. Robert Napier, the eminent
ship-builder of Glasgow, addressed to the compiler of
these Reminiscences in May of the present year, it
is stated that Mr. Smith first turned his attention
practically to the building of steam-vessels in 1829.
Mr. Napier prefaces his information with the following words:—" It will give me great pleasure if I can
be of service to you in regard to the late Mr. Assheton
Smith, for whom I entertained the highest respect on
account of his upright, kind, disinterested conduct in
all matters, and for his earnest and persevering exer-
tions to promote and improve steam navigation."

Before Mr. Smith communicated his design of building a private steamer to Mr. Napier, he had been for
many years a member of the Royal Yacht Club,
during which period he had built no fewer than five

sailing yachts. The last of these was the Menai. A proposition made by him to the club to admit steam-vessels to the privileges of the club was not favourably received, and some of the members went even so far as to taunt him with the insinuation that he intended to make any steamer he might build subservient to business purposes. Mr. Smith was, naturally enough, very indignant at so unjust an accusation, and subsequently withdrew his name from the club.

The history of the first steam-yacht he built, also called the Menai, shall be told in Mr. Napier's own words. "In the year 1829, I received a letter from Mr. Smith (at that time a stranger to me) requesting me to meet him at his house near Andover (not Tedworth*), which I did. He then informed me he had quarrelled with some of the members of the Royal Yacht Club, and was determined to leave the club, and build a steam-yacht; but that Mrs. Smith was very much against his doing so, and that *I must* overcome the objections to steam. To this I demurred, as I had never seen Mrs. Smith. He repeated, *I must do it.* At that moment dinner was announced, and I was introduced to Mrs. Smith. During dinner, Mr. Smith made many judicious remarks about steam and steam-vessels, others the

* He remained at Penton till 1830, at which time the house at Tedworth was completed.

reverse — the latter I explained when he was wrong. This was the only thing I did to overcome Mrs. Smith's objections.   Before parting, he asked me to come in the morning to breakfast (from Andover), which I did.   Mr. Smith then decided on building a steam yacht, with copper boilers, and gave me the order, saying, when I wanted money he would send it.   This vessel cost him about 20,000*l*., and during its construction he sent money as wanted; but he never came to see it, nor did he send any one, but left the whole to myself till she was delivered to him at Bristol.   What struck me most in this and the many other transactions I had with Mr. Smith, was the complete confidence he placed in me from first to last, to which I responded by doing everything I could to meet his wishes, and on the lowest terms I could, as I knew he did not build his vessels for mercantile purposes, but purely for the improvement of steam navigation.   So sensible was Mr. Smith that I wished to serve him in the most liberal manner, that he seldom would look at my accounts beyond the sum total.   This I did not like at first, as I knew he was very particular in his business dealings with others.   As another proof of his kindness and confidence, I may mention that he more than once volunteered to become my security when I was making heavy contracts for vessels or machinery with the Government or East India Company.   The fol-

lowing are the dates, names, tonnage, and power of
the eight steam-vessels supplied by me to Mr. Smith,
viz. :—

Date.	Names of vessels.		Tons.		Horse power.
1830.	Menai	about	400	. .	120
1838.	Glow-worm . .	„	300	. .	100
1840.	Fire-King . .	„	700	. .	230
1844.	No. 1. Fire-Queen	„	110	. .	30
1845.	No. 2. Ditto . .	„	230	. .	80
1846.	No. 3. Ditto . .	„	300	. .	120
1849.	Jenny Lind . .	„	220	. .	70
1851.	Sea Serpent . .	„	250	. .	80

"In 1843 I built for him the Water Cure, a very small
iron sailing vessel with two sliding keels. It is but
justice to state that every one of the foregoing vessels
was constructed entirely according to Mr. Smith's
own designs, and that with the exception of the Water Cure they were all successful, and realised the
objects he had in view. The Menai and Fire-King
were built of wood, all the others of iron. The
Menai had three keels, thus;
this was to prevent rolling,
which it did to a great extent.
Mr. Smith was always for
hollow water lines, and was
determined to prove their value on a large scale for
sea-going steamers. For this purpose he ordered the
Fire-King (1840) to be built according *to his own
model*, with long very fine hollow water lines. This
vessel was built at the Duke of Rutland's ship-

*Midship
Section*

building yard at Trorn, and lay on the stocks for about two years, during which time she was visited by many ship-builders and others interested in steam-vessels, by whom the model was uniformly condemned. After she was finished the speed and the ease with which she went through the water astonished every one ; and while the vessel's success wrought a complete change in the minds of all, it fully established the value of Mr. Smith's lines for all vessels, especially where great speed is required. I call them Mr. Smith's lines, for, although Mr. Scott Russell claimed them as his, I know that Mr. Smith, in 1829, wanted the Menai built with hollow lines, and that the Fire-King was the *first* steam-ship that practically proved the value of hollow water lines for great speed, &c." *

In this very interesting account given by Mr. Napier, we find him fairly and honourably acknowledging that, in planning these several vessels, he did but carry out Mr. Smith's designs; and this is the more extraordinary as, even allowing that the latter had taste and capacity theoretically for scientific pursuits, the practical application of his knowledge

* Mr. Napier says in another letter, " Mr. Smith had natural abilities of a very high order, with intuitive knowledge of a most varied and extensive kind, which, without any pretension to scientific acquirements, seldom, if ever, failed in enabling him to gain the objects he had in view. In everything his aim was to be the best and have the best."

to so intricate and delicate a subject as the construction of steam-vessels and their arrangements would almost seem impossible. It is certain that long previous to the building of the Fire-King Mr. Smith had studied the question of resistance to the waves by the prows and keels of vessels; and he used in conversation (for it was a favourite subject with him) to describe the difference of the hollow water lines from the old system of ship-building, by holding his two hands back to back. "This," said he, "illustrates the hollow water lines, whereas this," placing them palm to palm, and slightly bending the fingers, "exhibits the usual mode;" and he added that his first conception of the principle had been the result of observation made by him when a boy at Eton.

The question of priority in this discovery has been somewhat warmly discussed. There is no doubt but that Mr. Scott Russell obtained a prize from the Royal Society of Edinburgh in 1838 for a paper written by him, and published in the Transactions of the society for the preceding year. It is no less certain that he had built an experimental iron vessel in 1835, seventy-five feet long, called the Wave, to test the value of "wave" lines, as applicable to ship-building. But the Wave was never intended for practical purposes; nor do we find, until the success of the Fire-King, in 1840 (she was laid down in 1838), was

fully demonstrated on trial, that even so extensive
and eminent a ship-builder, and one who could not
have to wait long for opportunities to test the practical value of his theory, ever ventured to build a
vessel upon the new principle.   The fact appears to
be, that the discovery of the theory dates antecedently
to Mr. Scott Russell.   Mr. Smith always maintained
that he was cognisant of it long before he made the
experiment with the Fire-King.   He had, at all
events, previously to this altered the bows of one of
his sailing yachts, viz. the Menai; and it was his
confidence of success after this trial which induced
him to risk so large an expenditure on the Fire-
King, which, had the vessel been condemned, would
have been almost entirely thrown away.

We find, however, that as far back as 1830 the theory
of hollow water lines was tested on the Scotch canals
in much the same way as Mr. Scott Russell afterwards
experimented.   In 1830 Mr. Wood, of Port Glasgow,
constructed a boat for the Paisley and Ardrossan
Canal on the "hollow line" principle *forward;* and
in the same year Mr. Brown, boat-builder, of Brown
Street, Glasgow, built two for the Clyde and Forth
Canal on the same plan.   This was four years
before Mr. Scott Russell, in a letter which we now
proceed to give, says that he discovered the wave of
translation.   It is probable that the attention of
scientific men had been directed to this question for

some time before the experiments were applied to the Scotch canal boats; that Mr. Smith and Mr. Scott Russell, both men of great sagacity and practical talent, saw, it may be at the same period, but without communication with each other, the soundness of the theory projected. Mr. Scott Russell was the author of several valuable papers, and built a model vessel to demonstrate the principle; but Mr. Smith was the first to show, by the example of his sailing yacht Menai and of the Fire-King, that the superiority of the hollow water lines was an established fact. So little apprehensive was Mr. Smith of the failure of his plan that he sent a challenge to Bell's Life, to the effect that the Fire-King (whose speed had not been tried at that time) should run against anything then afloat from off Dover Pier, round the Eddystone Lighthouse and back, for 5000 guineas, or more money if required, the challenge to remain open for three months that the Americans might see it, and referring to the editor of Bell's Life, if accepted. That challenge was not accepted, and not a farthing would the editor charge for inserting so gallant an offer. On the first trial of the Fire-King in the Garloch, Mr. Scott Russell was on board, and was among those who expressed his admiration of her lines, and of the way she went through the water. In 1857 Mr. Smith, hearing that Mr. Scott Russell had claimed what he always called *his* lines, authorised Mr. Napier to ascertain upon what ground he rested that claim. Mr. Napier wrote according to Mr. Smith's direction, and the following was Mr. Scott Russell's reply:—

"37, Great George Street, Westminster,
"May 6, 1857.

" My dear Sir,—I wish you had sent me Mr. Assheton Smith's letter, as I should like to have known exactly what he now thinks on the subject of your letter, because his own statements to me personally have never amounted to any claim for himself of priority over me, or of my having taken anything from him. On the contrary, what he has stated to me is this, that he had long entertained a belief that hollow water lines were the best, but that he had never been able to try the experiment until the first trial of the Fire-King, in 1839, and this was after he had seen a full account of my 'lines' published in the Athenæum. You, on the contrary, seem to think that I had derived my knowledge of the subject through being present at the trial of the Fire-King, in 1839. I am glad you have written to me on this subject, because you must, in your own mind, have been doing me great injustice in supposing that I learned anything at the trial of the Fire-King that was new to me; on the contrary, I was delighted with the Fire-King, as an independent proof made by other parties of the advantage of hollow water lines. I have therefore referred back to the records of my early proceedings, which were published at the time in the Transactions of the Royal Society of Edinburgh, and also in the accounts of the Proceedings of the British Association for the Advancement of Science; and I find the following dates established beyond dispute:—

"'1834—I discovered the wave of translation in the summer of 1834, and I gave an account of its nature to the British Association at their meeting in Edinburgh in that year. 1835—I commenced the building of my first vessel on the wave principle in 1834, and completed it in 1835. It was an iron vessel 75 feet long, and was called The Wave, 1835. In 1835 I tried this " wave vessel" against three other vessels at equal speeds, and proved her resistance to be less than any of them.' I had this vessel moved at seventeen miles an hour, and I find the following record of the first trial of the wave vessel in 1835: 'It is a remarkable fact, that even when deeply laden and when urged to a velocity of seventeen miles an hour, there is no spray, no foam, no surge, no head of water at the prow, but the water is parted smoothly and evenly asunder.'

" I communicated these results publicly to the meeting of the British Association for the Advancement of Science, at Dublin, in the same year, 1836.

In this year I built an iron steam-vessel one hundred and twenty feet long by twelve feet wide and of thirty-horse power, on the wave lines, with numerous transverse bulk-heads, and with longitudinal stringers, and without frames. This vessel possessed the same qualities of perfectly smooth passage through the water, and of least resistance. From this time I made no further trials for my own satisfaction, but considered the wave principle established as a permanent truth. I reported the results to the meeting of the British Association, 1837. In April of this year, a full account of the wave principle, with drawings of the lines and the details of experiments, was published in the Transactions of the Royal Society of Edinburgh, 1838. In this year the large gold medal of the Royal Society was awarded to me for the foregoing paper. Now, if you will be good enough to refer to the above paper, which you will find in the College Library, you will there see the engraving of the vessel called The Wave; you will see the long hollow bow, the full after-lines, and the greatest section abaft the middle, and all the qualities of least resistance and of least disturbance, clearly and unmistakeably given, along with most accurate and laborious proofs by actual experiment of the true measure of resistance at various speeds up to seventeen miles an hour, made in 1834. When you have duly considered all this, I shall hope to

receive from you a statement that hitherto you
have done me *less than justice*, doubtless from not
possessing the means to verify dates.   That, however,
is no reason why I should do Mr. Assheton Smith
injustice.   He has informed me that he had for many
years believed that hollow water lines were best.
He assures me that he did so long before he saw any
published account of my experiments.   Whenever I
have had occasion to give the history of the progress
of the wave principle, I have mentioned Mr. Smith's
construction of the Fire-King, as a confirmation
of the truth of the wave principle, and as having
additional value from its being made by an independent party.   In return for these dates I have given
you, you will oblige me if you will look up the exact
date of the first trial of the Fire-King, at which
I was present.   I know it was 1839-40, but you have
the means of being quite exact.   Hoping to show
you the Big Ship when you come to London,

" Believe me to be

" Most truly yours,

" J. Scott Russell."

This letter was forwarded by Mr. Napier to Mr.
Smith, by whom it was returned to him with a letter
dated Tedworth, May 13th, 1857, in which he says,
" Mr. Scott Russell's letter *surprises me excessively*,"
and refers to the presence of the latter at the Fire-

King's trial.   There the matter rested, as far as Mr.
Smith was concerned, for he adds, "I'll take no further
trouble in the matter."   But an able letter was inserted
in the Times by his friend Mr. John Drummond,
in which Mr. Smith's claims to be considered the practical inventor of the hollow lines was established.
After the death of Mr. Smith, his widow, whose sole
interest and wish appeared to be to vindicate the
memory of her husband from the unjust aspersions
which had been cast upon him as regarded his general
pursuits, and feeling that full credit had not been
publicly given to him for his scientific improvements
in ship-building, applied, only two months before her
death, to Mr. Napier for a copy of the correspondence
which had taken place in 1857.   Hence Mr. Scott
Russell's letter just cited came into the possession of
the writer of this memoir, together with the one from
Mr. Assheton Smith, from which we have just given
an extract, and also with a letter from Mr. Napier
himself to Mrs. Assheton Smith, which we will now
proceed to transcribe :—

"West Shandon, 4th April, 1859.

"Dear Mrs. Smith,—Your much esteemed kind
letter of the 26th ult. I duly received, but could not
till this morning lay my hands on the accompanying
correspondence in 1857, regarding Mr. Scott Russell's
claims to the hollow lines of the Fire-King.   There

are two of the letters. I cannot find Mr. Smith's first letter requesting me to write to Mr. Russell, and the copy of the letter I did write. There is, however, enough to show your friend how matters stand with Mr. Scott Russell. All that Mr. Smith says to me about the trial of the Fire-King, in his letter of 13th May, 1857, is quite true, and I am sure Mr. Lloyd, the Admiralty chief engineer, who was on board at the trial, would corroborate the same. You will notice from Mr. Scott Russell that he claims the merit of the hollow lines, and that in 1834 he had read some papers on the subject before the British Association, and had also had a vessel, seventy-five feet long by six feet broad, built and experimented upon, &c. All this may be true, that these *theoretical* experiments had been tried; but so far as known to me, I never heard of a single *practical* result that ever flowed from these scientific experiments; and although Mr. Scott Russell says Mr. Smith had seen an account of his lines in the Athenæum, I never heard Mr. Smith say so, except with great disapprobation of Mr. Russell attempting to say the hollow lines were his plan.

"I am certain that hollow lines were a favourite plan of Mr. Smith long before he ever built a steam-yacht; for when contracting for the Menai steam-yacht, he told me that he had put a new bow with hollow lines on to his sailing yacht the

Menai, which had increased her speed greatly, and
he wished the same kind of bow put into the steamer.
If the plan of this new bow that was put on the
Menai could be got from the ship-builder it would
settle the matter at once, I think, in favour of Mr.
Smith for hollow lines, and that he wished them introduced into his steam-yachts before the Fire-
King.   On that occasion, however, Mr. Wood, the
ship-builder, being opposed to hollow lines, and Mr.
Smith at that time having had no experience of steam-
vessels, gave in to Mr. Wood, and adopted the lines he
recommended. But when Mr. Smith decided on building the Fire-King, he resolved the lines should be
hollow, according to his own plan, and she was built
exactly according to his views, with sharp hollow lines.
His plan being in opposition to anything that had been
done, created a great sensation among ship-builders
and scientific people, many of whom inspected the
vessel while building; and, singularly enough, almost
everyone condemned the plan, and continued of that
opinion till the day of her trial on the Garloch,
when her unexpected great success changed not only
the opinions but the practice of all connected with
steamers ; for from that day a rapid change took
place in the form of all steamers requiring speed, by
giving them hollow instead of round lines, &c.
From all that I know of these hollow lines, I am
decidedly of opinion that the *theory* of them may

belong to *this* or *that* person; *but that the practical
introduction and adaptation of hollow water lines to
steamers entirely belong to your late husband*, and
cannot, I think, be honestly gainsaid by any one.
Such being the fact, I would advise that the *theorists*
be allowed to fight for the honour of discovering the
lines, which I know does not belong to Mr. Scott
Russell. If I can be of any further use in this
matter, it would give me great pleasure to receive
your commands.

> "I am, dear Madam,
>
> > "With most sincere regard,
> >
> > > "Yours respectfully,
> > >
> > > > "R. NAPIER."

The following letter from Sir Roderick Murchison
ascribes originality of invention to both Mr. Assheton
Smith and Mr. Scott Russell, and thus analyses the
merits of each claimant:—

> "16, Belgrave Square, Nov. 25th, 1859.

"My dear Sir,

"In your letter of the 5th of November you
seek to obtain my opinion on the scientific knowledge
possessed by the late Mr. Thomas Assheton Smith,
and particularly as respects the discovery of the
'wave principle' in ship-building, which he claimed
as well as Mr. J. Scott Russell.

" In reply, let me first say that, when my old friend and myself were associated in Leicestershire, about forty years ago, neither of us talked much on any subject save 'the noble science,' in the pursuit of which Tom Smith had then been long '*facilè princeps.*'

" But when, after a quarter of a century of stone-breaking on my part, our intimacy was renewed, and I visited him both among his slate rocks of Carnarvon and at his seat in Hampshire, he often proved to me in conversation, that he could well handle, and even master, scientific subjects after his own shrewd practical manner.

" Among these subjects he spoke of his having been the first to carry out what he considered to be the wave line form in ship-building. His attention was, as he assured me, called to this form by reflecting upon the simple experiment pointed out to him, when he was a boy at Eton, by Mr. Walker, the lecturer on natural philosophy,— that when a flat stone was thrown into the Thames it made a gentle curve in sinking to the bottom of the river.

" Assuming that, in this case, the stone took the line of least resistance in water, he inferred, that the nearer he could approach to such a curve in the form of ships, the greater would be their speed. Following out his conviction he made, as his yachting acquaintances well know, many a costly experiment, and at length attained what he considered to be perfection.

"Whilst, however, there can be no doubt that Mr. Thomas Assheton Smith worked out this result entirely by his own ingenuity and indomitable perseverance, it is now admitted, I believe, by men of science that Mr. J. Scott Russell is the person who, by analysing the nature, forms, and movements of waves, arrived by philosophical induction at the correct application of the 'wave principle' to ship-building. The peculiar form which he has applied to steam and sailing vessels was, in truth, the result of very extensive experimental investigations into the theory of waves and the forms of ships, made during many years at the cost of the British Association for the Advancement of Science; the details of these enquiries being published in the Transactions of that body; the most important reports having been made in the years 1837 and 1844. Even, however, as early as 1834 Mr. Scott Russell read a memoir on hydrodynamics before the Association, to show, that the theory of the resistance opposed by fluids to the motion of floating bodies was in a very imperfect state; and in the following year he brought before us an account of a new form for the construction of ships, by which they should experience least resistance by the water in their passage through it. Again, in 1843, his views were illustrated and supported by 20,000 observations made on more than one hundred vessels of different shapes, accurate drawings of all of which were then exhibited.

"The principle established by these experiments led Mr. Scott Russell to fix upon the wave form, or that of least resistance. This form, however, is not constant, and its contour must be varied in accordance with certain rules to suit the velocity required. The author then observes, 'there is a second point in the wave system which is another element of its general usefulness; it partakes of the nature of a mathematical maximum or minimum. It is the peculiarity of a maximum and a minimum that deviations on either side of it to a moderate extent occasion deviations of magnitude that are comparatively very small. Thus it is that the wave line being considered the curve of least resistance, there are near to it an infinite number of approximate curves which are curves of small resistance, though not of least resistance, and out of them the constructor is free to choose those which shall best accomplish any other object at the sacrifice of the smallest amount of resistance.'

"'To the scientific investigator,' he adds, 'it gives precisely that latitude which he desires, to leave him free to work out the intentions of the owners and the uses of the ships he may have to build.'

" From what has been stated it would appear that the original thought and successful experiments of Thomas Assheton Smith, and the elaborate scientific enquiries and deductions applied by Scott Russell, stand on grounds widely separated from each other.

    " Believe me to be, dear Sir,
     " Yours very truly,
      "RODERICK I. MURCHISON.

" P.S.—Being wholly unskilled in ship-building, I cannot say anything on the hollow lines of Mr. Assheton Smith's vessels, on which he much prided himself. "

This question of the " lines " has occupied a considerable space, but is valuable as illustrating the character of Mr. Smith, and the inflexible firmness of purpose and self-reliance with which he prosecuted his plans. What remains to be told is even more remarkable. He was the originator of the gun-boats now generally introduced into the English and French Navies. Had Mr. Smith's advice and suggestions been taken advantage of when first offered, we should not have made the absurd spectacle we did, when lying helplessly idle off Cronstadt during the Russian war.

Some years ago, when the Duke of Wellington was staying at Tedworth, Mr. Smith communicated to the

great Captain his notions respecting gunboats. The
Duke listened, as he always did, with attention to the
squire's remarks, but gave no opinion at the time
respecting the subject of them. Next morning, as
they were both walking on the terrace after breakfast, the Duke said, " Smith, I have been thinking
that there is a good deal in what you said last night
about those gunboats, and I should advise your
writing to the First Lord of the Admiralty," then
Lord ———, which Mr. Smith accordingly did, but
received no answer. Some time after, when walking down Regent Street, he met the First Lord,
whom he knew personally, and asked him, in the
course of conversation, if he had received his letter
containing suggestions for the introduction of gun-
boats. The First Lord replied that he had, but that
the Admiralty could not pay attention to all the
recommendations made to them. Upon this, Mr.
Smith took off his hat, and turning away from him
with a stately bow, observed, " What His Grace the
Duke of Wellington has considered worthy of attention, I think your Lordship might at least have condescended to notice."

Yet within ten years from this interview, one fleet
of our formidable " vixen craft " is at sea, and another is being fitted out for service. Little perhaps
did the spectators, who proudly gazed not long
since upon the goodly swarm of these dark hulls at

Spithead, know that the projector of them was a fox-hunter, and that to a fox-hunter's clear head and far-seeing eye was the gallant Wildman mainly indebted for "the single little vessel" (the Staunch) with which he demolished four large junks in the Chinese seas. Yet it has been said that Mr. Smith was a fox-hunter and nothing more. The verdict of true Englishmen will be very different. His motto in many pursuits was, "Deeds not words." He did not make long speeches for the good of his country, but many a record of silent worth will place him high on the list of its benefactors.

CHAP. V.

GREAT MEET AT ROLLESTON IN 1840.— HEALTH OF MRS.
ASSHETON SMITH.—HE BUILDS THE GREAT CONSERVATORY.—
TRIES HYDROPATHY.—ANECDOTE OF THE FOX-HUNTER WHO
TRIED IT.—WORCESTER AND PORTHDYNLLAEN RAILWAY.—HE IS
FINED FOR AN ASSAULT.—HE HUNTS THE TEDWORTH HOUNDS
HIMSELF UNTIL A SHORT PERIOD BEFORE HIS DEATH.

> " Ruunt equites et odora canum vis."   VIRG.
> " Veteris stat gratia facti."   VIRG.

FROM 1830 to 1856 — viz. to the period of rather less
than two years before his death—Mr. Smith continued
to hunt his hounds regularly at Tedworth, generally
until the latter end of March, when the heat and the
London season made him hang up his hunting whip
till the autumn. His summers he spent at Vaenol, or
on board his yacht.

In 1840, he went into Lincolnshire on a visit
to Sir Richard Sutton, who had for some time
been disabled from following his favourite sport by a
severe accident. He was requested by Mr. Greene
of Rolleston, one of his best pupils in his Leicestershire days, to take his hounds once more into his
old country on his way thither, Mr. Hodgson, who
then hunted that country, placing the best fixture
at his disposal in the handsomest manner. Mr. Smith

accepted the invitation, and it would be vain to endeavour to commemorate the scene which took place when he met the field at Shankton Holt on Friday the 20th of March. More than two thousand horsemen were assembled. Men of the highest birth and station, men who had served their country with deeds of most daring gallantry by sea and land, men who in political or social life were the most brilliant in repute, thronged to do honour to the first fox-hunter of the day. They had come from remote counties, and more were pouring in along the grassy slopes and vales, or skirting the well-known gorse covers. As Dick Christian remarked, "the first lot were at Shankton Holt when the tail end wern't out of Rolleston gates." Cold must have been the heart of him who could behold without joyous emotion the crowds of grey-headed horsemen hurrying forward to shake hands with their old friend and fellow-sportsman, each calling vividly to memory some scene where he had acted the most conspicuous part. More than twenty years had rolled away since he had resigned the lead in that magnificent country. There had been splendid riders since his day; and while time had thinned the ranks of the veterans, younger men had either achieved or were achieving fame — Frank Holyoake, now Sir Francis Goodricke, well known for his splendid feats on Brilliant, Colonel Lowther, Lord Wilton, Lord Archibald Seymour, George Payne,

Little Gilmour, Lord Gardner, George Anson (*nemo ex hoc numero mihi non donatus abibit*), and a host of sportsmen well deserving of the reputation they had won in many a fearless exploit by "flood and field," but who were strangers to the doings of this hero of the Quorn, except through anecdotes familiar to them as "household words."

In the meantime the hounds were there, as fine a pack as in days of yore, when the squire's well-known "Hold hard!" or his more emphatic "Hi, hi!"* checked those who pressed too eagerly to the front. After some little delay a fox was found, but the finest huntsman in the world could never have hunted him. The whole country for miles around was studded with men and horses, the people having thronged on foot from all parts to see so grand a spectacle. What must have been the feelings of him to whom this cordial and memorable greeting was given? As far as hunting went, he for once had no sport; but deeply touched and gratified with his reception, he made light of the disappointment, and, as Dick Christian observed, "was quiet throughout the day." It was a great holiday, and as such written with red ink in the sportsman's calendar,

---

* It is said, in allusion to Mr. Smith's manner, which on this day was somewhat subdued by the warm greeting of his friends, that Mr. Haines, an old sportsman who always looked after Glen Gorse, remarked: "Ah, there is the old Hi, hi! but, alas! the *hemphasis* is wanting."

and ever afterwards mentioned with delight and enthusiasm by the old stagers of the Quorndon, the
Pytchley, the Cottesmore, Atherstone, and every
county for fifty miles round. Many of these had followed him when leading the van over Leicestershire,
or had ridden by his side in the front rank with the
Pytchley in Northamptonshire. The lines written
on one of the best of his hunters were not yet forgotten : —

> " On Ajax, a nag well in Leicestershire known,
> See the gallant Tom Smith make a line of his own :
> Though in dirt fetlock deep, he ne'er dreams of a fall,
> And in mounting the hill, why he passes them all."

They called to mind the far-famed exploits of
Dick Knight, when each country drew its parallel
between its favourite huntsman. Perhaps a little of
the ancient jealousy still remained, well described in
the following couplets, which referred to the squire's
father, who hunted with the Pytchley ; but on this
day, at all events, " the renowned Tom " was incontestably without a rival.

> " Now Dick Knight and Smith Assheton we spy in the van,
> Riding hard, like two Furies, to catch as catch can ;
> ' Now, Egmont,' says Assheton ; ' now, Contract,' says Dick,—
> ' By Jove, those proud Quornites shall now see the trick.'"

That such a compliment should have been paid to
the quondam master of the Quorn is the more remarkable, as he cannot be said to have been altogether per-

sonally popular either in Leicestershire or generally in
the hunting field.   There is no doubt that he wanted
the " *suaviter in modo* " which commended the
leadership of Lord Foley, Mr. Meynell, Sir Bellingham Graham, Sir Harry Goodricke, and others ; and
therefore by those who did not know the sterling
qualities of the head and heart which were encased
in this somewhat rough exterior, he had been more
admired than liked.   Was then, asks Nimrod, the
compliment paid to Mr. Smith exclusively, or in
part, to the noble diversion of fox-hunting ?   To
Mr. Smith entirely, he replies unhesitatingly to his
own question.   It was a spontaneous testimony to
the pre-eminence of an individual, and a day appointed to do him honour, rather than the public
celebration of a national sport.

Dick Burton gives a characteristic account of this
grand event.   " In the year 1840 I left Tedworth
with Mr. Assheton Smith's hounds for the great day
at Rolleston.   I went to Mr. Drake's kennel the
first day.   On the second I arrived at Mr. Hodgson's kennel, at Oadby, with the hounds.   On Friday,
the 20th March, met at Rolleston.   The day was
almost a failure as far as scent went.   We did not
find a fox until four o'clock, and then the scent was
bad : one hour and twenty minutes, and we lost him
pointing for Rockingham Castle.   Upwards of two
thousand people were out, and among them Prince

Ernest, brother to the Prince Consort (he had come over from Deane, the seat of the Earl of Cardigan). There never was such a glorious meet, and never will be again. One little incident I will mention. The horse Antwerp, which Mr. Smith intended to ride, got some skin knocked off his hips going by the train. I told Mr. Smith of the accident, as he was disfigured. He said, 'I will ride him and no other; can't you get some paint of the same colour?' So I did, and painted the place, and he did ride the horse that day. I rode a grey horse called Jem Crow, which Mr. Smith bought out of the New Forest. On Saturday, the 21st, I went to Sir R. Sutton's kennel, at Burton, with the hounds. We hunted five times, and killed four foxes. On Tuesday, April the 7th, the Duke of Rutland gave Mr. Smith a day in his country. We met at Ropsley Rice Wood, and had a very good day, but did not kill. On Thursday, the 9th, I went with the hounds to Lord Lonsdale's kennel at Cottesmore : he gave Mr. Smith one day. On Saturday, the 11th, we met at Owston Wood, and had a good day's sport, but got beaten. We had very large fields out every day. On Monday, the 13th, I started with the hounds back to Mr. Drake's kennel; and on the 14th reached Ted-worth. I had not much rest."

Dick Burton adds the following particulars respecting his master's and his own career in Leicester-

shire : " I lived with Mr. Smith at Quorn ten years.
I left him before he left Quorn. I then went to live
with Mr. Osbaldeston, and staid with him twelve
years ; and then I came back again to Mr. Smith
at Penton. I lived with him altogether twenty-two
years. The following horses were Mr. Smith's favourites when he hunted Leicestershire : — Minister,
Lazarus, Tom Thumb, Robin Hood, Shacabac, Gift,
Agonistes, Penknife, Gadsby, Newmarket, Old Jack-
o'Lantern, Young Jack-o'Lantern, Fitch, and Charlotte Lantern. I do not know what were his best
horses in Lincolnshire. There has not been so good
a sportsman at Quorn since Mr. Smith left, although
Mr. Osbaldeston was a first-rate sportsman, and I
think had one of the best packs of hounds I ever saw
or followed over any country : they were as stout
as the day was long, there was no tiring of them.
The grey horse that I stand by, in the picture painted
by Mr. Ferneley*, was called The Big Grey. In the
small picture at Tedworth †, my brother Will is
without his coat, and I think stands with a pair of
couples in his hand. Manager (the hound with him)
was heavier than Bill was at the time. — Yew Tree
House, Quorndon, Loughborough, October 6th, 1859."

The Bill here spoken of is Will Burton, who died
at Quorn of consumption, soon after the picture was

* One of the illustrations of the present Memoir.
† Also by Ferneley.

painted by Mr. Ferneley.   Mr. Smith set great store
upon the lad, as of great promise, and used to say,
observes the author of Silk and Scarlet (p. 280),
that, as he looked at it year after year in the ante-
room at Tedworth, he would have given ten thousand
pounds to save him.

An interesting account of the grand day at Rolleston was furnished by " The Adelphi" to the
Sporting Magazine of June 1840 (vol. xxi. 2nd
series), though " The Brothers" make a trifling mistake in saying that it had occurred on the 20th April.
Dick Burton's account is more correct in placing
the date at the 20th March ; for, after several days
in different counties, he says he brought the pack
back to Tedworth on the 7th April 1840.   It could
not very well be on the 7th May, and we know that
Mr. Smith very seldom took his hounds out after
Lady-day.   On the celebrated day at Rolleston, a
person counted seventeen hundred horsemen through
one gate alone.   Out of the two thousand, one third
were in pink.   In addition to these were a very
goodly display of carriages-and-four filled with ladies,
and pedestrians without number.   The hounds with
Dick Burton were drawn up on the lawn, while the
vast group of horsemen formed a circle, with the
carriages, and assembled crowd outside.   Mr. Smith
had brought eighteen couple of his best hounds, as
" The Adelphi" observe, "of great substance, par-

ticularly in the legs, open-chested, and in splendid
condition." The greeting between Mr. Smith and
his old friends the farmers was most cordial. Mrs.
Assheton Smith accompanied her husband in this
visit. After the friendly salutations were over, and
their enthusiastic character astonished no one but
the Illustrious Stranger present*, Mr. Smith took his
hounds to Shankton Holt, where he drew only the
bottom of the covert ; thence to Norton Gorse,
Stanton Wood, Glooston Wood, and Fallow Close, all
blank. It was an unfavourable day for scent,—a
bright sun with north-easterly wind, not a cloud to
be seen, and the cold intense. A fox having been
found by Mr. Hodgson, in Vowes Covert, as already
stated, away went the hounds towards Horringhold,
leaving Blaston to the right. Here Mr. Smith took
a strong flight of rails into a road, quite like a
" young un." The fox soon afterwards crossed the
Welland, and went away for Rockingham Park, where,
it being late, they whipped off. " We never saw,"
observe " The Brothers," " a handier pack, one more
completely under the command of their huntsman,
or quicker in getting to him at a cast." Of Mr.
Smith's horses they remark : " they were large and
powerful, extremely well suited to the country, and
getting cleverly over every description of fence, but
did not show the blood we should have thought

* Prince Ernest.

requisite to gallop over the Hampshire Downs."
Doubtless Mr. Smith, who was familiar with both
countries, had selected the horses for his Leicestershire and Lincolnshire visits which he well knew to
be best suited to the requirements of each country.

Mr. Greene of Rolleston, whose guest Mr. Smith
was on this occasion, had frequently followed him
close in Leicestershire, and was a pupil every way
worthy of his master. An excellent run has been
recorded by the author of Silk and Scarlet, from
Botany Bay, skirting the Coplow, but without
touching it, when they killed the fox in a field near
a covert at Schlawson windmill; the distance was
thirteen miles. Mr. Smith rode Gadsby, and Mr.
Edge Gayman. Besides these two, only Mr. Greene
on Sysonby, and Fryatt of Melton on Hastings, were
up. Mr. Smith pulled his watch out, and five
minutes elapsed before any other horseman was up.
Fryatt sold Hastings the next day for 400 guineas.
"On another day," says Dick Christian, "Mr. Greene's
horse Sysonby gave Mr. Smith and Shacabac a rare
showing up in the Harborough country ; it was a
strange wild day ; they found in a patch of wild
gorse near Gumley. The wind blew the scent, and
the hounds flashed over it. Mr. Smith rode Gadsby
first, and then Shacabac. They had an hour and
twenty minutes, racing all the way : there was only
himself and Mr. Greene left. All on a sudden
Shacabac starts a grunting and stops. Mr. Greene

got off Sysonby, and said, ' You get on my horse,
they are running to their fox.'   On Mr. Smith went
with Sysonby, and just at that time Mr. Greene fell in
with Gadsby, and got on him and finished.   There
they were at the kill, with the same horses they had
started on, only riders changed."   Mr. Greene was
the first *native* master of hounds in Leicestershire.

In 1845 the state of Mrs. Smith's health causing
him great anxiety, he was apprehensive of being
obliged to take her to a foreign climate for the winter.   Both were, however, unwilling to leave a spot
where each had so many objects of interest and enjoyment — he his favourite sport, and she her schools,
her poor, and the management of the house and
grounds, the details of which at Tedworth Mr. Smith
entrusted entirely to her.   The squire, therefore, determined to bring Madeira to England, rather than be
obliged to repair to the former in quest of health; with
this view he erected a magnificent conservatory, 315
feet in length, and 40 feet in width, where, with a tem-
perature always raised to a certain heat, Mrs. Smith
might take walking exercise during the winter months.
A Wiltshire farmer, on first seeing this building,
observed, he supposed the squire had it made in order to hunt there when a frost stopped him in the
field.   Along the whole length of this Crystal Palace in
miniature is a broad walk laid with the finest gravel,
and ranged on each side are thousands of the most

beautiful plants, even at Christmas time of the richest hues and fragrance. The conservatory is approached from an ante-room of the house by a corridor glazed on one side and 965 feet in length, forming with the conservatory nearly a quarter of a mile of glass, and warmed throughout with double pipes containing hot water. It was a melancholy spectacle to see the squire the winter before his death, when he could no longer join his hounds, mount one of his favourites — Euxine, Paul Potter, or Blemish — with the assistance of a chair, and take his exercise for an hour at a foot's pace up and down this conservatory, often with some friend at his side to cheer him up, and while away the time until he re-entered the house, for he was not allowed at that period to go out of doors. Even in this feeble condition, " *quantùm mutatus ab illo Hectore*," once on horseback he appeared to revive ; and the dexterity and ease with which he managed, like a plaything, the spirited animal under him, which had scarcely left its stable for months, was most surprising.

Before the conservatory however was built in 1845 on account of the health of Mrs. Smith, her husband had himself, vigorous and hardy as he was, been overtaken by indisposition. He was occasionally subject to attacks of asthma, for which he had tried homœopathy, under Dr. Quin. In 1834, "Dashwood," in the Sporting Magazine (September 1834), speak-

ing of him " as the most extraordinary huntsman perhaps whom England had ever produced," adds that he
was at that time " in indifferent health, and not again
expected to be able to take the field."   Nevertheless,
in the following year, when the great run took place
from Amesbury to Salisbury Plain, he must have
been in a great measure restored.   In 1843 the fame
of the founder of the water-cure, Vincent Preissnitz,
had reached England; and Mr. Smith having read
Captain Claridge's account of the cures performed
by hydropathy, consulted Dr. Weiss, who had studied the treatment under Preissnitz, at Grafenberg,
and was now in England, conducting an establishment for patients at Stansted Bury, in Herts.   His
own account of the relief he derived from the water-
cure has somewhat of the fabulous about it.   He
used to relate, that he went to bed labouring under
a severe attack of asthma, and having received
directions from Weiss to wrap round his chest the
wet bandage, or *umschlag*, since so celebrated in
assuaging pain and in healing sores, which he accordingly did, he slept soundly, notwithstanding the
chill which the damp application first occasioned, and
in the morning he jumped up with the exclamation
that his asthma was gone, and that he was perfectly
cured.   From this time Mr. Smith became an enthusiastic follower of Preissnitz ; he not only carried
out the treatment in his own person, barring his

three or four glasses of good sherry, which he never abandoned, but he sedulously recommended the water-cure to every sufferer within his reach. The writer was one of those whom he urged to submit to the discipline, and he has never seen cause to repent of it. Many instances occurred, where persons in the lower class of life were without adequate means to leave their homes or business in order to carry out the treatment; these he generously furnished with the necessary funds for that purpose. He was so convinced of the merits of hydropathy, that he introduced it into his stables, and used to have his horses sheathed in wet bandages after a severe run, or when any symptoms of swelling or disease showed themselves. His own habit was, after hunting, to undress and go to bed for an hour, or until dressing time, and then go into his bath, by which process he was thoroughly invigorated and refreshed. One day during the height of his zeal for hydropathy, he was returning with a friend across the downs from hunting, after a fine run and a "whoop," when he fell in with a shepherd who was ministering some nostrum to a sick ewe. "What is the matter with that sheep?" inquired the squire. "Giddy, sir," was the reply. "If you would just try the effect of cold water on her, she would soon recover." "Cold water," sneered the rustic (as Mr. Smith rode off), "why, what on earth else has she been drinking ever since she *were waned?*"

(weaned.) But although an ardent disciple of the water-cure — and we have seen that in that very year, 1843, he christened a sailing yacht after the treatment (as applicable, however, to the diversion of yachting as to hydropathy) — he used to relate with great zest an anecdote respecting the cure, which, as it was concerning a fox-hunter, may not here be inappropriate.

The story goes, that a lover of the chase who was somewhat addicted to the pleasures of the table, and loved more glasses of port wine than was quite good for him, consulted a hydropathic Galen respecting some symptoms in his kitchen department which were beginning to give him alarm. The doctor recommended the application of the wet bandage to his stomach at bedtime, there to remain until the following morning. "I will see you to-morrow," added he, "when I shall be better able to judge of your symptoms." At night our hero, having saturated the folds of linen in cold spring water, began the application as directed, but the shock to his internal economy being greater than he had bargained for, he bethought himself of taking off the chill by re-dipping the bandage into water in which there was a certain portion of his favourite beverage. Having thus made things rather more comfortable, he awaited the doctor's visit the next morning. "Show me your bandage," was almost the learned man's first exclamation. It was produced. The doctor regarded its discolorations

for a moment with feelings of lively satisfaction, and
then solemnly addressing his patient, who had some
difficulty in retaining his gravity, "I thought so, sir,"
he said; "this is the port wine you have drunk for the
last twenty years coming out."   But, although the
squire loved this story, he was always a very staunch
advocate of the water-cure, which he said could well
bear a laugh against it.   He was sixty-seven years of
age when he tried it, and must have had no common
vigour, and indeed the constitution of a man in the
prime of life, for it to have done him the good which
it did.   He used to say that till he became a hydro-
pathist he hunted four days a week, and six afterwards.   On these two days thus added to his meets,
Carter, his huntsman, used to hunt with a separate
pack; and sometimes, when master and man talked
over their day's sport together in the evening, the
squire used to say, "Well, you can give a better
account of your fox than I can of mine," for he never
grudgingly gave credit where credit was due.

The year 1845 is memorable as having witnessed
the innumerable schemes of railway enterprise which
terminated in the ruin of thousands.   Among the
lines projected was one intended to run from Worcester through Montgomeryshire and Merionethshire
to Porthdynlaen, a harbour well situated on the Carnarvonshire coast, and not far from Pwlheli.   The
advantages possessed by Porthdynlaen as a port of

departure for Ireland had not escaped the penetrating observation of Mr. Smith, and although the commissioners appointed to examine the harbours on the Welsh coast had reported in favour of Holyhead, he still remained convinced of the superiority of the former; and he ascribed its rejection to the working of undue influence.   With this conviction, and also foreseeing that the line would open up the mineral and other resources of the Principality, hitherto very imperfectly developed, he warmly espoused the design of the Worcester and Porthdynlaen Railway, to which he promised every assistance in his power, furnishing the promoters with an introduction to the leading landowners in North Wales, and allowing the prospectus to have his name appear in it as a patron of the undertaking.   At the same time he was wary enough not to join the Provisional Committee. The line was duly surveyed, and, except a very formidable tunnel at Llangunnog, looked very well on the ordnance map.   Scarcely, however, had the plans and sections been deposited, and those who remember the 1st of November 1845 will not forget the difficulties under which this was accomplished, when the panic set in; and the Worcester and Porthdynlaen, with, we venture to say, hundreds of other schemes, went to the bottom.   A month or two later there were sundry little bills to be paid, of engineers and their staff (in those days a surveyor could not

be got under five guineas a day), solicitors, &c.   Few
of the Provisional Committee of the Porthdynlaen line
were worth powder and shot; but the limb of the
law, who was without his costs, considered Assheton
Smith as well worth the experiment of a charge.   He
therefore sent his son, a youth of about twenty years
of age, who also acted as his clerk, to Hyde Park
Gardens, to serve the squire with a writ for work and
labour done by him the attorney for him the squire
aforesaid.   Mr. Smith's footman, hearing that the
bearer of the hostile missive had something important
to communicate to his master, introduced him into
his private study, when Mr. Smith, on hearing the
object of his message, under the pressure of injured
innocence, immediately knocked him down.   The
young man was glad to effect his exit from the
wrathful old gentleman of sixty-nine, and sent him a
summons to Marylebone Police Court for the assault,
on the following day.   Mr. Smith, upon receiving
this, went to the Temple to consult a friend learned
in the law upon the subject of his appearance before
the magistrate.   After hearing the squire's story,
which he with difficulty got through, being somewhat
out of breath with indignation at being called upon
for payment, and with having to mount four pair of
stairs in order to reach the lawyer's sanctum, the
representative of Blackstone on the rights of persons
ventured to suggest to him that he had somewhat

exceeded the bounds of decorum, and asked whether it would not be advisable, considering Mr. Smith's position in society, to offer the attorney's clerk a five-pound note and get him to withdraw the summons. Upon this counsel being tendered to him, the squire's anger, which had been hitherto kept under with an effort, burst forth, and looking at the ceiling, to the astonishment of the man of law, he exclaimed, "Good God, sir, your chambers let in the rain!" The fact was, that in the plenitude of his ire the perspiration trickled in large drops over his face, which he mistook for the moisture of the heavens. Precipitately leaving the chambers, he faced the charge next day before Mr. Broughton, nearly committed a second assault, was fined five pounds, and appeared on a subsequent morning in the columns of the "Morning Post," under the heading of "An irate Provisional."

The above anecdote proves that Mr. Smith occasionally gave way to his temper. He used to say that "his father was the worst-tempered man in the world except himself;" but in this saying he was a little hard upon both. In the hunting field as a master of hounds he had many things to contend against; sometimes against the wilful perverseness, sometimes the ignorance, of men who headed or rode over his hounds, sometimes the expressions of envy on the part of those whose riding he eclipsed, or whose want of nerve made them follow while he *led*. On these

occasions it is not to be wondered at if he was unable
to curb his temper.   On one occasion, on the borders
of the Pytchley country, a well-known parson, who
had the misfortune to be rather deaf, came through a
hedge (and he was afraid of very few) plump into
the middle of the hounds.   Smith called out, " Hold
hard, T——! you *can't* hear and you *won't* see."
The reverend sportsman was not so hard of hearing
as to fail in hearing the squire, who always uttered
what he did say pretty audibly ; he pulled up his
horse, and knowing that he had committed an error,
at once made an apology for it.

But although Mr. Smith was somewhat choleric
and impetuous, his ebullitions of temper were soon
over, and he always in a truly generous spirit
hastened to make amends where he felt that he
had been wrong.   He was like his favourite poet:
" Irasci celer, tamen ut placabilis esset."   In the
instance of the attorney's clerk he considered that
an attempt to extort money from him was made
under the guise and menace of legal proceedings,
and this he resented though in an improper manner.
Once when he hunted Lincolnshire, and his hounds
had drawn Kettlethorpe Wood, belonging to Sir
William Ingleby, without finding a fox, Mr. Smith
observed a man at a gate, in a shooting-jacket and
with a gun over his shoulder, who opened it for
him, and at whom, taking him to be the gamekeeper

and imagining him to have been beating the covert, he railed in no measured terms, saying he would tell his master of the blank which had occurred. The man listened quietly to the squire and touched his hat. After they had got through and were trotting off to Lee Wood, belonging to Sir Charles Anderson, at no great distance, Mr. Uppleby said to Mr. Smith, " Do you know who that was?" " No, indeed," was the reply, " and I don't care." When told that it was Sir William himself, and that he was merely passing through the wood in which he strictly preserved foxes, on his way to his shooting grounds, Mr. Smith was anxious to go back and apologise; but his friends said there was no occasion for this, for Sir William, they observed, was rather eccentric, and would be amused at being taken for one of his keepers.

After Mr. Smith gave up the Burton country, he resided in the Vale for several seasons, being frequently the guest of the Duke of Rutland, and joining the various packs in the neighbourhood from Belvoir Castle. " I've known him," says Dick Christian*, " come all the way from Belvoir to Gumley of a morning, two and thirty miles, to cover, and back again at night." To accomplish these long distances he was up early at the castle and breakfasted alone. On one occasion he was not satisfied

* Silk and Scarlet, p. 57.

with the breakfast prepared for him, and complained to the footman who waited upon him that he did not think he had the attention given to him to which he was entitled. The Duke's servant received the rebuke in silence, but on the following morning, when the sportsman came down to breakfast, he was surprised to see all the footmen in the castle enter the room in their state liveries, and take their station around the table. The Duke, to whom his guest's complaint had been reported, feeling satisfied that every attention had been paid to Mr. Smith, for whom he always entertained a sincere regard, took this effectual mode of reproving his testy humour. At another time he complained of the scarcity of muffins, upon which the servants received orders, when next the guests assembled at the breakfast table, to pour in upon him a perpetual stream of muffins. Each footman accordingly presented to the bewildered squire an unceasing succession of hot plates, the chorus being, " Muffins, Mr. Smith."

CHAP. VI.

HIS SEVERE ILLNESS AT VAENOL IN 1856, AND PARTIAL RECOVERY. — RELAPSE AND DEATH IN 1858.

> " Time, stern huntsman, who can baulk,
> Staunch as hound, and fleet as hawk ? "   *Walter* SCOTT.

UNTIL Mr. Smith had reached his eightieth year, which he did in May 1856, he showed no signs of physical or mental decay.   His head was as clear and his hand as firm as they had been twenty years years before.   If he felt himself not quite well of a morning, he used to plunge his head into cold water and hold it there as long as he could.   This, he said, always put him to rights.   He had returned to four days a week, it is true ; but on these days the farmers were delighted to see him vault on horseback as usual, and gallop down the sheepfed hill-sides with all the joyous alacrity of a boy of eighteen.

> "You yet might see the old man in a morning,
>   Lusty as health, come ruddy to the field,
>   And then pursue the chase."   OTWAY.

This enduring character of his riding is what renders it so essentially different from that of other men. He was still the same Assheton Smith, who had

L

hunted in the last century ; who had, for nearly
fifty years, been a master of hounds ; who had actually been in the saddle for a period of seventy
years—the ordinary life of man — who might have
hunted with Pitt and Fox, had they been sportsmen
— and who had outlived at least three generations of
fox-hunters. With most other men the best of the
spirit dies, or at all events waxes somewhat faint,
when the prime of active manhood has past. It
seemed never to desert Tom Smith. That adaman-
tine frame, the "robur et æs triplex circa pectus,"
appeared proof, not only against fatigue, but against
heavy falls which would have shaken younger men
all to pieces. Only two years before his death, on
his return from a hard run, he was telling some
ladies that he had encountered three falls on that day,
and felt none the worse for it. " Then, Mr. Smith,
you ought," said one of them, "when you die, to bequeath your skin to the British Museum to be stuffed,
as a particularly tough specimen ; " an idea at
which the squire laughed heartily. At another time,
as he lay on the ground after a tremendous purler,
a sympathising friend rode up and expressed a wish
that he was not hurt. "Thank you," said the squire,
not very grateful for his inquiry, as the hounds were
in full swing at some distance from the spot, "nothing
ever hurts Tom Smith."

" The last great run Mr. Smith was in," says

Dick Christian *, " was one of an hour and forty minutes, seven or eight seasons since, from Ham Ashley to Hungerford ; and he was so pleased with the chestnut he rode, that he gave Mr. Samuel Reeves 175 guineas for him. He christened him from the covert where they found, and ranked him ever after with the Amport, Rochelle, and Ayston of his Hampshire affections."

The time, however, was about to arrive when even that vigorous and hardy constitution, which had stood proof against such severe handling, and seemed to defy every " draw " upon it from toil, accident, or weather, was to succumb. He was approaching the shore of that dark strait,

> " Scilicet omnibus,
> Quicunque terræ munere vescimur,
> Enavigandæ." HORAT.

In September 1856, while at his summer residence in North Wales, Mr. Smith was seized with an alarming illness, which caused the greatest apprehension to his friends. The skill, however, of Dr. Stokes of Dublin, who was sent for, added to the unremitting attentions of Mr. Richards of Bangor, his usual medical adviser, who well knew his patient's constitution, brought him round after many weeks of protracted suffering, chiefly by the use of stimulants, to which he had never previously resorted, and which

---

* Silk and Scarlet, p. 283.

he was now most reluctantly persuaded to try. Mrs.
Smith was herself at this period in a very weak state
of health, but devoted herself most assiduously to her
husband, and greatly tended to his recovery.   Even
now, when he was in a most prostrate and debilitated
condition, the sight of his horse saddled at the door,
ready to carry him to the Port, only a mile distant,
seemed at once to cheer and revive him ; and the
man who had been five minutes before gasping for
breath on the sofa, under the powerful hold of his
old enemy, asthma, when once astride the animal
trotted off apparently by mechanical impulse, as if he
had more need of his hounds than of a physician.

Although he rallied from this attack in an as-
tonishing manner, he was no longer the same man.
The erect gait was bent, and the eagle eye had lost
its lustre.   He returned to Tedworth as usual ; but,
at the annual meet on the 1st of November 1857, the
hounds met without the accustomed centre-figure of
their master, who slowly rode up to them without his
scarlet.   He remarked, quite seriously, that if he had
worn his hunting gear, and his pack should observe
that he could not follow them, they would show their
sorrow by refusing to hunt the fox.   A universal
gloom pervaded the field ; he looked wistfully and
lovingly at his old favourites, the heroes of many a
well-fought field ; and, as he quickly went back into
the hall, shrinking almost from the outer air, while

the horsemen and pack turned away slowly towards the
shrubberies, every one felt with a heavy heart that the
glory of the old fox-hunter had at length departed.

The talented author of Silk and Scarlet thus
graphically describes the last time he was at the
covert side : —

" The covert side knew him no more after October
1857, when he just cantered up to Willbury on
his chestnut hack Blemish, to see his hounds draw.
Carter had had orders to bring the choicest of the
1858 entry, and he and Will Bryce arrived at the
usual rendezvous with five couple of bitches by the
Fitzwilliam Hardwicke and Hermit. He looked at
them for a short time, and exclaimed, ' Well, they
are as beautiful as they can be.' He then bade both
his men good-bye, and they saw him in the field no
more." This was only a week or two previous to
the grand annual meet already mentioned.

I passed a week with him at Tedworth, in the
course of the following winter. Although it was the
month of December, the season was mild, and, as
there had been very little shooting, I had some excellent sport with my gun in the spacious turnip-
fields which look down upon the village. One day
we came upon a fox lying quietly and unconcerned
among the turnips, as if he was aware that his old
enemy was disabled, and we had some difficulty in
making him stir from the spot. The keeper told me

that there had been a mortality among the foxes that
season, in consequence of the long continuance of dry
weather, and that the one in question was diseased,
or rotten, to use his own expression. I mentioned
the circumstance at the dinner-table in the evening.
A few intimate friends had been invited, and Mr.
Smith had asked me to take his seat at the bottom,
if it could be so called, of the round table at which
he usually dined, he taking his seat in a position
nearer the fire. He had been very silent during
dinner, and kept his head down, appearing not to
listen to what was going on, but to be intently occupied with the contents of his plate, which he was
devouring with much relish. When the anecdote of
the fox was mentioned, a lady present, looking at
him askance, remarked to me, " Why didn't you shoot
him?" In an instant the squire raised his head, the
lightning flashed in his eye, and he exclaimed, pointing
to me, " If he had, he would not have been there."
It was at this time he took his daily exercise for an
hour in the conservatory, as has been already related.
Hitherto Carter, his huntsman, and as good a one as
ever crossed a country, had been in the habit of seeing
his master every evening in the dining-room at nine
o'clock, to talk over the sport of that day, and to
settle what hounds were to run on the morrow, and
what horses were to go out. Now a short occasional
interview in the morning sufficed, when Mr. Smith

had taken his usual basin of soup with brandy in it, and when the pack was not out. Nevertheless, his intellect was unimpaired, and his head for figures as good as ever. He was investing largely at this period in consols, as the Welsh property was rapidly increasing in value, and within the last few years he had paid off every incumbrance on his estates.* What I was particularly struck with was his extreme neatness in his personal appearance, so unusual in an invalid, and the care he took never to come among the ladies, except *en grande toilette*, at those times when almost entirely without company, for even when he was most suffering, he could never be prevailed upon to enter the drawingroom in his *robe de chambre*.

His gallantry and the respect he showed to the fair sex were always remarkable. To them the loud and often boisterous sportsman was gentleness itself. When dressed for the evening, in his white silk stockings and well-fitting pumps, (for he was not a little proud of his foot,) he looked the pattern of an old English gentleman. He studiously avoided giving trouble, and seemed annoyed at being obliged to ask any one to perform any little service for him. In this way he lingered on till the autumn of 1858, when he died rather suddenly at Vaenol, on the 9th of

---

* His father had left large fortunes to each of his sisters, which were charged upon the property in Hants and Carnarvonshire, and which he had all paid off.

September, after a second attack of the same symptoms which had shaken him so severely in 1856. He had only a few weeks previous to this event completed his eighty-second year. He bequeathed to his widow the whole of his vast possessions. No other person was named in his will, which was found written on half a sheet of writing paper, except a few old servants, to whom he bequeathed legacies; and Mrs. Smith inherited the estates both in England and Wales, to do exactly as she pleased with them, without any direction, recommendation, or suggestion of a wish on his part as to their ultimate disposition. The funeral took place at Tedworth, and his remains were interred in the village churchyard, the mausoleum in the grounds intended for both husband and wife, and also for Mrs. Smith's mother, Mrs. Webber, who had died a short time previously, not being then finished. There had never been any issue of his marriage.

The following minute account of his illness in 1856 has been furnished by an eye-witness and very old friend, who also received the particulars of his last attack from the wife who so devotedly attended him.

"When Dr. Stokes arrived from Dublin in September 1856, he gave little hope to those about Mr. Smith that he would last long, but strongly advised a free use of stimulants, which Mr. Smith firmly resisted for some time, saying he had always been a very temperate man, to which he believed he owed his vigorous constitution. However, he yielded to the solicitation of his friends, and when apparently at the last gasp, found relief from half a wine-glass of brandy. During this autumn, his kind neighbour and highly esteemed friend, Colonel Douglas Pennant, two or three times sent his pack of beagles for Mr. Smith's amusement. Even the sight of them turning into the gate appeared to give him new life. On one occasion, he had been very ill all the morning, and was threatened with one of his fainting attacks, when looking up in agony into his wife's face, he gasped out, 'I am going.' Nevertheless, brandy, ether, and other stimulants revived him. About an hour afterwards the hounds arrived, and, much to the astonishment and dismay of all about him, he crawled, with the help of his valet and butler, to the hall-door, and was soon in the saddle. Once there, he looked immediately ten years younger. Observing a horse belonging to Colonel Pennant which he fancied, he dismounted from his own, and though told the other was rather restive, he determined to mount it and follow the hounds. His groom had strict orders to keep very close to him, with a vial of brandy in his pocket. Some anxious friends followed on foot, and from a piece of high ground watched his movements. They were soon terrified by seeing him thrown off. He was not hurt, and wished to continue the chase, saying, 'it was curious how he had lost his *gripe* on a horse,' which he always said was the secret of his riding; but at last was persuaded to return home in the carriage. There is great reason to believe that stimulants prolonged his life, but his sufferings were very great. He used to say, the feeling of 'sinking away' was the most painful of all; and yet he never murmured, but used often to repeat, 'It is the will of God,' and, as soon as he was relieved from momentary pain, make a slight bow, and exclaim, 'Thank God!' His valet, Attwell, who had been with him many years, nursed him with the tenderest care night and day; but poor Mr. Smith was so anxious not to disturb him unnecessarily at night (when he had to take medicine at stated hours), that he tried several ways of making the light reflect on his watch, so that he might reach the medicine bottle himself. Many of these failed; at last, he and his clever carpenter, John Jones, devised a me-chanical contrivance which answered admirably. When he had been unusually restless, and had been obliged to call up his servant, he used to say to him in the morning, 'I am sorry to have disturbed you so often; you will find a sovereign on my table, take it.'

"His death was at last rather sudden. He was very ill when he left London in August 1858; but bore the day's journey to Vaenol better than was ex-pected, and in a week seemed to rally considerably.

In the meanwhile, all his anxiety seemed to be cen-
tred on Mrs. Smith, who had been very ill for some
months, insomuch, that he had written to beg her
sister, Mrs. Heneage, and her family, to give up their
tour in Scotland and come immediately to Vaenol,
which they did, and found her in a most anxious
state, but the squire far better than he had been for
some time. However, on the Thursday after their
arrival, Mr. Smith complained of feeling very weak,
and said he should not go down stairs, which was so
unusual an act of self-indulgence that Attwell for the
first time gave him up ; and, sure enough, he never
left his room again. On the Saturday morning he
fell into a stupor, from which the medical men and
those about him had no hope of his rallying.
When this sad conviction was gently broken to his
wife, it was unexpected by her, for she had seen his
sufferings so much greater that she could not, and
would not, believe he was to pass away without one
kind word to her. After remaining in this state
throughout the day, he suddenly opened his eyes,
and in his usual powerful and firm voice he asked
for something to drink, to the amazement of all
about him. The next day he was better, and wrote
a cheque for money that he ought to have given the
day before, remembering it of his own accord. The
three following days he remained placid, apparently
not suffering much, and at times insensible. In a

moment of consciousness, evidently aware of his approaching end, he said to his devoted wife, 'Take care of that man,' pointing to his faithful valet; and when Mrs. Smith left the room, he said to her maid, 'Watch over your mistress; take care of her.'

"About nine o'clock on Thursday evening Mrs. Smith left him to lie down for an hour, leaving her sister to watch by his side, and exacting a promise that she would not take her eyes from his face. A faithful and kind watcher she proved, for in less than an hour she fancied she perceived a slight change in his countenance, and called her sister, who immediately came to his bedside; but before his valet and the doctors could be summoned, he had breathed his last in a gentle sigh. Thus departed, in an enviably peaceful death, the spirit of him who for eighty-two years had led a most stirring and energetic life. His virtues were many; a noble, generous, kind heart, always prompt to hear the tale of woe, and only too ready to relieve it: his numberless acts of liberality known to few, but his cheque-book bearing testimony to beneficent deeds. His faults were those to be expected from his education: his father was a very stern man, and yet over-indulgent in some things; and his mother a weak, vain, selfish woman, little caring for her children, and leaving them early to their own devices. He therefore too early became 'lord of himself, that heritage of woe.'"

CHAP. VII.

HIS CHARACTER. — PERSONAL APPEARANCE AND HABITS. — IM-
PETUOSITY OF TEMPER. — GENEROSITY OF DISPOSITION.—SKILL
IN GAMES AND SPORTS.

> "His saltem accumulem donis, et fungar inani
> Munere."   VIRG.

THE character of Mr. Assheton Smith has already
been so fully drawn in the course of this narrative,
that it may appear superfluous to add anything to the
portrait. Some traits, however, have been purposely
passed over, or imperfectly sketched, in order that we
might follow him with less interruption through his
lengthened career. We should be doing him much
less than justice if we omitted them altogether.
There are some details, in themselves insignificant,
which impart its chief interest to biography, and
bring it closely home to men's " business and bosoms."
We naturally wish to know all about the personal
appearance, the habits of life, the friendships of the
individual, whose life we have been perusing, and the
want of these particulars is a gap which we cannot
afterwards fill up. After the lapse of a short time,
so rapidly do other prominent figures come upon the
stage, the most vivid personal reminiscences of any individual, however illustrious in any pursuit or profes-

sion or grade of life, fade away from recollection. Let us therefore, while our memory of the lamented squire of Tedworth is as perfect as when he lived, while the hoof-mark is fresh and deep upon the soil, subjoin in recapitulation a short description of him.

Mr. Assheton Smith was of the stature best adapted to exertion and endurance, about five feet ten inches in height, with a frame athletic, well-proportioned, and muscular, but rather slight than the contrary. His weight was latterly about eleven stone ten; in his Leicestershire days, Dick Christian says he was not above ten stone. He was fond of weighing himself, and had scales both at Tedworth and at his seat in Wales. His features were plain, and not in any way indicative of high breeding, but intelligent, the whole countenance denoting a powerful and resolute will. A rival once in Leicestershire said, " he is snake-headed, with a dash of the bulldog." He used to say of himself that he was the plainest man in England, but generally added, " that fellow Jack Musters spoilt my beauty." His ordinary dress was a blue coat with brass buttons, and a buff waistcoat; during the hunting season he dined in scarlet, the inside of the coat being lined with white silk. In his living he was particularly abstemious as regarded drinking: in eating he indulged more freely, and his appetite was surprising. The immense exercise which he was daily in the habit of taking, and his early

hours in the morning, required an adequate supply
of nourishment, and after his severest day's work he
was never "off his feed." The copious plate of
hashed mutton, which was his constant breakfast
before going out to hunt, even to the last hastily
eaten while his horse was at the door, and digested
in the saddle, was a proof how well he was able to
set all rules of diet at defiance: unlike the more careful and no less celebrated Meynell, whose hunting
breakfast was a pound of the best veal condensed
to as much soup as would fill a small tea-cup. In
Tom Smith's bachelor days, relates an old friend who
saw a good deal of him at that period, his usual
dinner was mutton soup of the best description, and
a couple of glasses of claret. "I once rode with him
to Hungerford," he adds, "in a bitter cold frost, and
our luncheon was tea and toast." The fact was, his
hearty breakfast served him for the day, and he
seldom took anything, until quite latterly, between
that meal and his dinner.

In his friendships he was warm, generous, faithful,
and noble-hearted; on the other hand, like all men of
ardent temperament, he had his dislikes, and never
took any pains to conceal them. Where he had once
conceived an aversion, he could be seldom brought to
overcome it. This he inherited from his father, who
used to say of himself, "No man was ever in my company twelve hours without fully perceiving whether

I liked or disliked him." "And no man," rejoined the friend to whom the remark was made, "if you disliked him, would wish to be with you for five minutes."

As has been already remarked, the son was hasty and excitable; "*impiger, iracundus, et acer*," like Achilles, but not "*inexorabilis*." He was of a liberal and benevolent disposition, and as his means enabled him to gratify his inclination in this respect, he gave without ostentation, not unfrequently in quarters where his liberality could never be spoken of abroad, and where the situation in life of the parties precluded their asking for assistance. To the poorer classes he was always open-handed.

About the year 1847, after a severe frost, so sudden and rapid a thaw succeeded that a whole line of villages in the valley of Salisbury Plain was inundated, and the poor inhabitants were exposed to the greatest dangers and privations. Mr. Smith was the first to ride down, and leave 100*l.* with the clergyman for the immediate relief of the sufferers. The noble example thus set was so successfully followed, that in a short time funds were raised, not only sufficient for the purpose intended, but a surplus was handed over to Salisbury Infirmary. At another time an old colonel, broken down by years and misfortune, was reduced to the last climax of distress by having an execution in his house, and all his little property put up to auction. Mr. Smith desired his agent, Mr. Northeast, who always most effectually carried out his master's generous impulses, and well repaid the confidence placed in him, to buy the whole and return it to the late owner; not as a *gift*, but as a *loan*, lest it should again be seized and sold.

"I was one day riding not far from Tedworth," writes the friend and fellow-sportsman to whom the reader is indebted for many of the interesting anecdotes related in these pages, "in a contrary direction to where the hounds were fixed to meet, when I met the squire, and the following conversation occurred. 'Why are you not going out with me to-day?' said he. 'I have just heard of the death of an old friend and relative,' was my reply (mentioning his name), 'and I am now going to see his son and hear when the funeral is to take place.' 'Your relative, it is true, always opposed me in the Craven Hunt; but he was a bold rider and a gallant sportsman. I hear his grandson is just going out to India, so pray tell the boy's father I will give him 100*l.* for his son's outfit, which will make your visit less painful to him.'"

On another occasion, during a violent storm on his return from hunting, Mr. Smith was standing under a tree for shelter in the village of Chute. A poor man came out from his house, or rather hovel, for it was in a miserable condition, with a sack which

M

he asked permission to put over the saddle, while the
squire retired under his roof for shelter.   Both offers
were accepted, and the man was liberally rewarded
for his attention.   His surprise, however, was not dis-
agreeable the next day on the arrival of a bricklayer
and carpenter, who, at Mr. Smith's expense, entirely
rebuilt his cottage for him.   It was a remark of the
celebrated Samuel Johnson, that no man could be
under a gateway with Edmund Burke during a shower
of rain, and not be at once convinced that he was
talking to the most extraordinary man it had ever been
his good fortune to encounter.   It would be difficult to
analyse the feelings of this poor labourer respecting
his visitor of the previous day; for it may be safely
asserted, that no other man could be named, who
ever did a more generous act for so insignificant a
favour.

On being once thanked by a friend for a liberal
donation to a young man about to seek his fortune
in Australia, Mr. Smith asked, "Is the young fellow
a lad of spirit?" and on being assured that such
was the case, he put his hand in his pocket and said,
" Then here is ten pound more for him."

During the short time he was on the turf, he was
once at Newmarket, where he had two horses training, Cracker and Cantator.   While attending a meeting of the Jockey Club, to which he then belonged,
a bill for 300*l.*, drawn by an unfortunate brother-

sportsman, was handed round the room, but at such a discount that it was offered to any one for 30*l*. On Mr. Smith's inquiring the name of the drawer, and finding that it was that of an old schoolfellow of his, he requested to see the bill, and having immediately drawn a cheque for 300*l*., which he handed to the holder, put the bill behind the fire.

The following incident may appear too trifling to record, but it is characteristic of his kindness of heart. When he was a patient of the famous Dr. Jephson of Leamington, the doctor happened to mention that he had experienced great difficulty in procuring grapes, at that time out of season, for a fair invalid, having sent in vain for them to London, Birmingham, and other places, when Mr. Smith, with whom the lady was only slightly acquainted, exclaimed, " Why did you not tell me of this before? I would have sent your dear patient a cart-load." Within as short a time as possible, a large hamper of fine grapes arrived for her from Tedworth.

Although Mr. Smith's name was not often to be found heading public subscriptions, or in the lists of charities, he was never known to refuse an application for aid to promote a truly charitable purpose. Mrs. Smith has been heard to say, that she never asked him for money for the advancement of religion or to promote the comfort and welfare of the poor, but it was cheerfully granted to her, and to any

amount. The almshouses at Tedworth were kept
in comfortable repair entirely at his expense, in
order that the funds for the maintenance of the aged
inmates might not in any way be diminished. In
1857, only a few months before his death, a new
village school was completed near the Hampshire
Cross, a handsome building, capable of holding a
hundred children. The sight of the girls in their red
cloaks on a Saturday afternoon, and of the noisy
urchins rushing from the porch to commence their
various pastimes, would gladden the heart of a
" Times " commissioner.

Mr. Smith's well-knit and manly frame, combined
with great activity in the use of his limbs, rendered
him successful in all athletic sports. In his youth
he had been a first-rate swimmer, rower, and shot.
To his powers as a cricketer, this memoir will hereafter give ample testimony. His eminence as a fox-
hunter has, however, thrown into the shade the fact
of his having excelled in these diversions. He said
he should like to ride, shoot, play cricket, and box
with Mr. Osbaldeston, but he would begin with the
last, in order to disqualify his opponent from obtaining the victory in the other three exploits. From
his love of boating at Eton, doubtless, sprang his taste
for yachting in after life. Everywhere at Tedworth
might be traced indications of his favourite science.
Along the ledge of the shelves in the library were

ranged, and still remain, the models of some favourite steam-yachts, Fire Queen, Screw Queen, Glowworm, Jenny Lind, and Sea Serpent. Of the last, a beautiful water-colour drawing hangs over the mantel-piece. Of his qualities as an amateur shipwright we have already spoken, and the science he displayed in the various vessels he built, both sailing and steam-yachts, evinces no ordinary skill and aptitude for mechanics; his acute observation frequently enabling him to make suggestions of great value in the construction and improvement of ships. He used to say that his knowledge of building sailing-vessels was derived from observing how low wild-ducks swam in the water.

The quickness of eye and steadiness of hand, which made him a good shot and a good cricketer, served him also at billiards. He mentioned that in Paris he was backed to play a celebrated marker, whom he beat, upon which he was challenged by the same individual to play for a very large stake. This he wisely declined, never being a gambler. Once at Tedworth, after a large party had finished a game at pool, a constant evening's amusement at the beautiful slate table there, he came into the billiard-room, and challenged to play the winner. This happened to be the then Marquess of Douro, no common performer. The game went pretty even, the one in constant practice, the other quite the reverse. At last the squire put his adversary's and his own ball into the pocket. He had then to play at the red ball, which was just below the middle pocket. "Who says I cannot pocket the red ball in the middle pocket?" observed the striker. A friend, who stood by, knowing his man, made a bet to that effect; and the way in which Mr. Smith did it showed at once what a player he must have been when in practice, and astonished every one present. He hit the further end cushion with his ball, which, on its return, gently deposited the red in the middle pocket, winning the game for the player, and the bet for his friend.

The squire loved hospitality, and at Tedworth, during the season, there was a constant succession of visitors. His table, his equipages, his appointments, the domestic arrangements of his establishment, were all in first-rate style, and in excellent keeping. To Mrs. Smith's suggestions for the laying out and improvement of the grounds he almost always deferred; once, however, the squire was determined to have his own way, even as regarded landscape. This occurred at Vaenol, when an artist was commissioned to take a sketch for a picture from a certain spot which Mr. Smith had selected, and which proved that he had an eye for the picturesque. With his usual quick perception, the owner of the property inquired whether a clump of large trees standing immediately before the house, did not obstruct the view; upon the

artist's replying that he did not think their removal
would be an improvement, and appealing to the ladies
of the party, among whom of course was Mrs. Smith,
for the preservation of the timber, he hastily drew
him aside and whispered, " Pray hold your tongue;
I want these trees down, but if you say another word
I shall not get leave." Leave was granted, and in less
than half an hour, ropes, ladders, saws, and axes were
at work. Mr. Smith knew that ladies *do* sometimes
change their minds, and by the rapidity of his movements he placed the permission beyond the " power
of revocation." The event proved the correctness of
his decision; the undulations in a park of 500 acres
can now be seen, and the gap, formerly filled by the
trees, lets in as fine a prospect as can be seen in
North Wales. During the last year of his life, a
friend riding with him and Mrs. Smith, by the Tedworth Lodge, observed to the latter, how much nobler
an appearance the chestnut trees would present, if all
the scrubby bushes lying under them were removed.
Mrs. Smith acquiescing in the remark, the squire,
without further comment, said to two men who were
painting the fence, " Put down your brushes, and
get axes, and let me find all these bushes cut
down on my return from my ride." This was accordingly done, much to the improvement of the
landscape.

The squire's love for science influenced even the

arrangements of his household. At Tedworth, at Vaenol, and at his London house, he devised a railroad from his kitchen to his dining-room, along which the dishes passed and repassed, and thus he obviated the necessity of his servants quitting the room, and the consequent delay. At Vaenol, the train arriving with its savoury load opened a trapdoor at the end of the dining-room; this closed of itself immediately after the admission of the course, and thus no inconvenience arose from the smell of cooking which frequently penetrates open doors and passages in the largest houses. The weight of the empty dishes going down, as in the case of the slate waggons at Llanberris, brought upon the platform within the dining-room, by means of diminutive connecting ropes, the hot and smoking trucks coming up. This process, if not the only one of the kind in England, was at all events invented and introduced entirely by Mr. Smith. Latterly, in London, when suffering from asthma, he had an ingenious mechanical contrivance, by which he was raised to his bedroom on one of the upper stories, as he always entertained a great objection to sleeping on the ground-floor.

His attachment to all animals (we are afraid foxes would demur to being placed in the category), especially to horses, dogs, and birds, was remarkable. We have already instanced his care and kind treatment of the gallant hunter who carried him close to the

hounds. He never would permit his coachman to
use the whip with his carriage-horses, and if the in-
junction happened to be forgotten, he would start up
in his carriage and severely reprimand him. His
lady's pet dogs were always sources of great interest;
Flash, Dandy, and Fop shared his regard and were
privileged favourites. Poor Dandy came to an un-
timely end, being badly bitten by one of the fox-
hounds whom he had in his wantonness attacked, and
his sad fate was severely felt and lamented. Mrs.
Smith was no less fond of animals than her husband,
and there was always a favourite hunter whom she
coaxed and fed. Once hearing that the son of a
friend had a tame magpie at school, which he resisted
all solicitations to sell, although his pocket-money
was entirely exhausted, she immediately sent him a
sovereign. Birds were objects of especial interest
to the squire; he loved to remark their habits, and
his country amusements afforded him ample opportunities of observing their instincts. He had at
different times several pet robins, whom he constantly
fed in the conservatory, and his favourite rooks, who
used to come close to the library windows during
the severe weather, and were never sent empty away.
These incidents may seem too insignificant to mention, but men are more thoroughly known by trifles
than by serious actions; in the former the disposition
is far more faithfully reflected than in the latter. At

one end of the conservatory he had a beautiful cocka-
too, which was sure of a kind word from him at every
turn of his horse when he took his daily rides there,
during the last winter of his life. He took no small
delight in watching the innumerable flocks of starlings
that always in the severe season roosted in the laurel
plantation abutting on Ashdown Copse, and used to
say, how wonderful it was, that when these countless
myriads all on a sudden turned as it were on a pivot,
without any previous signal, they never by any chance
in their gyrations struck against one another, or
interfered with their respective evolutions in the
air. These birds were by his strict orders never
molested.

The natural kindness of disposition which thus
manifested itself towards inferior creatures, shone
out as a feature in his character, only with greater
strength and intensity, in his treatment of those
around him. No master, peremptory as he was in his
commands, and exacting in having his orders at once
executed and to the very letter, was more beloved
than he was by his servants. If he was violent and
tyrannical, as has been sometimes represented, how
was it that years after the same individuals composed
his household, and that the retainers on his estates in
Hampshire and North Wales had grown grey-headed
in his service? In his friendships he was a man of
strong affections, as has been already observed, and of

a childlike tenderness of heart. Dictatorial, impetuous, and overbearing as he occasionally was, and these failings sprang as much from his self-confidence as from his ardent temperament, it is recorded of him that he never lost a friend. He had survived almost all his contemporaries, but among those who enjoyed his intimacy latterly, out of his own family, were the Duke of Bedford, the Hon. Philip Pierrepont, Sir John Pollen, Mr. John Drummond, the Rev. Henry Fowle, Mr. Charles Bell Ford, Admiral Montague, and Sir Richard Sutton; of these Sir Richard, so many years his comrade and fellowsportsman in the hunting field, held the place nearest to his heart. When he heard of his death* he was overwhelmed with grief, and burst into a flood of tears; and afterwards, when he commenced telling a story about Sir Richard, he suddenly threw up his hands in strong emotion, exclaiming, "Oh, my poor friend!" and could not proceed. The regard he entertained for the Duke of Wellington has already been adverted to, and his friendship was warmly reciprocated. Once a report getting abroad that Mr. Smith was dead, his Grace, who was then in London, despatched the Marquess of Douro immediately from Strathfieldsaye to Tedworth, to make enquiries, and finding to his satisfaction that the squire was enjoying his usual robust health, the Duke wrote to him the following letter:—

* In 1856.

"London, Nov. 12, 1851.

"My dear Smith,—They have killed you again in these last days! But I have been happy to learn that the report is without foundation.

"They treat you in this respect as they do me. I conclude that it is in your capacity of Field Marshal of Fox-hunting.

"Ever yours, most sincerely,

"WELLINGTON."

Another note written by the Duke is characteristic of the writer:—

"London, May 11, 1840.

"My dear Smith,—I have received your note. I attend in Parliament four days in the week. At the Ancient Musick on Wednesdays. There remain Sunday and Saturday.

"Every animal in the creation is sometimes allowed a holiday, excepting the Duke of Wellington. There the days are, take any Saturday or Sunday that you please.

"I should certainly like to have occasionally a day's leisure, while the Ancient Concerts are going on, and the pressure of business is so heavy in Parliament.

"But my convenience, likings, or dislikings, have nothing to do with the matter; they are not worth discussing. I would prefer doing anything, rather than have a discussion on the subject.

" Remember me most kindly to Mrs. Smith, and believe me ever yours most sincerely,

" W."

A strong sense of justice was one of his prevailing characteristics. He constantly took the part of persons who were total strangers to him, when subjected in his opinion to injury and oppression. He threw himself warmly into any case of injustice recorded in the public journals, both using his interest on behalf of the sufferer, and contributing money for his relief. Once, when he saw an Irishwoman beating her child on the high road, he tried to expostulate with her in order to dissuade her from that method of correcting it; but finding his entreaties had no effect, and that the virago opened on him for his interference, he left the spot, but not without giving five shillings to a labourer, who happened to be present, to see that the violence was not repeated. As a proof of his acute observation and discernment of character, I will mention the following anecdote.

He had two small green boxes in his study at Tedworth, in one of which he kept his letters and papers, and in the other what money he had in the house. The first of these was one morning missing, the thief having by mistake taken the wrong box, both being exactly alike. Mr. Smith, considering that the fact of his keeping his cash in one of these boxes would be more likely to be known to the servants who were in the habit of waiting upon him in his study than to any one else, caused a search to be made throughout the premises, and the missing box was at length discovered open in one of the shrub-beries. Mr. Smith, upon this, had his whole phalanx of men-servants drawn up in line before him, and put the question direct to each. All having strictly denied any knowledge of the transaction, were dis-missed by their master to their several duties. But shortly afterwards one of the footmen entering his study to put coals on the fire, Mr. Smith went straight up to him, and collaring him said, " It is you, sir, who took the box; here is a five-pound note, take it, return me my papers, and begone this moment." The man, guilty and thunderstruck, and at the same time overpowered by his master's kindness, imme-diately owned to having committed the theft, and said, trembling, that it was the first time in his life he had done so dishonest an act. Mr. Smith said after-wards that he had remarked this man's countenance, as he stood before him with the other servants, and that his suspicions then excited were strengthened into certainty of the man's guilt by the peculiarity of his manner as he entered the room with the coals.

Mr. Smith was always most precise and regular in his appointments. When he gave Mr. Ferneley his first sitting on Jack o'Lantern at Quorn, in 1807, he said he should allow the artist thirty minutes. He sat patiently during that time, looking occasionally at his watch, and the instant it had expired, as Mr. Ferneley relates, he was "off the saddle." The sketch was first seen by Tom Jones, his groom, who said it was an excellent likeness. He always rode Jack o'Lantern with a slack rein. This portrait was painted the first year Dick Burton came to him, being at that time only fifteen years old.

Religion is a topic upon which Mr. Smith was generally silent, and certainly, beyond a regular observance of the Sabbath, he made no particular external profession of it. But one who knew him best, said that he had a most simple and devout faith, his favourite motto being, "Whatever happens, all is for the best;" and whenever he saw any one in sorrow or distress, he always said, "We must submit to God's will, whatever it is." During his severe sufferings in both his attacks of illness, he evinced the most tranquil patience and resignation, and whenever he felt easier, or in any way relieved, his exclamation was, "Thank God for everything!" On one occasion a friend happened to say, heedlessly and jokingly, in a letter to him, that he felt much distressed in mind, and was almost inclined to commit suicide. Mr. Smith replied to him with a severe admonition never to speak lightly upon so serious a subject.

CHAP. VIII.

HIS CHARACTER AS A MASTER OF HOUNDS, HUNTSMAN, AND RIDER.
— TESTIMONY OF CONTEMPORARY SPORTSMEN. — ANECDOTES OF
HIS HORSEMANSHIP.—HIS VAST ESTATES ARE LEFT ENTIRELY TO
THE DISPOSAL OF HIS WIDOW, WHO SURVIVES HIM ONLY A FEW
MONTHS.

> " Si petis exemplar mentis, vitæque virilis,
>   Cùm fortes animos Anglia voce ciet.
> Sive feraris equo, seu magna incepta sequaris,
>   Dux tibi, quicunque es, vir sit hic, ' ire viam.'
> Nec malè, Venator, campi rapis ardua cursu ;
>   Addunt se comites Mars, nemorumque Dea."
>
> WICCAMICUS.

To come at length to his qualities as a fox-hunter,
it may appear superfluous to contend for what has
been already conceded by every sportsman. His fame,
as far back as the beginning of the present century,
is matter of history. The Emperor Napoleon the
First, who somewhat disconcerted the vanity of the
great orator Erskine, by the observation, " Êtes-vous
légiste? " honoured Mr. Smith by addressing him as
" Le premier chasseur d'Angleterre." He was called
by the Parisians, " Le grand chasseur Smit." There
has not a book been published in his time which does
not allot to him the highest place as a master of

hounds, a huntsman, and a rider. To say nothing of
the celebrated Nimrod, whose pages are familiar to
all lovers of the chase, the testimony of Mr. Delmé
Ratcliffe, in his work on the " Noble Science of
Fox-hunting," is perhaps the most complete. " I
could nowhere find a more fitting model for the
rising generation of sportsmen. . . . He was an
instance of the very rare union of coolness and con-
summate skill as a huntsman, combined with the
impetuosity of a most desperate rider; and not only
was he the most determined of all riders, but equally
remarkable as a horseman. His practice as a huntsman was that which is best followed in any, but
especially in a good, country, — that of leaving
hounds very much to themselves, although ever on
the spot to render assistance if required."* Among
the best of the songs in which his feats are mentioned
is a capital one by Lord Forester, " On a Run with
the Duke of Rutland," the third verse of which runs
thus : —

> " The hounds had not been there a minute,
>   When the Duke cried, ' Hark! halloo! away!'
> Not a hound was there left behind in it,—
>   You'd swear they would show him some play.
> Th' hard riders jump'd off in a crack,
>   Not one of them minding his neck,
> And for Belvoir were running him back,
>   When Tom Smith rode the hounds to a check."

---

* Noble Science of Fox-hunting, p. 202.

N

I cannot resist the temptation of here inserting the language of Nimrod, it is so hearty, genuine, and unmistakable. " I have a long list in letter S," says he, in his alphabetical catalogue of eminent riders, " and of course lots of Smiths. But Theodore Hook says 'they should be numbered :' and there can be no hesitation as to the best claim to 'number one,' namely, T. Assheton Smith, Esq., of Tedworth House, Hants, late owner of, and huntsman to, the Quorn Hounds, and at present (1841) hunting a very good pack of his own in Hampshire. Now I am not going to give merely my own opinion of Mr. Thomas Assheton Smith, as a horseman and rider to hounds, but shall lay before my readers that of all the sporting world, at least all who have seen him in the field ; which is, that taking him from the first day's hunting of the season to the last, place him on the best horse in his stable or on the worst, he is sure to be with his hounds, and *close to them too.* In fact, he has undoubtedly proved himself the best and hardest rider England ever saw, and it would be vain in any man to dispute his title to that character. But we might as well attempt to make a blind man an optician, a lame man a dancing-master, or a one-armed one a fiddler, as to suppose that any gentleman could arrive at this ultra state of perfection in a very difficult art, which horsemanship undoubtedly is, unless nature had been prodigal of the requisites.   Setting

aside the daring, undaunted, the not-to-be-denied *
determination of Mr. Smith to get to hounds, despite
of any and all difficulties which may have opposed
him,—the result of strongly braced nerves and great
physical powers,—let us look at him in his saddle.
Does he not look like a workman ? Observe how
lightly he sits ? No one would suppose him to be a
twelve-stone man. And what a firm hand he has on
his horses ? How well he puts them at their fences,
and what chances he gives them to extricate themselves from any scrape they may have gotten into.
He never hurries them then; no man ever saw Tom
Smith ride fast at his fences, at least at large ones
(brooks excepted), let the pace be what it may ; and
what a treat it is to see him jump water! His falls,
to be sure, have been innumerable ; but what very
hard-riding man does not get falls ? Hundreds of
Mr. Smith's falls may be accounted for : he has
measured his horses' pluck by his own, and ridden at
hundreds of non-feasible places, with the chance of
getting over them somehow. Bravo! Mr. Smith, you
must be number *one*, for, by Heavens! there will never
be such another Mr. Smith as long as the world
stands." †

To go back to writers contemporary with the feats

---

* No word so thoroughly describes his character as the English
word "pluck."

† Hunting Reminiscences, p. 294.

of which they spoke, when criticism and censure would have soon exposed and overwhelmed any attempt at exaggeration, let us listen to the testimony of "Dorset," writing in November 1836. After expressing his astonishment at the difficulties Mr. Smith contended against and overcame in Hants, where, to use his own forcible expression, he " screwed odd ends of a country together," he thus proceeds :—" Of Mr. Smith, as a huntsman, it is needless to speak here, or indeed anywhere. He ranks with the first professors of this noble science; and as the *first horseman of the age,* as well as the most *accomplished huntsman* of the present day, his name will be enrolled historically in the deathless pages of the chronicles of the chase, and among those who have advanced and aided the political economy of his country in one of its most important departments." *

The testimony of Dick Christian, and of "The Druid" in Silk and Scarlet, is perhaps the most unreserving of any. "No man," says Dick †, "that ever came into Leicestershire could beat Mr. Smith, I do not care what any of them say : " while " The Druid," after giving some very interesting anecdotes of him whom he styles "the great master of the nineteenth century," thus speaks of him " at the finish :" —" However hasty in temper and action he might be in

* Sporting Magazine, 2nd series, Nov. 1836, p. 168.
† Page 58.

the field or on the flags, he was the mightiest hunter that ever 'rode across Belvoir's sweet vale' or wore a horn at his saddle-bow."*

Beckford says, in his celebrated work†, that it is as difficult to find a perfect huntsman as a good prime minister, and he proceeds to enumerate the requisite qualifications for excellence in the former as follows: — A clear head, nice observation, quick apprehension, undaunted courage, strength of constitution, activity of body, a good ear, and a good voice. We may observe that every one of these qualities was to be found in Mr. Assheton Smith. He was particularly careful in making his casts‡, often three in number, each one wider than the other, and spreading like a sky-rocket. He was averse to lifting his hounds, which he said made them idle, and too dependent on the huntsman. He preferred seeing them work out the scent and improve gradually upon the line; — here a hit and there a hit, now a challenge from a trusty old hound, ("Hark to Ringwood! he has it,") when the willing pack rush with headlong eagerness to their leader; then a general dash which bursts forth at the same moment into hard and determined running. No huntsman ever laid hounds on the line with greater quickness than Assheton Smith. Yet

* Silk and Scarlet, p. 284.
† On Hunting, p. 6.
‡ "Cecil" in the Sporting Magazine, March 1840.

he would sometimes lift his hounds, when he was
desirous of getting away from the large fields of
sportsmen out in Leicestershire; to effect which
he would also perform the following stratagem.   It
is usual after drawing a cover, if no fox is found, to
proceed to the one next adjoining, but Smith would,
in order to get rid of what he called the Spring Captains (for he was never very partial to young sportsmen), gallop off at a splitting pace to some wood five
or six miles off, over every hedge and ditch that came
in his way.   His system of hunting differed essentially from that of Mr. Osbaldeston in this respect,
that he was as silent as possible until the fox was
found, whereas Osbaldeston thought to make him
break cover by the noise he made.*   Mr. Osbaldeston's
system was the more popular of the two, as that of
Mr. Smith put too great a restraint upon the field.
The latter did not even always carry a horn, especially in his earlier career.   He always put the most
entire confidence in his hounds, and often mentioned
the story of the Belvoir huntsman, who followed his
pack to the door of a barn, when every one in the
field supposed the fox had gone on.   "If he is not
in *here*," said he, " my hounds deserve to be hanged,"
and sure enough they found Reynard hid under
the boltings of straw, and killed him.   It was a

* Among the ancients it was considered an ill omen if any one
spoke while hunting.

splendid sight to see Mr. Smith throw his hounds into cover, although he was sometimes in the habit of drawing too quickly.   At the great meet in Leicestershire in 1840, he did not half draw Shankton Holt, and if it had not been for Mr. Hodgson, who waded into Vowes Gorse in his jack-boots, he would not have found a fox there.   If Mr. Smith had a fault as a huntsman, it was that he was too impatient.

When he went into Leicestershire he found Lord Foley's hounds not of large size, but he soon raised the standard, dog hounds to twenty-five inches in height and bitches to twenty-three.   Some sportsmen considered his dog hounds, although of enormous power, too heavy for his light and Alpine country, and too large for his great woodlands, but all acknowledged his bitch pack to be perfect.   " They're beauties," he used to say himself, pointing to Dairy-maid, Pastime, and Blowsy, " and John Mills* might well write their lives."   The late Duke of Beaufort drew largely from Mr. Smith's packs, with the assistance of his huntsman, Will Long.   The squire was fond of breeding from hounds of various qualities; the combination of strength, swiftness, and nose thus formed the perfect hound.   As to mixture of colour, he was fond of that in which the blue or grey predominated, although he was of the same opinion as Foote, namely, that a good dog could not be of a bad colour.

* Author of The Life of a Fox-hound.

How he loved the thrilling melody of his pack!—

"Match'd in mouth like bells, each under each,"—

and how he would turn round in his saddle, even before he was half over his leap, to catch all he could of the joyous ecstasy of their voices—

"Vocat ingenti clamore Cithæron,
Taygetique canes, domitrixque Epidaurus equorum,
Et vox assensu nemorum ingeminata remugit."   VIRG.

As an instance of the enthusiasm Mr. Smith always evinced for his favourite diversion, and of the value he set upon a participation in it, an anecdote may be mentioned of the Rev. Francis Dyson, now rector of Cricklande. Mr. Dyson's father was the clergyman at Tedworth, and gave his son a title to orders as his curate on his being first ordained. Mr. Smith was so pleased with his first sermon, that, on coming out of church, he slapped the young man on the back, and said, "Well done, Frank! you shall have a mount on Rory (Rory O'More) next Thursday." Young Dyson had many a run afterwards out of the squire's stables, for his performances in the field pleased as much as those in the pulpit.

Among Mr. Smith's sporting congregation were not a few of the clergy, and these were never far in the rear of the squire. He was once entering the house of a certain divine, where his hounds met that morning, accompanied by the late Lord G. Bentinck. "What profession is this gentleman of?" said his

Lordship, as they entered his drawingroom. " A parson," replied the squire, and pointing to the pictures of eminent sportsmen which adorned the walls, added, " Don't you see the portraits of his favourite bishops?" Dr. Coplestone, bishop of Llandaff, had loved fox-hunting in his youth, and always looked on these " clerical errors" with some indulgence. When he was provost of Oriel, a needy curate wishing to ingratiate himself with the Oxford dignitary, pointed out to him, as they sauntered together down High Street, a worthy parson of Jesus College, who was riding leisurely along on his way to meet the hounds, and remarked, with a shrug of religious horror, " Sic itur ad astra." " It is not the white breeches," replied the provost, with greater discernment and liberality, " that the Church need be afraid of, but your long-coated, black-gaitered gentlemen."

Doubtless Mr. Smith had vast advantages of physical strength, of extraordinary nerve, and a constitution never bending under fatigue. These are important adjuncts to success in the hunting-field, but they are not the ruling elements, and Mr. Smith shared them with many other men. Cassius complained with envy, that the weakly temperament of Cæsar overcame the world. The secret of Mr. Smith's great success lay in his unbounded ardour for his favourite pursuit, and the unremitting energy he brought to bear upon it.

The reason why there are no great men among us
at the present day, in the senate, the forum, and in the
camp, is, that there is no enthusiasm. The prevailing
symptom of our age is a lack of abiding earnestness.
We have become so refined in our tastes, and there is
such a reduction of intellect, education, habits, and
consequently of character, to the same level, that the
word enthusiasm has almost become one of reproach.
An ardent or enthusiastic man is held out as a mad-
man; and yet it might be said of Tom Smith, as it was
of the heroic admiral, " I wish we had five hundred
men as mad as he was." By this quality, be its estimate
what it may, he achieved his renown; and, what is
more extraordinary still, his ardour never flagged nor
abated. Whether it be ambition or any other passion
stimulating the senses or quickening the understanding, most men gradually tire of the pursuit. The
attainment and fruition of an object gradually lessens
our excitement, and we seek a renewal and revival of
our activity in varied interests and in fresh pleasures.
But we see Mr. Smith year after year following the
same pursuit, in the highest degree animating, but
having no very great novelty or variety to recommend
it, with unabated ardour, with almost increasing zest.
Can it be wondered at, with such constancy of purpose as this, and talent to execute co-extensive with
it, that he carried the science of hunting as near to
perfection as it is capable of, and retained for it its

national distinctiveness?   It would be difficult, perhaps, to separate from each other any of the numerous ingredients which, combined with and assisting
the enthusiasm we have described, went to raise
Mr. Smith to the high rank he will ever possess
among British sportsmen.   Bacon says, in his admirable essay on State Government, that boldness is the
first in civil despatch, boldness second, boldness third;
meaning that, for all practical purposes, all other
qualities are immeasurably subordinate to this.   In
like manner it may be said of fox-hunting, that
boldness in riding makes up three fifths of eminence
in it.   The fourth and fifth parts wanting may mar
the other three.   Not so in the case of Mr. Smith.   He
was fully master of the details and minutiæ of the
sport, and his judgment was equal to his courage.
His observation was so quick, and his intuitive
knowledge of the animal he pursued so ready, that he
never hesitated a moment at a check what to do, and
always could give a good reason for what he did.
" Quickness of decision," observes an excellent judge,
" is the life and soul of fox-hunting."   Mr. Maxse was
heard to say that the reason why Mr. Smith showed
such famous sport in Leicestershire was, that when
his hounds came to a check he would just as soon ride
over any high gate or tremendous fence, if he thought
that the scent lay that way, as make his cast over the
open field.

" As a huntsman," said one who well knew what a
combination of qualities is necessary for the attainment of excellence in that department of the science
of fox-hunting, "I fearlessly put Mr. Smith in the
first class. He has *even to this day*" (in 1841, when
the squire was sixty-five years old) "all the requisites
to make him such; zeal, quickness of perception,
untiring perseverance, a ready judgment when in
difficulty, and horsemanship quite unequalled for
daring and duration by any man of this or any other
age. For example, what said his brother-sportsmen
of him only last season in Lincolnshire? Why, that
there was no man who could get over, or out of when
in, the wide and deep drains of that country, so
cleverly as Tom Smith did. When too wide to be
cleared, as I was informed by an eye-witness, he
would force his horse into them diagonally, then,
alighting from his saddle and scrambling up the bank,
he would pull his horse after him; and this when
past his grand climacteric."*

The following anecdote was related by Mr. Child,
a Hampshire yeoman of the right sort, who always
had a fox for Mr. Smith in Wilster Wood. " The
first time Mr. Smith ran a fox into the Newbury
Vale, I and some friends, seeing he pointed for the
meadows near East Woodhay, got forward to a tremendous leap that had often stopped the whole

* Nimrod's Hunting Reminiscences, p. 298.

Craven Hunt. 'It was a stile, bank, and hedge, and a liberal allowance of water on the far side. Down came the squire on Screw-driver, and took it in his stroke. This did not so much surprise us, but what *did* was, that he *never once turned round to look at it;* whereas, had one of our fellows got over it, he would have looked at it for a week and talked of it for a year."

His notion of a huntsman was that he should always be with his hounds. On this principle he invariably acted ; for he well knew that unless a master of fox-hounds, hunting them himself, had head, hand, and heart, and could be close to his hounds when they were close to their fox, he could not do his duty as it should be done. One day when he had the Quorndon, after a sharp affair of forty minutes, the fox, quite beaten, ran into a small covert with a lane half round it. The field kept the lane; the squire, exclaiming, " They will have him in five minutes!" leapt into the adjoining paddock, at the further end of which there was a tremendously thick bullfincher. Unused to denial, he rode at it, and fell with his horse on a heap of rough stones on the other side, tearing his white cords most piteously. He was up again in a moment, and as unconcerned as if he had fallen out of his arm-chair, and *did* kill his fox within the five minutes. Mr. Smith had a great contempt for a man who attempted to hunt a pack of fox-hounds and could not ride to them; and he never scrupled to express his opinion whenever any such instances came under his own observation, as no man was more fairly entitled to do. The following anecdote of his courage was related by Nimrod at the time when the circumstance occurred. It was during the last year Mr. Smith hunted Leicestershire. He had a run of nineteen minutes, point blank, known to the present time by the name of the Belvoir Day. It happened that the pace was so good, and the country so severe, that no one was with the hounds towards the last except the squire of Tedworth and Mr. John White, a well-known sportsman of that day. These two came to a fence so high and so strong that there was apparently only one place at all practicable, and this was in the line Mr. White was taking. Mr. Smith consequently was obliged to turn his horse to this place, expecting to find White well over; but instead of this he found him well " bullfinched," that is, sticking fast in the hedge. " Get on!" says Mr. Smith. " I cannot," replies Mr. White: " I am fast." " Ram the spurs into him!" roared out the squire, " and pray get out of the way." " If you are in such a hurry," rejoined Mr. White, " why don't you charge me?" Mr. Smith never spoke, but did charge him, and sent him and his horse into the next field, when away they both went again as if nothing had happened, the squire of course soon making to the front.

Another remarkable run with Mr. Smith's hounds, when in Leicestershire, is also thus chronicled by Nimrod :—" I will mention a day's sport which I had when Mr. Smith (*the* Mr. Smith) had the Quorn hounds, which I have no doubt is fresh in the recollection of many who witnessed it, for it was a brilliant one, and such as no other country in the world could have shown *on that day*. It was on the 17th of April, and as Tom Wingfield (the whipper-in) observed, 'a kind of day more fit for growing cucumbers than for hunting.' It was, however, allowed to be the second best day's sport of the year. We had had one good burst of sixteen minutes without a check, best pace, heads up and sterns down. *The* fox of the day, however, was found in Holt Cover, and took us away twelve miles in fifty-eight minutes, with only one trifling check of eight minutes, before he died. The country he went over could only be compared to Newmarket Heath, enclosed with strong fences. That there was distress among the horses it is needless to observe, after the above description. Mr. Smith rode his famous Jack-o'-Lantern in his usual style. Seeing Mr. Lindow on 'The Clipper,' encouraging the hounds to a scent at a gateway, he was beginning to rate us, saying 'that the hounds had been pressed upon, and that we only wanted a puff for our horses.' At this moment the chase was resumed, and Lindow turning round, aptly remarked, 'that he had had *his* puff, or he would not have been there.' The fox lived about eight minutes longer, and Mr. Smith, seeing two couples of his young hounds leading, appeared transported with delight. He never turned his horse's head so much as ten yards to the right or to the left for an open gate, or for a gap, but rode by the side of his pack, cheering them to their fox (which he knew must die) in a manner and at a pace that I shall never forget."

Most people know what a number of brooks there are in the Quorn and Belvoir counties, and most sportsmen, if they were never out with Mr. Smith, have at all events heard what a capital hand he was at getting over them. He once charged the river Welland, which divides the counties of Leicester, Northampton, and Rutland, and is said to be altogether impracticable, at the end of one of the most desperate runs ever known. This knack he had of getting across water is to be attributed to his resolute way of riding to hounds, by which his horses knew that it was in vain to refuse whatever he might put them at. A remarkable example of this occurred in the Harborough country. He was galloping at three parts speed down one of the large grass fields which abound in that district, in the act of bringing his hounds to a scent, and was looking back to see if they were coming. Exactly in the middle of the field, and in the line immediately before his horse, was a pool of water, into which the animal leaped, thinking it useless to refuse, and of course being unaware that he was not intended to take it. This horse would doubtless have jumped into the Thames or the Severn in a similar manner, had they been before him. His wonderful influence over his hunters was strongly exemplified at another time, but in rather a different manner. He had mounted a friend, who complained of having nothing to ride, on his celebrated horse Cicero. The hounds were running breast-high across the big pasture lands of Leicestershire, and Cicero was carrying his rider like a bird, when a strong flight of rails had almost too ugly an aspect of height, strength, and newness, for the liking of our friend on his "mount." The keen eye of Assheton Smith, as he rode beside him, at once discerned that he had no relish for the timber, and seeing that he was likely to make the horse refuse, he cried out, "Come up, Cicero!" His well-known voice had at once the desired effect, but Cicero's rider, by whom the performance was not intended, left his "seat" vacant, fortunately without any other result than a roll upon the grass.

"I have said," remarks Nimrod, "that Mr. Smith's make and shape, together with a fine bridle-hand, have assisted him in rising to perfection as a horseman; and I will produce one or two proofs of the use he made of these by no means subaltern endowments. I have seen him riding horses which scarcely

o

required a bridle, such as his large Grey Horse, Jack-o'-Lantern, Gift, Tom Thumb, Gadsby, and others equally temperate and agreeable ; and I have seen and heard of him riding some that no other men could have ridden *as he rode them*. Mr. Lindow's Clipper was, for example, so hard a puller with hounds that the bit, called ' the Clipper bit,' was made purposely to suit him ; and a most severe one it is. On a proposal being one day made, that Lindow and Smith should exchange horses for the day, the latter, previously to mounting the Clipper, put his curb chain into his pocket. ' Good-bye to you !' said his friend, as the hounds were finding their fox, ' we shall never see you again.' He rode, however, in his usual place, — alongside the pack." *

I once saw, relates a friend, a fine specimen of Mr. Smith's hand and nerve in the going off of a frost, when the *bone* was not quite out of the ground. We were running a fox hard over Salisbury Plain, when all at once his horse came on a treacherous flat, greasy at top, as sportsmen say, but hard and slippery underneath. The horse he rode was a hard puller, and very violent, named Piccadilly ; and the least check from the bridle, when the animal began to blunder, would have to a certainty made him slip up. Here the fine riding of the squire shone conspicuously. He left his horse entirely alone, as if he were swimming ; and after floundering about and swerving for

* Hunting Reminiscences.

at least a hundred yards, Piccadilly recovered himself and went on as if nothing had happened. I saw him, he adds, on the same horse on another occasion, when a fox was sinking, and his horse so beaten that he could scarcely ride at a fence, charge a stiff wattled hedge. The horse got over, but came down on his head, nevertheless was quickly righted again. The same fence, with a ditch *from* him, was to be encountered again at going out of the field ; and here the squire's address was no less remarkable than had been his cool courage. When within about twenty yards of the fence he had a pull at his horse, and after a slight pause sent him at the fence as if he were riding at water. The impetus carried him over the ditch, and he landed safely in the next field, bringing the best part of the fence along with him. A timid rider, or one with less presence of mind, in either of the above positions, would inevitably have met with what is known in sporting parlance as " a case."

He was once drawing for a fox on his famous horse Fire-King (his horse and yacht of that name did him alike good service), when he came to a precipitous bank at the end of a meadow, with a most formidable drop into a hard road. " You cannot get out there, sir," said a polite farmer. " I should like very much to see the place where *we* " (patting Fire-King) "cannot go," was the reply : and down he rode, to the astonishment of the field. This circumstance occurred at Martin, near Wexcombe, and is spoken of to this day as a most dangerous leap.

Mr. Smith's character as a master of hounds has been ably and faithfully drawn by Mr. Newdegate, member for North Warwickshire, himself an excellent sportsman and daring rider. " Mr. Smith was in the field sometimes very rough-tempered, and cared not whom he offended. He thus made many personal enemies, or rather exasperated those who were jealous of his pre-eminence ; but he was almost always just in his anger, and only fell foul of those who were spoiling sport. He had one great characteristic ; he was determined that hunting should be a sport worthy of gentlemen, and of which ladies need not be ashamed. As master of a country he would not countenance, nay more, he very actively *discountenanced*, gambling, drinking, and debauchery. He was not foolish enough to set himself up as a severe moralist, but he was steadfastly opposed to what might be called the ostentation of vice. He was, in fact, a good man, with all the qualities of a first-rate soldier ; and these, I believe, produced the cordial friendship which the late Duke of Wellington always extended to him.

" There can, I think, be little doubt that Mr. Smith would have made a first-rate cavalry general ; in all his conduct, at home and in every country, he manifested a sincere desire to promote the best interests of all classes within his reach, and did this effectually, but without the slightest ostentation; while his quickness, foresight, and determination were undoubted. His devotion to hunting was, no doubt, exaggerated; but beneath it lay the purpose of fostering the manly qualities of his fellow-countrymen of all classes; an object of the deepest importance at the period of peril to this country which existed when he first became distinguished as a sportsman (1805 to 1815). I heartily wish we had a Tom Smith now."

The greatest riding period, observes the author of the Post and Paddock, with the Quorn is generally allowed to be that of Lords Jersey, Germaine, and Forester, and Messrs. Cholmondeley (afterwards Lord Delamere), Assheton Smith, Lindow, and his twin brother, Mr. Rawlinson, who was as famous over Leicestershire on Spread Eagle as he was on the turf with Coronation. It used to be said that Mr. Rawlinson's riding was the better for his horse, but that Mr. Lindow sold his horses better.* "Mr. Meynell," says Dick Christian, in his Post and Paddock lecture, "was like a regular little apple-dumpling on horseback; Mr. Assheton Smith and Lord Forester, they were the men for me. Lord Jersey, too, my word! he was very good; and Sir Charles Knightley,

* P. 298.

he was one of Lord Jersey's stamp. How he would
go, to be sure ! he *would* be with the hounds, to see
them do their work. Blame me, but I've seen him,
at the end of a run, all blood and thorns. Mr. Smith
never galloped his horses at fences, he always
drew them up. He had little low-priced horses when
he first came into this country, but he rode them so
as no man ever will again, and they would do
anything; get into bottoms and jump out of them
like nothing. My eyes ! he made them handy. Those
were different days ; you might find at Melton Spinney and run to Billesdon Coplow, and not cross a
ploughed field."* "I have seen Mr. Holyoake go
like distraction for fifteen minutes, but Mr. Smith
and Mr. Greene, and Mr. Gilmour, and Lord Wilton,
they are the men to go when others are leaving off." †

Among the foremost of Mr. Smith's field, the last
season he hunted Leicestershire, was Colonel Wyndham of the Scotch Greys, who had returned to England after the battle of Waterloo. Wyndham was a
very powerful man, and could even in those days
get no change out of sixteen stone, but no fence ever
stopped him. When he could not get *over*, he got
through ; where a bullfinch seemed impenetrable, the
horsemen would cry out, " Where's Wyndham ? " and
he soon made a gap big enough for almost a whole
regiment to pass. Nor was it less extraordinary how,

* Post and Paddock, p. 359.   † P. 365.

with the Leicestershire pace, and with his heavy
weight, he got to his fox. On one occasion, when
Tom Smith thought he had it all his own way,
and the hounds were running into their fox, Mr.
Smith turned round to see how far he was ahead of
the field, and to his surprise saw Wyndham close at
his heels. " How the d——l did *you* get here ? " exclaimed the squire, who had some difficulty in retaining the lead. That lead his fellow-sportsmen occasionally endeavoured to snatch from him, but very
seldom with success. Sir F. Goodricke, then Frank
Holyoake, a very dashing rider, and others, rode
against him in a memorable run, but Smith went
clean away from them all, and Baronet, Sir James
Musgrave's horse, on which Holyoake was mounted,
was killed in the attempt. A steak from this renowned horse was afterwards served up at Melton,
and after William Cooke had partaken of it, his friends
jokingly asked him if he knew what he had eaten.
When informed it was a slice of his old friend Baronet,
instead of being disgusted, as they expected, he immediately replied, " Give me another cut off the same
steak." Once, after a severe run in Leicestershire,
when the fox was sinking, and Mr. Smith found his
horse in a like condemnation, " Oh, if I had but a
fresh horse," he exclaimed, " I would soon settle him."
" Get upon mine," said Mr. John Cook, who was riding
Lancet, a famous horse of great value. This offer

was at once accepted, and the whoop soon followed.
Instead of the expected panegyric when the horse
was restored to the owner, the remark of the squire
was, "I heard that he was a *plater*, but he is as slow
as a donkey." The fact was, he was annoyed at his
own horse being beaten.

The Post and Paddock, however, records in the
following terms an occasion on which Mr. Smith was
fairly conquered. "George Marriott once, on old
Prince, in a well-remembered run, played first to Mr.
Smith. The hounds had just found at Whetstone
Gorse, when Sir Robert Leighton said to Marriott:
"Don't ride to-day, as Mr. Canning wants to settle
about a match for you to ride with the old horse
against all comers at sixteen stone for a thousand
guineas." "You are too late," replied George; "he
would break my neck if I tried to stop him now."
Away they both went, side by side, Sir Robert and
George, till they reached a wide brook, which old
Prince cleared in a stride, pricking his ears up as
usual, while his companion floundered and fell in.
The old horse went for fifty minutes without a check,
and Mr. Smith could only take a second place with
him."[*]

Occasionally Mr. Smith read a severe lecture to his
field in pithy terms. A groom in the service of a
worthy baronet was riding his master's hack home,

_____
[*] Post and Paddock, p. 281.

when it broke away with him, and ran slap through the body of the pack, who were trotting up to draw "Carthanger" in Conholt Park. Old Cruiser, a splendid hound, was the victim, and lay sprawling on his back. The servant, having at last stopped his runaway horse, came back intending an apology, when he was thus addressed by Mr. Smith: "If you think, sir, you have *not* done quite mischief enough already, pray ride through my hounds again; but if you think you *have*, go home as quickly as you can." At another time, "Bob," the second whip, hallooed a hare away by mistake for a fox from Everley Gorse. The squire and the hounds were soon at the spot, and, of course, not a hound would speak. "I do not know, sir, whether you are ashamed of yourself, but my hounds, you see, are heartily ashamed of you," was the remark.

"Will you not wait for Captain Coldstream?" said an officious yeoman, as Mr. Smith was moving on to draw Clatford Oakcuts. "I have had three hundred captains out before now, sir," was the response, "but never better sport for it." "Why do you lie there, howling and exposing yourself?" said he to a rustic, whom his horse had slightly kicked. "My dear Tom," said his more feeling friend, Mr. Henry Pierrepont, "the man is hurt, and why so rough to him?" "On *principle*," rejoined the squire; "if I had *pitied* him, he would have been there for a week, but *now* you see he is up and well already."

During the winter of 1815, or the spring of 1816, in a run from Barkby Holt, while in the heat of the chase, Parson B., a well-known character in those days, fell in taking a large fence. A bold dragoon coming too quickly after him, drove out of the body of the reverend divine what little wind was left in it, by making a stepping-stone of the prostrate man. Mr. Smith, who beheld this transgression, instantly attacked the offender in no measured terms, when he excused himself by saying that it was not his fault, but that of his horse, as he had on only a snaffle bridle.   " Then, sir, the sooner you go home and get a double one the better," replied the Nimrod of unquestioned authority ; thus giving good advice to every one who could trust himself to a single rein instead of two.

" I like to see Squire Smith with the horn on his saddle," said Marsh, the sporting shoemaker ; "for he does things as *should be*. If he kills a fox, he kills him, and if he loses him he *loses him*. He does not do as Ben Foot (the Craven huntsman) does—go muttering after him all day long, and *worriting* him to death at last." Persons in Marsh's sphere of life form a very accurate estimate of men and things, and as they can feel no jealousy, there is no faintness in their praise.

When Mr. Smith purchased Sir Richard Sutton's hounds in 1827, they were brought up to Penton

Lodge by Jack Shirley and George Gardener, Sir Richard's huntsman and whip. Gardener remained as whip at Penton, and Dick Burton returned to his old master, with whom he had lived ten years in Leicestershire. A neater or better horseman than Dick could not be seen, nor one more active either in the kennel or field. His quickness in getting hounds to cap and halloo from such big spinnies as Collingbourne, Doles, and Doyly woods was marvellous; and his hark halloo, or as he pronounced it, *yaick haller*, hit a hound as hard as whipcord. Tigress was his especial plague, who, though first-rate in chase, was "such a one for hare," and always *hanging*. Once, when the hounds were running short with a sinking fox, a person clad in a long black coat, with a very missionary look about him, and evidently thinking scorn of the fun, inquired of Dick what the *dogs were then doing*. "Why, sir," said Dick, throwing a keen glance down the inquirer's person, "they are preaching his funeral sermon."

At another time, after a capital run, those who were lucky enough to be up, came to a sudden, and as they feared, a fatal check; when Dick perceived a shepherd's boy with his hat off, pointing forward. Dick rode up, caught the boy up before him on the saddle, galloped on to the point, where the fox was viewed, and killed him just getting into a large covert. Nothing but quickness would have saved the run. Dick lived twenty-two years with Mr. Smith; his other masters were Mr. Osbaldeston, Lord Southampton, Earl Ducie, and Lord Henry Bentinck. He is now enjoying a green old age, "frosty but kindly," at his old haunts near Quorndon. When Dick heard that Mr. Smith had been to see Rarey and his tamed zebra, he observed, "Ah! if Mr. Rarey had known my old master at twenty-five, to have tamed *him* would have been much more wonderful a task. I recollect him in those days," added the old huntsman, "riding a horse in Leicestershire called Agonistes. He gave him four falls before we found a fox. The last fall was over four strong draw-rails into a slow hole. The gentlemen laughed at him. Mr. Smith says, 'If I find a fox in Keythorpe spinnies, I will beat every one of you.' They found, had fifty minutes without a check, and killed." (This is like Cæsar's description, "Veni, vidi, vici.") "He did beat every one of them. He went as straight as the crow flies."

Mr. Smith was once running a fox hard by Tangly, when the hounds turned up a footpath into a field; just before them was an old woman carrying a bundle of sticks. Seeing the hounds in full cry close to her quarters, the old girl lashed out right and left with her heels. "Ware hounds," shouted Dick Burton. "What, ain't you steady from riot at your time of

life ? I *jest* wonder what you'd have done when a
filly !" When Dick and Tom Day whipped in for
Mr. Smith, nothing could be more perfect than the
tout ensemble of master and men. All had the same
jaunty balance seat, all were light good hands, all
first-rate horsemen ; and a fox, when they conspired
against him, had about as much chance of escape as
a felon, when Brougham or Scarlett held the adverse
brief. Exceptions, however, occurred sometimes,
and one must be noted, when the "imperiosa libido"
of the master saved the fox's life. The hounds had
been running with a holding scent in Collingbourne
woods, when at the extremity pointing for South
Grove, they came out of cover with a swing, and
after one swerve round, away they went like a flock
of pigeons for some time mute, as if they had not
time to say a word; and then every tongue in the
pack joined chorus. Unfortunately Mr. Smith did
not see them break covert, and when he came up,
they were running hard as if in view, and a hare
before them. Immediately he blew his horn, and
Dick had to ride for his life to stop them ; and when
he headed them, it required something stronger than
rate and whipcord to turn them. The squire sat
still blowing his horn, but the old hounds, instead of
going back to him, kept trying to get forward, and
then when rated remained where they were. "How
is this?" said a sportsman present to Dick, when at

last he got them back. "If that was not a fox, sir," was the reply, "I and those old hounds (pointing to Trimbush, Trimmer, Watchman, and Vanquisher) ought to be hung up to the kennel door without judge or jury." It was afterwards remarked to Mr. Smith, that the hounds were a long time coming back. "Yes," said he, "I see how it is, but it is too late to rectify it." It was very seldom that he showed this want of confidence in his hounds. In the well-known picture of Mr. Smith by Ferneley, Dick Burton appears the pattern of a smart huntsman.

George Carter came to Mr. Smith with the Grafton hounds, when purchased in 1842. At Tedworth he hunted the young and old hounds on the Wednesdays and Saturdays, Mr. Smith hunting on the other four days. Carter was generally confined to the big woods, Wednesday's fixture being always Wherwell Wood, containing upwards of 3000 acres, in which George said he had passed time enough to qualify him for a settlement as a parishioner. Whenever any hound in Mr. Smith's pack misbehaved himself, he was handed back to Carter's academy. The pack, which, as "the Grafton," were notorious for being hare-runners, improved wonderfully under the judicious management of Carter ; and when in his latter years he was left to breed them according to his own selection of sires, they became more level to the eye, and, like the sisters described by the poet,

"Facies non omnibus una,
Nec diversa tamen, qualem decet esse sororum."—Ovid.

Mr. Smith was much pleased with an original expression of Carter's, who liked to see his hounds draw a covert clean, and as much in line as possible. Mr. Smith seeing him once not very well pleased, asked him what was the matter. "If you please, sir," said he, "they are zedding" (a word coined by him from the letter z) "about after their fox." George was not a dashing rider, but was seldom far from his hounds. It was his favourite remark, "*I ride to hunt; master hunts to ride.*" In the last days of the poor old squire, he sometimes came out and hunted Carter's pack, which a Wiltshire farmer observing remarked to his companion : " They be at it *double-handed* to-day, neighbour ; how's that ? " " Why," replied the other, " Carter, he finds the fox; and our squire, he loses 'un."

N.B. *Double-handed* is a term used by farmers when very busy in their harvest, at which period two pitchers and two loaders are used.

No man ever displayed more patience and temper with young hounds than Carter. When a puppy spoke there was no rate, and when a fox was viewed at finding, there was no hallooing ; all was done *quietly.* As a rule, Carter held that you could not, in a close-lying large covert, say too much in cheering hounds *before* a fox was afoot, or too little afterwards. He once did a clever thing under Doyly large covert. The hounds had been running hard for some time, and all at once flung outside ; when an officious farmer cracked a whip in their faces. "What are you doing ?" said Carter. "I saw a hare break just before at that spot," he replied. "Pray let them alone," said George ; "they have noses, and what is their use if they cannot distinguish ?" In the meantime the hounds, after one flash round, settled on their fox, and a good run was the result. Had he listened to the farmer, this chance would have been lost, as the fox had slipped away before he saw the hare.

One or two more anecdotes of George will not be inappropriate. He was sitting with Will Long and Tom Sebright, enjoying the fun at Stockbridge races, when a notorious fox-killing keeper, named Watkins, thus addressed him : "Come, Mr. Carter, I will spend five shillings on a bottle of wine, if you will drink it with me." "I will spend half a crown on a rope," replied George, "if you will promise to hang yourself on the next tree." Jack Fricker and T. Bryce are the present whips under Carter. Jack is a very promising sportsman, and when George was ill, did credit to the horn on his saddle. Indeed, if there is anything in education, Jack could not escape being eminent, inasmuch as from a child he

was under Dick Burton and Mr. Smith, and afterwards
took his degree, a first class, under George Carter,
a combination of advantages which might well be
envied by the most aspiring youth at our universities,
or by the most distinguished pupils of old Meynell.

George Carter was always a famous runner and
dancer, and used particularly to distinguish himself
at the servants' Christmas Ball, given every year
at Tedworth. He could, they said, put more steps
into a figure than any man within the limits of
the Tedworth Hunt. He performed an extraordinary
feat, as a young man, in the following manner :—An
overflow of the river had enabled the deer to escape
out of some gentleman's park in Warwickshire, with
whom Carter then lived. He and four other young
fellows started on foot on the slot of a buck, and
determined to take him. They first came up with
him in a slough half full of water, out of which he
bolted, and took pretty straight across the country,
with his pursuers at a respectful distance. On, however, they went, seldom viewing him, but never losing
his track. Carter at last became the leading hound,
and marked him up to some pales, along which was
a deep wet ditch, tangled with briars and rushes.
Carter saw by his track that he had hesitated to
jump the pales, and had gone down the ditch to the
right and then to the left. This satisfied him that
the buck was somewhere " harboured ; " and, looking

P

very closely, he at last espied his nose and eyes just peering out of the water. Without waiting for hound No. 2, who was just coming up, in he went, and a fearful struggle took place, Carter clinging to him as if wrestling ; and at last, with the assistance of the rest of the party, they secured him, and walked him back in triumph among them to the Park, whence they had started in the morning, after an animated chase of nearly twenty miles.

George used to say a good thing sometimes in a quaint, quiet way. A certain nobleman in the Tedworth Hunt, a good friend to foxes, was sometimes so excited, as to ride too near, and press hounds. One day when the " venandi immensa cupido" was very strong upon him, he rode too close to them at a check, when Carter thus imparted his ideas to a friend who rode beside him : " I heartily pray" (quoth he) " that the day may come when his Lordship may hunt a pack of hounds of his own ; and have another Lord, *just exactly like himself*, as one of his field."

Mr. Smith had a very high opinion of Tom Wingfield, who was with him in Leicestershire. He had been first whip to Lord Sefton on the death of Jack Raven. Mr. Smith said he was the cleverest fellow he ever had with hounds, but not of an amiable temper. He is still alive, and in his eighty-fifth year; he resides at Ashbourne in Derbyshire.

An anecdote of Tom Wingfield was related with

no little zest by the squire himself. When both master and man were bordering on eighty years of age, they happened to meet, after a long lapse of time, when the following conversation arose: " May I be so bold as to ask, sir," said Tom Wingfield, " whether you can manage *them there* big places as well as you used to in Old Jack-o'-Lantern's days?" " I hear no complaints," was the squire's reply, " and I believe my nerve is as good as ever." " Ah, sir," said Tom, sorrowfully, " it is not so with me; for although my sight is dim, *them there big places looks twice as big to me as ever they used to.*" " Is that a favourite horse," inquired a young aspirant to honours of Tom Wingfield, when out once with Sir Thomas Mostyn's hounds in the Brill country. Before replying, Tom threw his keen single eye over the person of the youth, and observing how green he was about the boots and breeches, and how redolent of Alma Mater (he had just entered at Oxford), " They be *all* favourites," he said quietly. " Can *you* say so much of your *larning books?* "

The recollections of these eminent huntsmen respecting their master would be incomplete without those of him who still heads the Tedworth pack. George Carter gives the following account of his arrival at Tedworth:—" I came to Tedworth on the 1st April, 1842, and on my arrival with the Grafton

hounds, both old and young, when added to Mr.
Smith's old hounds and young ones, I never saw so
many together before nor since. We had upwards of
two hundred couples. In the spring we drafted them
to about one hundred and four couples, and that
number we kept to begin the season with. Mr. Smith
had a dog pack and a bitch pack, and in each he had
twenty-six couples. I hunted the old hounds and the
young, and my pack amounted altogether to about
fifty couples. Mr. Smith hunted Mondays, Tuesdays,
Thursdays, and Fridays; I hunted Wednesdays and
Saturdays, and that we did for fourteen years; and
very often, if Mr. Smith had a short day on Thursday,
he would hunt the same pack on Saturday. He
would go six or eight miles north of Tedworth, and
I went ten or twelve miles south. This we did for
many years.

"David Edwards was Mr. Smith's first whip; he
hunts the Cheshire pack at the present time. William
Cowley was his second man. George Rutt rode Mr.
Smith's second horse, and John Fricker rode his
third; he generally had out three horses a day.

"His favourite horses when I first came to him
were Rory, Cracker, Election, Hailstone, Hungerford,
Pantaloon, Rochelle, Netheravon, Ham Ashley, and
Fire-King. About the latter part of Mr. Smith's
time, he rode a favourite horse which he bought of
Sir Richard Sutton, and called Paul Potter. There

was also a little chestnut mare which was a great
favourite.   Mr. Smith called her Blemish.   She was
a very nice animal.

"Mr. Smith did not think so much about favourite
hounds as some gentlemen.   He certainly had a few
favourites, such as Royalist, Conqueror, Purity, and
Charity.   There was also a favourite dog hound
which we called Nigel.   He once found a fox in a
spinney and killed it himself.   We had a stud hound,
a Belvoir-bred dog, Bertram by name, a wonderful
good one.   We now have an old dog, Nelson, which
Mrs. Smith wished me to keep as long as he lived,
quite a favourite of Mr. Smith.   This hound would
choose to go to him, and did to the last, and was the
only one Mr. Smith knew at last.

"I know but little of Mr. Smith's good runs, as I
very seldom went out with him; but for ten or twelve
years he had excellent sport for such a nasty flinty
country.   I must tell you that he had first-rate sport,
by the number of foxes killed in a season.   We never
began cub-hunting until September, and left off by
Lady-day.   We have killed sixty and seventy brace
of foxes in a season.   I went every night to see Mr.
Smith at nine o'clock P.M., and that I did for fifteen
seasons.   I should think that no man in the world
rode more miles than Mr. Smith did, for he would
ride miles round a covert when other people were
standing still."

Side by side with George Carter's narrative may
be inserted the Tedworth entry of young hounds for
May 1859.

Names.	Sires.	Dams.
Benedict Bonny Lass	Paradox	Birdlime.
Fair Maid Frolick	Ditto	Folly.
Pilot	Ditto	Florence.
Rocket Rufus Romulus Rosebud Rachel	Nautilus	Rosebud.
Juniper Jewess	Nigel	Jessie.
Barnabas	Nigel	Beldam.
Broker	Ditto	Boundless.
Nimrod Nelson Notable	Lord Yarborough's Nimrod	Fatal.
Brilliant Betsy	Ditto, Nestor	Benefit.
Comrade	Ditto, ditto	Crafty.
Favourite Fickle	Blazer	Frantic.
Roderick	Leveller	Rosy.
Lionel	Ditto	Termagant.

There are at present thirty couple of dog hounds
in the kennels at Tedworth, and twenty-five and half
couple of bitches. The height of the dogs ranges
from twenty-three and a half to twenty-four inches,
and that of the bitches averages about twenty-two

and a half.   In the days of Solyman, Conqueror, and
Watchman, the hounds were much larger, but Mr.
Smith found that the Hampshire country required a
smaller hound than Leicestershire.

Speaking on the subject of hounds, we are naturally drawn to contemplate the splendid picture of
the Hunt at Tedworth, painted at Penton in 1829, by
Mr. Ferneley, who came expressly from Leicestershire into Hants, and was the squire's guest for a
fortnight, for this purpose.   Mr. Smith, as has been
elsewhere already mentioned, is on Ayrton, with Dick
Burton, his huntsman, standing at the side of the
Big Grey; Tom Day, the first whip, on Reformer;
and Bob Edwards, the second whip, holding Anderson,
Mr. Smith's second horse.   The numerous hounds
in the picture are all portraits.   Among those most
famous are Rifleman, standing close to Dick Burton,
who has a pair of couples in his hand, Watchman,
Dimity, Chorister, Dabchick, Trimbush, Tomboy,
Traffic, Reginald, Rubicon, Roundley, Rosy, Commodore, and Clinker.   Trimbush is looking up at Mr.
Smith, while Chorister stands under his horse's head,
and Rifleman with the huntsman is at his side.   In
front of the picture are Commodore and Watchman,
while Rarity is gamboling towards her master.   Under
the tree, in the background, sits Remus, a well-known
hound.   In the left is Tedworth House.   The sportsman in the green coat just about to mount his horse

in the distance is Mr. Northeast, the agent of the Tedworth estates, famous for his judgment and experience in the breeding of south-down sheep.   Speaking
of this picture, and of the principal figure in it,
Mr. Ferneley says in a letter written on the 23rd of
October last : " It gives me much pleasure to hear
of the publication of a memoir of so excellent a
sportsman and so good a man.   It is now fifty-
three years since I first saw him; he was riding his
horse Jack-o'-Lantern.   I saw him near Frisby
Gorse, trying to get his horse over a flight of rails
six or seven times, but he refused, and Mr. Smith
had to take him to another place before he could
succeed."   Mr. Ferneley adds : " He was the *first red-
coat* I painted, and on Jack-o'-Lantern.   The picture
was bought by Mr. Mayler, and at his death it was
sold, and I do not know what became of it.   This
was in 1806, the year Mr. Smith first took the Quorn
hounds.   I also painted his portrait, with his hounds,
for the Earl of Plymouth.   In the same picture were
portraits of Lords Plymouth, Aylesford, and Dartmouth, Messrs. P. Mills, J. Bradshaw, Paris, J. W.
Edge, Hinton, &c.   This was in 1819; and I fear
never again will Leicestershire boast the assembling
together of such thorough sportsmen, as well as kind
noble-hearted men."   Mr. Ferneley is in his seventy-
seventh year, and, as he observes, as well as can be
expected at that age.   In another celebrated picture
Mr. Smith is conspicuous, viz. in that painted for

Sir Richard Sutton by Mr. Frank Grant.   Although
Sir Richard and his sons, together with the Duke of
Rutland, Colonel Lowther, and others, occupy the
most prominent position in the picture, yet the circumstance of their all wearing hunting-caps, while
Mr. Smith has the usual well-known hat, makes it appear as if the hounds were his, and those around him
his huntsmen and whippers-in.   The horsemen in
this picture are all portraits of eminent sportsmen.
A fine engraving of it has been made by Bromley.
Another excellent likeness of Sir Richard Sutton on
horseback hangs in the ante-room at Tedworth.

Let us proceed to enumerate some remaining
qualities in Mr. Assheton Smith's character as a
huntsman and master of hounds.   He was scrupulous
in all that appertains to the etiquette of hunting.
He was jealous of his rights, and would allow no
hounds but his own to draw a covert, however
outlying, which he believed to form part of his
country: on the other hand no man was more cour-
teous than he was, on any occasion of packs clashing.
His commendations of a master of harriers (Mr.
Willes of Hungerford Park) on a memorable occasion
were unbounded.   The squire's hounds had met some
fifteen miles off, but had run their fox into the country of the merry harriers; the blue mottles were immediately locked up in a barn, and their field joined
the fox-hounds.   No sooner had they met than Mr.
Assheton Smith rode up to Mr. Willes, and shaking him

heartily by the hand, said: " This is the most sports-
manlike conduct I ever knew in my life; I saw you
order your hounds home as we came over the hill. You
must come and dine with us to-day and stay two or
three more, for such things require to be talked over."
Some masters of fox-hounds have a dislike and contempt for harriers, but this famous sportsman knew
that in skilful hands they were very useful in keeping
foxes at home and making them avoid hedgerows.

Mr. Assheton Smith hunted the Tedworth country
for thirty-two years, during which period no subscription of any sort or kind was ever asked for ; but only
a request made to land-owners to preserve foxes. He
was hardly ever known to dig a fox, and would not
have a terrier in his kennel, his opinion being that a
good fox might save himself if he could. Unless he
was " a dirty ringing rascal," he would never allow
him to be disturbed, after he went to earth [*]; yet had
he killed as many foxes, perhaps more than any man of
his time, and all were fairly hunted, without any mob-
bing or unfair riding for the sake of blood. The order
he kept the field in greatly facilitated this, as he was
always in his place to see what was going on; and it
was a treat indeed over a well-fenced grass country to
watch his hounds trying in vain to run away from him.
His average of noses was fifty brace, as George Carter
can testify who rode with him for seventeen seasons.
One season he killed seventy brace, the last " worry "

[*] Beckford used to say that digging a fox was *cold work.*

having taken place on a winding-up day under a broiling sun. These are pretty good proofs of his popularity with all classes, and his liberality to keepers, which last indeed almost amounted to profuseness. He always was prone to discredit complaints of the disappearance of geese and turkeys in consequence of the abundance of foxes, but where claims for poultry really slaughtered by Reynard were fairly made out, he made ample compensation: indeed, the gentlemen of the Tedworth Hunt always took care that the farmers should be no losers by the care they took in keeping up the breed. His respect for the animal who contributed so essentially to his health and diversion made him lean to his side. If a fox came to his death unlawfully, and it became known to the squire, he would dwell upon it with feelings of the greatest indignation. Once at the breakfast-table at Tedworth, he was intent on reading the newspaper, when suddenly he uttered an expression of horror, and visible concern overspread his countenance. The ladies present supposing some great European calamity had occurred, hastily asked him what was the matter, when he replied, looking over his spectacles, " By Jove, a dog fox has been burnt to death in a barn."

The country which he found so bare of foxes he has left most amply stocked. When no longer able to hunt his hounds himself, he curtailed his hunting days, and presented twenty couple of first-rate hounds

to the Craven, a neighbouring pack. For the last
two years of his life, the hounds may be said to have
been kept entirely for the amusement of his friends,
for although he did go out occasionally in 1856, subsequently to his first severe illness, it was rather as
a spectator than a master of hounds. At the time
of his decease, there were ninety couple of hounds
in his kennel, fifty more at walk in Wales, and
thirty in Wilts. They used to come up in a caravan
by railway to Andover. When Carter first entered
Mr. Smith's service, so great was the number of
hounds in the kennel, that much nicety of judgment
and discrimination was requisite; for it was no easy
matter to decide which hound to choose and which to
reject, where every one was valuable. The two veterans (for neither master nor man was at that period
exactly in the bloom of youth) succeeded by their
united skill in kennel discipline, in forming a pack of
fox-hounds which have been unrivalled in the world.

Mr. Horlock, himself an eminent sportsman and
first-rate judge of hounds, thus comments on the
Tedworth pack. "For a draft of young hounds, I
think I should select the pack of the wonderful squire
of Tedworth, for several reasons. First, he has some
good old blood, having bought the Duke of Grafton's
hounds, and before that, he had been breeding largely
from Mr. Warde's kennel. His hounds have a rough
flinty and woodland country to contend with, where

they must hunt as well as run. In their performances they are, like their master, second to none. They are not hallooed and hustled about by whippers-in, although the squire occasionally is very cheery when things go well; and that happens so often, that I hardly ever saw a day with him when he was not cheery. His hounds, however, are left to do their work pretty much by themselves, and I may venture to say, that no pack of hounds in England, Scotland, or Ireland can beat them in any respect. They can show their speed at a racing pace over the downs, and push along through the large woodlands and over the flinty hills (which rattle like broken bottles) at a splendid rate indeed; the wonder is they do not cut their legs off. The squire hunts six days a week; and therefore has a large body of hounds in kennel, sometimes nearly a hundred couples; he breeds largely also, and judiciously; the result of great knowledge and long experience." *

The number of foxes killed by Mr. Smith during his mastership of hounds savours somewhat of the marvellous. He assured a brother-sportsman that he had cut off fifteen hundred brushes with a pocket knife which he afterwards lost in West Woods. These brushes were his by right, both as master of hounds and huntsman.

Of many of the best horses in his stable we have

* The Management of Hounds, by Scrutator, p. 14.

already spoken.   The arrangements of his stud were
in no wise inferior to those of his kennel.   He would
have no man about him who did not thoroughly
know his business, and his grooms exhibited the style
and smartness of their master.   No man saw more
rapidly the good points of a horse, however out of
condition he might be.   This talent enabled him
often to purchase for trifling sums what appeared
" screws" to a less practised eye : the owners of
these could not recognise their own animals when
the latter headed the field with Tom Smith in the
saddle.   To have seen him on Ham Ashley, Nether-
avon, Rory O'More, or Jack-o'-Lantern, would re-
mind us of that splendid passage in Shakspeare's
"Venus and Adonis," in reading which we almost
fancy our immortal bard must have acquired his
knowledge of horseflesh with the South Warwickshire hounds :

"Look where a painter would surpass the life
    In limning out a well-proportioned steed,
His art with Nature's workmanship at strife,
    As if the dead the living should exceed :
So did this horse excel a common one,
In shape, in courage, colour, pace, and bone.

"Round-hoofed, short-jointed, fetlocks shag and long,
    Broad breast, full eyes, small head, and nostril wide,
High crest, short ears, straight legs, and passing strong :
    Thin mane, thick tail, broad buttock, tender hide.
Look what a horse should have, he did not lack,
Nor a proud rider on so proud a back."

In the last line we have taken a liberty with the

poet, in substituting the word *nor* for *save*, to make
the picture exactly represent the squire and his steed.

When Mr. Smith's horses had grown old, or were no
longer equal to their work, they were permitted to
roam at large in the park, for he never sold an animal
when worn out, to be subjected, as he said, to the
chance of ill-treatment.

After his death, no hunter was sold out of his
stables; all were given away by his widow among his
intimate friends. Paul Potter, Ham Ashley, Euxine,
and Blemish thus passed into the possession of those
who would value them for their master's sake, and
never part with them. His noble pack of hounds was
presented by her to the county of Hants, but still
continues for the present to inhabit its old quarters.
A committee has been formed, comprised of the leading land-owners of Hants and Wilts, and with the assistance of liberal subscriptions, for which are to be
found and put down the names of the largest game-
preservers of the district, and under the able management of Mr. Northeast, whose services are entirely
gratuitous, in the commissariat department, the sport
is destined to be kept alive, and long may it be kept
alive, with George Carter as huntsman, assisted by
Jack Fricker and Will Bryce, to do honour to the
memory of the most renowned fox-hunter of his day.

Did Mr. Smith then live alone for his favourite pastime ? Let the reader answer that question who has

accompanied him in these pages throughout his gallant and honourable career. Is it not rather to him,—whose keenness and unswerving resolution, the "vivida vis" or ardour of whose mind, so essential to success in enterprises whether great or small, whose singleness of purpose this memoir has endeavoured faithfully to delineate,— is it not to him, I repeat, that we owe in a great measure the high tone and character of the chase, and that fox-hunting has continued, in spite of our refinement and civilisation, the powerful element in our social system, which it was described to be at the outset, and which serves, together with other ingredients, to make the Englishman respected throughout the world, for his courage, his perseverance, and the independent freedom of thought and action inseparable from his nature? For there is one circumstance which must not be lost sight of. The intemperance which formerly was associated so frequently with this amusement, and gave a handle to its opponents to detract from its merits, no longer exists. It is as disgraceful at the present day for a man to be a drunkard as to be a coward; while that a free indulgence in wine and stimulants is not necessary, either for a man's reputation among his fellows, or for his nervous energy and strength, is clearly proved by the example before us. While Mr. Smith's habits were temperate, almost amounting to abstemiousness, "quicquid vult valdè vult" was his motto in every business he undertook. Whether it was the chase, or the improvement of ship-building, or the development of his quarries, or the amelioration of the comforts and condition of his Welsh labourers, whatsoever his hand found to do, he did it with his might.   As has well been observed by the Editor of The Field, it is only by such enthusiasm in the pursuit of fox-hunting as he evinced, "that with the improved state of husbandry, and the increasing system of enclosures, added to the large field of thorough-bred horses pressing upon the hounds, it is kept from degenerating into a second-rate sport."   His country, therefore, is the real gainer by the line that he pursued, "for if," adds the same writer, "hunting or any other diversion is really useful in a national point of view, it is of the utmost importance that it should be vigorously carried out, and that a few of the leaders in it should devote their time, their minds, and their fortunes to render it something more than a mere gentlemanly amusement, although to the great bulk of mankind it presents no other feature whereby it may claim their attention."

There will perhaps be some who still remain sceptical.   These we refer to Lord Bacon's essay on the "True Greatness of Kingdoms and States," already quoted, from which we extract the following passage : "It is certain that sedentary and within-door arts, and delicate manufactures" (in which as a nation we are chiefly engaged) "requiring the

* Q.

finger rather than the arm," (and it may be added, laborious studies and professions,) "have in their nature a contrariety to a military disposition; and generally warlike people are a little idle and love danger better than travail; neither must they be too much broken of it, if they shall be preserved in vigour." *

If, therefore, hunting, with its perils, its enterprises, and its ambition, has been truly styled "the image of war,"—if it has a direct tendency to remedy this natural effect of our national habits and employments, — long may the noble youths of our country cherish a passion for this and other manly exercises! Thus will their bodies be best inured to toil, and their nerves best braced to encounter dangers, wherever they may be found. Thus will they be less liable to turn aside to the allurement of vicious indulgence, while we shall look up to them with firm reliance against foreign aggression. Ill will it fare with Great Britain when her children shall peruse such a life as that of Mr. Assheton Smith, except to see in it a model for their example. Should such a day arrive, our best national defences would serve us little against an invader, and our empire would soon cease to maintain that proud pre-eminence it has so long held among mankind. But, if I know my countrymen rightly, that day

* Bacon's Essays.

need not be apprehended.   Rather will this narrative of some passages in the life of a true Englishman touch a chord in every heart, and find its home in every clime where British resolution to overcome obstacles, where British courage and emulation find congenial spirits.   If the prevailing defect of our age be indifference of purpose*, in our politics, in our moral and social sympathies, ay in our very sports, no more powerful spur to rouse our slumbering energies, and to revive us to a generous warmth of sentiment and action, than to behold the almost certain success attending every pursuit and undertaking which enthusiasm pervades, as well as the honour we ungrudgingly hasten to pay to a great and shining quality, even though we may be wanting in it ourselves.

> "Illum nulla dies unquam memori eximet ævo:
> Dum domus Æneæ Capitoli immobile saxum
> Accolet, imperiumque pater Romanus habebit."

Soon after the death of her husband, Mrs. Assheton Smith retired to Tedworth, where she remained in strict privacy, until the state of her health, which, at all times delicate, had undergone a considerable shock from the anxiety and fatigue consequent upon his long illness, obliged her to spend the winter of

* When this was written, the Rifle movement had not attained its present full strength.

1858 at Torquay. At first the society of her sisters*, the change of scene, and the mildness of the climate in that beautiful spot, appeared to give her relief : but her spirits never rallied after the closing scene at Vaenol, and happening to take fresh cold in March last, she grew rapidly worse.

Feeling a strong desire to return to Tedworth, she was moved with difficulty from Torquay, but got no further on her journey than Compton Basset, near Devizes, the residence of her brother-in-law, George Heneage, Esq., where she expired on the 18th of May, 1859. Having had entrusted to her by Mr. Smith the sole disposition of his princely fortune, it was a matter of great interest and curiosity to know to whom she would bequeath it. The event proved that she was animated by the same strong sense of justice which had been so predominant a feature in the character of her husband. By her will she left the whole of his Welsh property, exceeding 40,000l. a year†, to one of his nearest relations, whom she had never seen, the son of Captain and Mrs. Duff, and grandson of Mrs. Astley, Mr. Smith's sister. Having thus done her duty to the family of her husband, she bequeathed the Tedworth estate to her favourite nephew and godson, Francis Stanley, the son of

---

* Mrs. Heneage, Mrs. Sloane Stanley, and Mrs. Ker Seymer.

† Mr. Smith stated to a friend, two years before his death, that the Llanberris Slate Quarries cleared on an average, after payment of all expenses, 30,000l. per annum. The landed property produces 15,000l. per annum.

one of her sisters. To the other members of her
own family she left personalty and legacies varying in amount, not forgetting some of Mr. Smith's
and her own oldest friends. Many of the old
family servants and retainers were left handsomely
provided for. The Will, made, as it must have been,
in the hour of acute suffering and sorrow, strongly
exemplifies those Christian principles which had
been the rule of her conduct through life. A con-
scientious desire to discharge her duty, great warmth
of kindness to those whom she loved, deep devotion
and respect for her husband's memory, who had
shown her so signal a mark of his confidence and
affection, added to an anxiety to carry out what she
considered would have been his wishes, all these
influences enabled her to perform an act of great
difficulty in such a manner, that its justice must be
universally acknowledged and admired.

Mrs. Assheton Smith was buried by the side of
her husband, in the church-yard at Tedworth, on the
26th of May, 1859, little more than eight months
after his death.

APPENDIX.

PUGILISTIC PROWESS.

Page 9.

ORATOR HUNT.

ORATOR HUNT was a bold rider, and, like Mr. Smith, well able to use his fists. Mr. Warde's hounds were once drawing South Grove, when some remark of Mr. Hunt's provoked a sneer from Tom Smith. Fierce words ensued on both sides, and they were in the very act of dismounting to settle it then and there, when fortunately a fox was hallooed away, an attraction which neither could resist. "I always regretted this interruption," said an eye-witness of the scene, "for depend upon it this fight would have been well worth seeing, although Hunt had the advantage in weight and height; but for all that," he added, "I would have backed the squire."

Mr. Smith's father was once riding about his farm, when he heard the report of a gun. Galloping up to the spot, to ascertain who was the trespasser, he found Orator Hunt, who had just shot a hare. While the latter and old Mr. Smith held no very friendly parley, Hunt's brother, who was deaf and dumb, came up and offered the old squire the hare. This was, in Mr. Smith's mind, an additional insult, and, not knowing that the man was dumb, he mistook his attempts to make himself understood for mockery, which he was about to resent, when his brother, seeing his mistake, observed sarcastically, "Are you not ashamed thus to insult a deaf and dumb man?" This appeal to his feelings, which were always most sensitive, immediately cooled the old gentleman's ire; the trespass was at once forgotten, the amends made, and the squire and the dumb sportsman kept bowing to each for five minutes, like a couple of Chinese mandarins. The Orator, however, continued to shoot away as merrily as ever after Mr. Smith's departure, while the keepers did not dare to inform their master, for fear of a second explosion.

MELTON MOWBRAY, 1813.

Page 16.

THE following song was composed about the year 1813, by the Rev. Dr. Ford, Vicar of Melton Mowbray for forty-five years. He was a native of Bristol, and was very popular with the members of the Melton Hunt for his wit and social qualities. The song has reference to the period when Mr. Smith was "King of Quorn." Mr. Ferneley, who found it among some old papers, and to whom the reader is indebted for it, remarks, "That was the best time I have known at Melton, where I have been a resident since 1813."

THE MELTON HUNT.

> "I must have liberty
> Withal, as large a charter as the wind,
> To blow on whom I please; for so fools have;
> And they that are most galled with my folly,
> They most must laugh." SHAKSPEARE.

I sing Fox-hunting, and the gen'rous rage
Which spurs the noble youth of this new age,
With careless toil, all for their country's good,
To rid us of those vermin of the wood

That nightly steal, and for their luncheon hoard
The *poultry* which should smoke upon our board
Such feats advent'rous through the hard run day,
From dull *November* to all charming *May*,
Call for the poet's best and readiest rhyme
In strains at once familiar and sublime.
Oh! could my muse resemble such a chase,
And with the riders keep an equal pace,
Though cautious, bold; cool, yet with ardour fired
Free, without check; impetuous, yet untired.

Ye knowing sportsmen, foremost of the lead,
Who keep no turnpike, and no fences heed;
Who crack the echoing whip, go off in style,
Enjoy the sport, and pace through every wile —
Now found, now lost, and now again in view —
The cunning fugitive ye close pursue:
Ye *booted senators*, who for me *frank*,
Claiming post after post an unpaid thank;
Who, with yourselves, bring thousands yearly down
To glut the cravings of this sharp-set town,
Whose trickful tradesmen, farmers, rogues in *grain*,
Thrive by your wants, and by your losses gain,
Scramble who most at sight your *bills* shall share,—
"Take in a hunter," and the booty's fair:
Be candid, hunters, if, once famed in Greek,
Faintly your foreign dialect I speak,
Up to your phrases, if I'm found unable,
Not tutor'd in the science of your stable.
Besides *our* tribe you know scarce hunt at all
Save for *preferment*, and the well cribb'd *stall*;
Yet by your partial notice made thus rich,
Raised by your favours to my *honour's* pitch,

I'll try to set the table whilst you quaff,
If not on roar, on a facetious laugh,
Whilst spice of Latin shall with harmless jest,
Like poignant *Cayenne*, give my olio zest.

  Not as their fathers erst " with early horn,"
Our modern hunters now " salute the morn,"
'Tis noon, ere these in scarlet bright array
Commence th' achievements of the dubious day,
Each on his steed, sleek-coated and high fed,
From *sire* to *dam* in *calendar* well bred;
For in the *jockey's heraldry* the stud
Must boast descent from *ancestry* of blood ;
As well you might a *hobby-horse* bestride,
As mount a *roadster* of no lineal pride.
Here blacks, browns, bays, and chestnuts, most re-
    nown'd
For spirit, temper, shape, price, fill the ground ;
Each brags his favourite's prowess in the field,
" My *grey mare* to no better *horse* shall *yield;* "
But Forester's fine eye and single glance
Finds out the latent blemish as they prance ;
Deep skill'd to scan the solid worth that lies
In horses, men, and their true qualities.
Hear him but talk, what music on his tongue !
It cheers the old, it fascinates the young ;
Look in his face, no doubt the counterpart,
The honest, liberal sentiment of heart.
Hark ! forward how they bear ; nor them restrains,
Or driving blast, or storm with drenching rains.
What springs they make, o'er ditches, post and rail,
And dash and plunge through *Belvoir's stick-fast vale!*
In at the death 'tis glorious to arrive ;
To claim the *brush* no mean prerogative :

Thrown out, and some thrown off, besplash'd with mire,
A motley group — peer — parson — grazier — squire.

Home safe return'd, how changed! studious they dress,
In newest fashion for the sumptuous *mess;*
Set out with Lucry's complete bill of fare:
Fish by the mail — delicious, costly, rare;
High-season'd dishes, — fricassees — ragoûts,
All that the sav'ry pamp'ring art can do.
They eat like hunters, frequent bumpers drain,
Of flavour'd claret and of brisk champagne.
Flush'd with the grape, like Persia's prince grown vain,
They thrice each bullfinch charge, and thrice " they slay
      the slain,"
WHERE SMITH WOULD DRAW, what lengths with *freshmen*
      go,
To break them into service passing show!

" Saddle white Surrey for the field to-morrow."
But ah! unlook'd-for, to their spleen and sorrow,
The next day " comes a frost, a killing frost,"
All's at a stand, and all their pleasure cross'd.
To town some scamper, and the odds are even,
Who first get seats in *Chapel of St. Stephen,*
To do their duty there, State flaws detect,
Invent new laws, and trespasses correct;
The frost now gone, they're down again in mind,
And motion quicker than the verging wind.
To sober whist, some *soberly* betake,
Though deep the rubber, deeper yet the stake,
Fix'd as *staunch pointers* to a practised set,
Well read in *Hoyle,* on every deal who bet:
And cards play'd out, what a confused din
Of blame, or praise, as the sets lose or win!

"You play'd the *Knave*, you might have play'd the
    Deuce." —
"You drew and *forced* my *Queen*." — "Pray, spare
    abuse."
"You cut my hand to pieces, threw away
Your highest diamond, and you call this Play?" —
"There a cool fifty goes! Before we part,
Take my advice, get Bob Short's rules by heart."
So oft began the midnight conversation,
So closed as oft in mutual altercation.

But now a scene how brilliant hath ta'en place,
Where beauty, elegance, and softest grace,
Of highest female rank — resistless can
Charm and control that lawless creature, *man ;*
Improve his morals, harmonise his heart,
And *tenderness* to *fortitude* impart!
School of Politeness, be our club hence named,
For kindest conjugal attention famed,
Each well deserving that pure bliss of life,
The sweet endearments of a lovely *wife ;*
Be Benedict of Beatrice possess'd,
Like Cavendish, Powlett, Worcester, Plymouth bless'd,
Like Forester .   .   .   .   .   .
.   .   .   I leave a lengthen'd space
Where *bachelors forlorn* may find a place ;
Aylesford and Dartmouth, gallant Craven, May,
All-polished Mayler, and Sir Robert Gay.

This round of labour ruddy health insures,
To courage stirs, to hardiness inures ;
Thus train'd, my masters, you would meet the foe
Furious to battle, as to covert go.
A *cavalry already* form'd the French to rout,
And Tally-ho! your frantic war-whoop, shout.

But hold! our furrows in the blade look green,
Our burden'd ewes their tender lambs 'gin yean,
Timely you cease, of damages afraid,
Nor injure lands for summer crops new laid;
Pastures revive—foxes shall breed and rear
Strong and inviting *cubs* for next LEAP year.

SHALLOW.

THE LATE SIR HENRY PEYTON.

Page 17.

LEPIDUS was one of his best horses.

CAPTAIN WHITE.

Page 18.

"WHAT a one the Captain's Merry Lad was for rails in a corner! he popped over for all the world like a deer." *

CRICKET MATCHES.

Page 20.

IT will be interesting to the lovers of cricket, to see in detail the celebrated matches in which Mr. Smith took a distinguished part. We have not been able to find any especial record of his prowess at Eton or Oxford; but in 1802 we find him playing on the side of Surrey, against all England, in a match which came off at Lord's, on the 25th of August in that year. The respective sides contained the names of

* Silk and Scarlet, p. 20.

the most eminent players of the day. Lord Frederick Beauclerk heads the eleven of the England side, and going first to
the wickets as soon as play was called, he did not quit them
before he had placed 54 runs upon the score; in fact more
than half the innings of his side. He was, however, well
supported in the second innings by Fremantle, Hammond,
Bennett, and Fennex, who made between them 155 runs,
the whole innings amounting to 211, which Surrey was unable to fetch up. England therefore proved the winner by
83 runs. Mr. Smith scored 1 in his first innings, and 10 in
his second. From this period until 1820, we find his name
in all the prominent matches of the day, and always more or
less distinguished. He was no less active and hard-working
in the field, than when he held his bat.

In the year 1803 he played with Hants against Nottingham.
The game took place at Lord's on the 4th, 5th, and 6th July,
Hants coming off with flying colours. The match is well
worth recording in full.

The County of Hants against the Counties of Nottingham and Leicester, with Lord Frederick Beauclerk.

NOTTINGHAM AND LEICESTER.

	First Innings.		Second Innings.	
T. Warsop	18	run out	6	st. Fremantle.
Lord Beauclerk	34	b. Clair	74	c. Jas. Bennett.
Dennis	12	b. Bennett	5	b. Bennett.
R. Warsop	0	b. Clair	3	b. Jas. Bennett.
Leeson	24	b. Purchase	4	c. Ditto.
Street	2	b. Goddard	6	b. Smith.
Chapman	4	c. Small	7	b. Goddard.
Jeffries	4	b. Goddard	2	b. Jas. Bennett.
M. Morgan	1	not out	7	c. Goddard.
Smith	6	ct. Smith	0	not out.
Stringer	5	b. Purchase	0	c. Purchase.
Byes	6	Byes	3	
	116		117	

HANTS.

First Innings.

Fremantle	-	-	-	- 22	c. Beauclerk.
Pointer	-	-	-	- 32	c. T. Warsop.
T. Smith, Esq.	-	-	-	- 23	c. Dennis.
Bennett	-	-	-	- 33	c. Smith.
Small	-	-	-	- 8	c. Beauclerk.
Goddard	-	-	-	- 14	c. Leeson.
Jas. Bennett	-	-	-	- 73	not out.
Parker	-	-	-	- 43	c. T. Warsop.
Howard	-	-	-	- 4	c. Morgan.
Purchase	-	-	-	- 0	b. T. Warsop.
Clair	-	-	-	- 1	b. Ditto.

253

Hants won in one innings by 20 runs.

On the 8th of June, 1804, we find Mr. Assheton Smith engaged in a game played at Lord's, between 11 of Marylebone, and 10 of the Homerton Club with Beldham. The Marylebone Club won by 24 runs. Mr. Smith scored 5 and 58 in his two innings. On the 27th of June following, the Marylebone and Homerton Clubs played Hants. The former were victorious by 24 runs. Mr. Smith scored 13 and 9. In this game Lord F. Beauclerk played on the Marylebone side, and got 50 and 42 runs. On the 2nd of July in that year, the Marylebone Club played all England. After much excellent play, Mr. Smith on the side of England scoring 59 and 4, and Lord F. Beauclerk 15 and 94, the match was given up in favour of Marylebone. The following is an account of the game : —

MARYLEBONE.

	First Innings.				Second Innings.	
G. Leycester, Esq.	14	b.	Pontifex	-	6	c. Barton.
Capt. Cumberland	7	b.	Ditto	-	15	c. Beeston.
T. Smith, Esq.	- 59	b.	Barton	-	4	b. Warren.
Lord F. Beauclerk	15	c.	Burgoyne	-	94	b. Pontifex.
Colonel Maitland	- 2	c.	Beeston	-	0	st. Barton.
Hon. A. Upton	- 15	b.	Tanner	-	35	b. Burgoyne.
J. Laurell, Esq.	- 1	b.	Barton	-	20	b. Pontifex.
Capt. Beckett	- 6	b.	Tanner	-	34	b. Ditto.
T. Mellish, Esq.	- 5	not out	-	-	14	b. Barton.
Colonel Onslow	- 6	b.	Tanner	-	—	absent.
Turner - -	- 0	b.	Ditto	-	3	not out.
Byes -	0		Byes	-	0	
	130				235	

ENGLAND.

	First Innings.				Second Innings.	
J. Tanner, Esq.	- 34	b.	Beauclerk	-	7	absent.
Pontifex, Esq.	- 9	b.	Ditto	-	0	c. Upton.
Warren, Esq.	- 27	b.	Ditto	-	—	absent.
F. Ladbroke, Esq.	0	b.	Cumberland	-	—	Ditto.
Wells - -	- 10	b.	Beauclerk	-	—	Ditto.
Beeston	- 0	b.	Ditto	-	—	Ditto.
Burgoyne, Esq.	- 8	not out	-	-	47	not out.
Barton - -	- 0	ct. Laurell	-	-	44	c. Upton.
Booth - -	- 1	b.	Beauclerk	-	1	c. Laurell.
E. H. Budd, Esq.	- 0	b.	Ditto	-	—	absent.
Abbott -	- 0	b.	Ditto	-	—	Ditto.
Byes -	- 0		Byes	-	7	
	89				106	

In this game we first find the name of Mr. Budd, afterwards one of the cleanest hitters and finest batsmen of his day.

On the 9th of July, 1804, we find Mr. Smith playing on the side of all England against Surrey. England won in one innings by 4 runs, Mr. Smith's bat obtaining 10. In the following year, Surrey again met England at Lord's on the 24th of June, when England won by 10 wickets; Mr. Smith obtained 12 and 3 runs, and was not out in the second innings. He took part in no other important game during that year; but in 1806 he distinguished himself in a great match played at Lord's on the 16th of June, between 9 of Hants, with Lord F. Beauclerk and Lambert, *versus* all England. Here he scored 17 and 30 runs, Lord F. Beauclerk making 40 and 1; England won by 87 runs.

ENGLAND.

First Innings.			Second Innings.		
T. Walker	- 41	c. Howard	- 0	st. Lambert.
J. Hampton	- 10	st. Ditto	- 0	b. Beauclerk.
Robinson	- 24	run out	- 9	hit wicket.
Hammond	- 39	b. Bennett	- 0	st. Howard.
Beldham	- 53	c. Pointer	- 1	c. Fremantle.
G. Leycester, Esq.	- 1	st. Lambert	- 10	b. Bennett.
Hon. A. Upton	- 27	st. Ditto	- 24	not out.
H. Bentley	- 8	c. Ditto	- 6	c. Beauclerk.
Fennex	- 2	b. Beauclerk	- 5	st. Howard.
Strudwick	- 13	c. Lambert	- 0	leg before wicket.
Sparkes	- 0	not out	- 5	b. Lambert.
Byes	- 9	Byes	- 1	
	227		**60**	

HANTS.

First Innings.			Second Innings.		
C. Warren, Esq.	- 0	b. T. Walker	- 4	c. Beldham.
Small	- 0	c. Sparkes	- 1	c. Howard.
T. Smith, Esq.	- 17	b. Hampton	- 30	c. Bentley.
Lord F. Beauclerk	40	b. Ditto	- 1	st. Hammond.
Lambert	- 27	b. Ditto	- 29	b. T. Walker.
Bennett	- 9	c. Beldham	- 1	c. Strudwick.
Fremantle	- 8	c. Howard	- 3	c. Beldham.
Pointer	- 8	b. T. Walker	- 3	c. Strudwick.
Hon. E. Bligh	- 10	not out	- 1	b. Fennex.
Howard	- 2	b. Hampton	- 2	not out.
Goddard	- 0	st. Hammond	- 3	b. Fennex.
Byes	- 0	Byes	- 1	
	121		**79**	

It is worthy of observation how very few byes there were in these times, the days of swift and round bowling not having then commenced.

On the 30th of June in the same year, Mr. Smith played in a match at Lord's, between Surrey and England, and again distinguished himself, obtaining 86 runs in his first innings, and 7 in his second; Lord F. Beauclerk scoring also 40 and 31. England won by 93 runs. The 7th of July following was remarkable as being the first occasion on which the gentlemen of England contended against the players, but this they did not anticipate they could accomplish without the assistance of Lambert and Beldham, two of the most celebrated players of the day. Nevertheless they were victorious in one innings by 14 runs; Mr. Smith's score showing 48, when he was run out. The details of this game will be interesting to all lovers of cricket.

PLAYERS.

	First Innings.				Second Innings.	
T. Walker	- 14	c	Upton	-	- 24	c. Upton.
J. Hampton	'- 18	st.	Lambert	-	- 4	c. Ditto.
Robinson	- 13	c.	Bligh -	-	- 15	b. Beauclerk.
Bennett	- 1	c.	Beldham	-	- 13	c. Upton.
Hammond	- 0	c.	Lambert	-	- 2	c. Beldham.
Howard	- 2	c.	T. Smith	-	- 13	c. Upton.
Small	- 0	c.	Beldham	-	- 21	not out.
Ayling	- 1	b.	Wills -	-	- 8	c. Bligh.
Fremantle	- 14	not out	-	-	- 1	st. Lambert.
Fennex	- 5	b.	Beldham	-	- 0	c. Upton.
H. Bentley	- 0	c.	Bligh	-	- 8	leg before wicket.
Byes	- 1		Byes	-	- 3	
	69				112	

GENTLEMEN (WITH LAMBERT AND BELDHAM).

First Innings.

Hon. Gen. Bligh	22	c. Hammond.
Pontifex, Esq.	14	b. Howard.
Lambert	57	st. Hammond.
T. Smith, Esq.	48	run out.
Beldham	16	c. Howard.
Lord F. Beauclerk	1	c. Bennett.
Wills, Esq.	1	c. Hampton.
G. Leycester, Esq.	14	c. Walker.
Hon. A. Upton	11	run out.
Nyren, Esq.	4	c. Ayling.
Warren, Esq.	2	not out.
Byes	5	
	195	

The great success attending this effort on the part of the gentlemen, induced them to make another trial of their strength with the players. On the 21st of July, in the same year, when assisted only by Lambert, they entered the lists again at Lord's, and were victorious by 82 runs. The gentlemen went in first. Lord F. Beauclerk made a splendid score in each innings.

GENTLEMEN (WITH LAMBERT).

	First Innings.			Second Innings.	
Pontifex, Esq.	2	b. Howard	16	c. Sparkes.
Nyren, Esq.	1	b. Wells	1	absent.
Lambert	2	b. Ditto	43	b. J. Wells.
Lord F. Beauclerk	58	b. Howard	38	b. Hammond.
G. Leycester, Esq.	4	b. Bennett	5	run out.
T. Smith, Esq.	4	b. Ditto	8	c. Bennett.
Hon. Gen. Bligh	15	b. Howard	3	b. J. Wells.
Wills, Esq.	1	st. Hammond	5	st. Hammond.
Hon. A. Upton	4	leg before wicket	6	absent.
Burgoyne, Esq.	1	c. Sparkes	0	Ditto.
E. H. Budd, Esq.	0	not out	5	b. Walker.
Byes	4	Byes	2	
	96		132	

PLAYERS.

	First Innings.			Second Innings.	
Small -	- 3	c. Nyren -	- 0	b. Wills.
Sparkes	- 8	b. Lambert	- 27	run out.
Howard	- 6	b. Ditto -	- 4	not out.
Ayling -	- 1	c. Bligh -	- 0	c. Leycester.
T. Walker	- 18	run out -	- 5	c. Ditto.
Robinson	- 15	hit wicket	- 1	c. Beauclerk.
Beldham	- 0	b. Wills -	- 1	st. Leycester.
Hammond	- 2	c. Lambert	- 8	c. Budd.
Bennett	- 6	b. Ditto -	- 0	st. Lambert.
Fremantle	- 3	not out -	- 26	st. Ditto.
J. Wells	- 0	b. Lambert	- 4	c. Wills.
Byes -	- 3	Byes	- 4	
	65		81	

In the following month, viz. on the 5th of August, we find
Mr. Smith taking part in a game in which his own county, Hants,
with Beldham and Lambert, contended against All England,
and won by 10 wickets. The match came off on Stoke
Down, not far from the squire's own residence at Tedworth.
Here we find his great rival, Lord F. Beauclerk, playing
against him.

HANTS.

	First Innings.			Second Innings.	
Fremantle -	- 49	b. Wells.			
Lambert -	- 0	b. Ditto.			
T. Smith, Esq.	- 12	run out -	- 3	not out.
Beldham -	- 30	c. Beauclerk.			
Small -	- 25	b. Hammond.			
Howard -	- 13	b. Wells.			
Hampton -	- 0	b. Beauclerk.			
Parker -	- 1	c. Sparkes.			
Pointer -	- 4	c. Hammond.			
Stewart -	- 1	not out -	- 3	not out.
Windebank -	- 6	b. Fennex -	- 0	b. Fennex.
Byes -	- 0	Byes -	- 0	
	150		6	

ENGLAND.

	First Innings.			Second Innings.		
Hardy - -	-	1	leg before wicket	-	9	st. Howard.
Ayling - -	-	0	b. Howard	-	0	b. Ditto.
T. Walker -	-	1	st. Ditto	-	13	c. Ditto.
Lord F. Beauclerk		0	b. Lambert	-	11	b. Ditto.
Robinson -	-	6	b. Howard	-	1	b. Ditto.
Hammond -	-	11	b. Lambert	-	25	c. Beldham.
Hon. Gen. Bligh	-	3	run out -	-	22	run out.
Sparkes -	-	26	b. Lambert	-	3	c. Beldham.
J. Wells -	-	0	b. Howard	-	0	not out.
Bridger -	-	6	hit wicket	-	6	c. Beldham.
Fennex -	-	4	not out -	-	4	c. Hampton.
Byes -	-	2	Byes -	-	1	
		—			—	
		60			95	
		—			—	

In 1807 the batting of Mr. Assheton Smith was no less
distinguished than in the preceding years. On the 25th
of May, 9 of Hants, with Lambert and J. Hampton, played
England at Lord's; but on this occasion the latter was
victorious by 47 runs. Mr. Smith scored no notches in
his first innings, but made 24 in his second. Beldham,
on the side of England, ran up to 79 in his first innings,
and was not out, but was caught by Lambert in his second,
without adding a single run to the score. Lord F. Beauclerk did not play in this game. On the 2nd of June
following, in a match played at Lord's, between the Marylebone Club, with Lambert, Beldham, and Hammond, against
All England, Mr. Smith played on the Marylebone side,
and scored 6, and 26, and not out; Marylebone won by
9 wickets. It is a remarkable fact, that in looking at the
records of these great matches, as furnished us by Mr. Bentley,
we find that almost invariably, the winning side was that on
which Mr. Smith played. Lord F. Beauclerk obtained 53

runs for Marylebone in his first innings, and did not go in a second time. Mr. Smith was again victorious shortly afterwards in a match between the Marylebone and Homerton Clubs, played at Lord's on the 25th of June. The game is remarkable for the long scores obtained by the Marylebone players; and also as being one of the first appearances of the late Benjamin Aislabie, Esq., one of the most staunch supporters and most liberal patrons of cricket. Even in our own time no great game was complete without the presence of this highly respected secretary of the Marylebone Club. On the occasion we refer to, he played on the Homerton side, and obtained 22 runs, and was not out in his second innings. The Marylebone Club, however, came off the winner by 354 runs. The insertion of the score needs no apology.

MARYLEBONE.

	First Innings.				Second Innings.	
Hon. Gen. Bligh	- 48	b. Walpole	-	- 0	b. Holland.
G. Leycester, Esq.	- 62	c. Peppercorn	-	- 80	c. Walpole.
Col. Maitland	- 64	b. Nyren	-	- 18	c. Warren.
Capt. Beckett	- 14	b. Ditto	-	- 21	b. Ladbroke.
R. Leigh, Esq.	- 12	b. Ditto	-	- —	absent.
C. Onslow, Esq.	- 32	b. Aislabie	-	- 13	b. Holland.
T. Smith, Esq.	- 35	b. Hicks	-	- 17	b. Peppercorn.
T. Mellish, Esq.	- 5	b. Aislabie	-	- 12	b. Ditto.
Hon. Col. Upton	- 26	c. Nyren	-	- 18	run out.
J. Laurell, Esq.	- 4	b. Peppercorn	-	- 22	not out.
Gen. Onslow	- 4	not out	-	- 10	leg before wicket.
Byes	- 14	Byes	-	- 2	
	320			213	

HOMERTON.

	First Innings.			Second Innings.	
Peppercorn, Esq.	0	c. Onslow		9	b. Upton.
T. Vigne, Esq.	45	b. Smith		0	b. Smith.
Hicks, Esq.	2	b. Onslow		—	absent.
F. Ladbroke, Esq.	20	run out		—	b. Smith.
C. Warren, Esq.	0	c. C. Onslow		—	absent.
Nyren, Esq.	13	c. G. Leycester		—	absent.
Sir H. Martin	0	c. Bligh		13	st. Leycester.
Holland, Esq.	6	b. Smith		10	b. Upton.
R. Walpole, Esq.	1	b. Upton		12	b. Smith.
B. Aislabie, Esq.	0	not out		22	not out.
Bridges, Esq.	0	b. Smith		12	run out.
Byes	2		Byes	4	
	89			90	

Marylebone won by 354 runs.

In the above match we observe that Mr. Smith distinguished himself successfully as a bowler. On the 6th of June previous, eight of the Marylebone Club, with Beldham, Robinson, and T. Walker had contended at Lord's with eight of the Homerton Club, with Lambert, Hammond, and Small. On that occasion also victory had declared itself in favour of Marylebone by 156 runs. Mr. Smith made his greatest innings in this game, viz. 58, and not out, in his first innings, and 20 in his second. He was now thirty-two years of age, and in the prime of manly vigour and activity. Three matches were played in the course of this year at Lord's between Surrey and England, in which he took part. Surrey, however, was the victor on all three occasions, although the fine play of Lord F. Beauclerk on the side of England was very conspicuous. He scored 52 and 7 in the first match, 24 and 16 in the second, and 24 and 57 in the third. Mr. Budd also showed some fine play on the same side, making 30 in the first match, and 14 and 45 in the second. The part of Surrey was, however, too powerfully supported by Beldham, Robinson, Lambert, and Tanner. They severally obtained 62, 68, 86, 36, and 30, in one or other of these matches; while to Mr. Smith's bat we find set down in the second match the respectable figures of 10 and 25, and in the third of 11 and 19.

In 1809 Mr. Smith did not play in the match between Surrey and England, which came off at Lord's on the 27th of June, Surrey being again the victor by 6 wickets. He does not appear to have taken part in many of the matches played during this season, although we find his name in a game played at Lord's on the 13th of June, between eight of the Marylebone Club, with Lambert, Beldham, and H. Bentley, and All England. Mr. Smith played on the Marylebone side, and scored 5 and 28; England won by 3 wickets. In this game the name of the celebrated George Osbaldestone first appears, so long afterwards renowned in sporting circles, not only as a cricketer, but a rider with foxhounds, steeplechase rider, and pedestrian; in fact, in every department of British sports. He was the first gentleman in England who rode a steeple-chase. In almost every athletic sport requiring muscular strength, pluck, and power of endurance, he found a competitor worthy of his prowess in Tom Smith. In the game above-mentioned between Marylebone and England, Lord F. Beauclerk greatly distinguished himself on the side of the former, scoring 32 and 114, and on each occasion being caught by Hammond. In 1810, Mr. Smith may be said to have attained his highest reputation as a cricketer. He was then in his thirty-fourth year, and once more brought victory to the side of England in a match with Surrey, which was played at Lord's on the 18th of June, when after some splendid play on both sides, England was declared the winner by 6 wickets. Mr. Smith obtained the largest score to be found on both sides, viz. 47, although Lambert, Beldham, and Robinson were enlisted on the side of Surrey. The following is the account of the game; Surrey going in first, and putting in Walker and J. Wells, who reckoned 80 runs between them before they parted, and cutting out some **tough** work for Mr. Smith and his companions in arms.

SURREY.

	First Innings.		Second Innings.	
Walker - -	- 38	run out -	- 7	c. Budd.
J. Wells -	- 42	c. Budd -	- 10	c. Ditto.
Lambert -	- 42	run out -	- 0	run out.
Beldham -	- 15	c. Beauclerk	- 27	c. Beauclerk.
Robinson -	- 18	b. Howard	- 0	c. Howard.
J. Tanner, Esq.	- 14	not out -	- 6	b. Ditto.
Harding -	- 1	st. Hammond	- 1	c. Budd.
Bridger - -	- 4	b. Budd -	- 6	b. Howard.
G. Sparkes -	- 0	c. Howard	- 4	c. Carter.
Goldham, Esq.	- 0	b. Beauclerk	- 4	not ont.
Hampton -	- 0	b. Howard	- 1	c. Fremantle.
Byes	- 18	Byes -	- 5	
	192		71	

ENGLAND.

	First Innings.		Second Innings.	
Bennett -	- 39	b. Wells.		
Small - -	- 8	c. Beldham.		
Hammond -	- 32	b. Ditto.		
Howard - -	- 1	c. Lambert.		
E. H. Budd, Esq.	- 12	b. Ditto	- 11	c. Walker.
T. Smith, Esq.	- 16	b. Ditto	- 47	st. Beldham.
Lord Beauclerk	- 14	b. Ditto	- 3	b. Ditto.
H. Bentley -	- 0	c. Harding	- 10	not out.
Fremantle -	- 12	c. Hampton	- 29	c. Beldham.
Carter - -	- 9	not out	- 4	not out.
Osbaldestone, Esq.	- 11	c. Beldham.		
Byes	- 3	Byes -	- 3	
	157		. 107	

England won by 6 wickets.

A fortnight afterwards the gentlemen and players under 38 years of age contended at Lord's, against those above that age, when the former won the game with ease by 10 wickets. Mr. Smith contributed 37 runs to the first innings, and was put in first with Lord F. Beauclerk in the second to win the game. They were both not out. Lambert scored 69 on Mr. Smith's side. In this, as in the preceding game, his opponents had won the toss and gone in first, when they did not leave the wickets without marking 156. Lovers of cricket will not find fault with the whole score being given.

ABOVE 38 YEARS OF AGE.

	First Innings.		Second Innings.	
J. Wells	- 3	run out	- 6	c. Harding.
T. Walker	- 1	c. Howard	- 4	c. Bennett.
Robinson	- 52	c. Bridger	- 7	st. Howard.
Hammond	- 27	st. Howard	- 0	run out.
Beldham	- 4	c. Beauclerk	- 5	c. Beauclerk.
Fremantle	- 17	c. Bridger	- 10	b. Lambert.
Hon. Gen. Bligh	- 0	b. Lambert	- 0	c. Smith.
Small	- 32	c. Beauclerk	- 14	b. Budd.
Ayling	- 5	c. Budd	- 0	b. Ditto.
Ray	- 12	b. Lambert	- 5	b. Lambert.
Collins	- 0	not out	- 3	not out.
Byes	- 3		Byes - 1	
	156		**55**	

UNDER 38 YEARS OF AGE.

	First Innings.		Second Innings.	
H. Bentley	- 4	b. Collins.		
Bridger	- 3	b. Ditto.		
E. H. Budd, Esq.	- 21	b. Wells.		
Lambert	- 69	c. Beldham.		
Lord F. Beauclerk	5	b. Hammond	- 1	not out.
T. Smith, Esq.	- 37	b. Collins	- 5	not out.
Bennett	- 3	b. Robinson.		
Howard	- 38	b. Wells.		
Harding	- 16	c. Ditto.		
T. Tanner, Esq.	- 8	not out.		
Carter	- 0	b. Hammond.		
Byes	- 2		Byes - 0	
	206		**6**	

Under 38 years won by 10 wickets.

On the 24th of July following, the players *above* 38 years of age took Mr. Smith into their ranks, when it will be seen he caused the tide of fortune to turn with him. No greater proof could be given of his skill in the game, as well as of the repute in which he was held by his brother-players. The game was interrupted by the unfavourable state of the weather, but was finally played out on the 17th of August, when what were termed the old 'uns won by 90 runs. Lambert did all he could to maintain the prestige already obtained by the preceding match, but Mr. Budd did not play this time, nor was Lord F. Beauclerk fortunate enough to mark a double figure in either innings. The following is the score :—

ABOVE 38 YEARS OF AGE (*WITH T. SMITH, ESQ.*).

	First Innings.		Second Innings.	
Wells	1	b. Beauclerk	15	b. Lambert.
Ray	2	b. Ditto	0	c. Harding.
Robinson	62	c. Howard	16	c. Carter.
T. Smith, Esq.	10	st. Lambert	20	c. Bridger.
Hammond	27	b. Bennett	64	b. Howard.
Fremantle	0	b. Ditto	0	st. Ditto.
Hampton	2	b. Beauclerk	3	not out.
Small	0	b. Howard	12	st. Lambert.
Ayling	1	b. Lambert	10	c. Howard.
Reed	5	not out	1	b. Beauclerk
Winter	4	b. Beauclerk	2	b. Lambert.
Byes	5		Byes 6	
	119		149	

UNDER 38 YEARS OF AGE.

	First Innings.		Second Innings.	
J. Tanner, Esq.	0	b. Wells	9	not out.
H. Bentley	5	c. Ray	3	hit wicket.
Howard	18	b. Wells	11	b. Reed.
Lambert	5	c. Hampton	45	c. Winter.
Bennett	11	b. Wells	6	b. Hammond.
Lord F. Beauclerk	5	b. Ditto	0	b. Wells.
Harding	19	b. Hammond	0	c. Fremantle.
Carter	17	c. Fremantle	6	b. Wells.
Bridger	6	c. Reed	2	b. Hammond.
Pointer	0	b. Wells	—	absent.
Shearman	4	not out	3	b. Hammond.
Byes	3		Byes 0	
	93		85	

The Old 'uns won by 90 runs.

In 1812 Mr. Smith played in one or two matches, but of no great consequence. He was now known as one of the best and hardest riders in England, and his attention, even out of the hunting season, was doubtless much absorbed with his kennel and his stud. In 1813 his place on Lord's Cricket Ground was worthily filled up by the greatest cricketer within the memory of the last half century, the late W. Ward, Esq. We find Mr. Ward's name first in the record of a match played at Lord's, on the 7th of June, 1813, between two select Elevens of England, the Hon. General Bligh and Lord F. Beauclerk being their respective Captains. Mr. Vigne also was at that period coming into play. Lord F. Beauclerk remained on the cricket field long after Mr. Smith had quitted it, and continued to maintain his reputation till 1825, in which year his name is to be found in several matches. He did not, however, play with the gentlemen in that year, when fifteen met the players of England at Lord's, on the 4th of July, and were winners by 72 runs. It was on this occasion Mr. Ward obtained his celebrated innings of

102, and then left the wicket in consequence of being hurt.
The play of the present Mr. Henry Kingscote was remarkably
fine in this game. He scored 22 and 38. On the part of the
players the hitting of Saunders, Broadbridge, and T. Beagley,
was deservedly admired. Saunders scored 99 in his first
innings, and was run out; T. Beagley scored 54, and not out;
and Broadbridge marked 52 and not out in his second innings.
The first innings of the players reached the large number of
243, while that of the gentlemen only marked 143, but they
made up 272 in their second innings. The year 1825 is
also memorable in the annals of cricket, as being the first
that saw the matches between the Public Schools at Lord's.
The Winchester Eleven on this occasion beat Harrow by
140 runs, while the Etonians also won in their match with
Harrow by 7 wickets. These matches have been regularly
continued until the present time, with the exception of one
or two years, when they were stopped by the head-masters, in
consequence of complaints made by some of the parents of
the boys, on account of the expenses and temptation their
sons incurred by remaining in London. A general expression of public feeling, however, in favour of the restoration
of these popular matches, which always attracted a very large
concourse of spectators and excited the warmest interest,
caused the veto to be taken off, it being generally considered
that the evil of one or two boys being dragged into the vortex
of dissipation and expense, was more than counterbalanced
by the stimulus thus given to manly and athletic exercises.
Consequently, when Dr. Vaughan, the late head-master of
Harrow, who was always most favourable to the continuance
of the Public-School matches, a year or two ago entered Lord's
Cricket Ground to witness the prowess of his own scholars,
his appearance in the cricket field was hailed with enthusiastic
cheers by the vast multitude of spectators assembled to watch

the game. In 1820, Mr. Smith once more entered the cricket lists, being then 44 years of age, to play on the side of Hants against England, but he appears then to have been out of practice, for he was bowled out in the first innings by Powell, without scoring a run, and in the second only obtained 2, when he was stumped by Shearman. England won on this occasion by 82 runs. In 1820, the three Pilches first played in a match at Lord's on the 24th of July, between the Marylebone Club and the county of Norfolk, with Messrs. E. H. Budd, F. Ladbroke, and T. Vigne. N. Pilch succeeded in scoring 52 runs in his second innings. The other two bowled with success on the Norfolk side. Mr. Ward made the great score of 278 for Marylebone in his first innings, and Lord F. Beauclerk 82 and not out. The whole innings reached 473, and the game resulted in Marylebone winning by 417 runs. The four innings of both sides amounted to 745. The batting of Fuller Pilch, who subsequently resided at West Malling, in Kent, afterwards attained the highest excellence, while his fielding was most admirable. Twenty years afterwards, viz. in 1840, he was the finest and most powerful hitter in England, while the extraordinary reach with which he covered the field at point or middle wicket, and the wonderful manner in which he picked up the ball, never failed to elicit the warmest plaudits from the spectators. Nothing could have been more splendid than the attitude of Fuller Pilch, when, taking his place at the wicket, he opened his broad chest and threw back his well-knit shoulders to receive the ball from the bowler, and if it came to leg, turned it over without apparent effort into the distant part of the field. The writer of this memoir gladly pays the tribute of admiration, not only to his skill, but to his manly yet always respectful deportment, and to the invincible pluck which he always evinced while contending against a stronger side than his own. For the above brief record of Mr. Assheton Smith's feats in the cricket field, the reader is indebted to the Register of Cricket Matches from 1786 to 1823, drawn up by Henry Bentley, and published in the latter year. The volume was printed by T. Traveller, 43, Park Street, New Road, and is now extremely scarce. A copy, which formerly belonged to Caldecourt, but is now in the possession of Frederick Lillywhite, has furnished the foregoing details.

BILLESDEN COPLOW POEM.

Page 23.

THE run celebrated in the following verses took place on the 24th of February, 1800, when Mr. Meynell hunted Leicestershire, and has since been known as the Billesden Coplow Run. It will only cease to interest, says a writer in the Sporting Magazine, when the grass shall grow in winter in the streets of Melton Mowbray. They found in the covert from which the song takes its name, thence to Skeffington Earths, past Tilton Woods, by Tugby and Whetstone, where the field, as many as could get over, crossed the river Soar. Thence the hounds changing their fox, carried a head to Enderby Gorse, where they lost him, after a chase of two hours and fifteen minutes, the distance being twenty-eight miles. A picture descriptive of this famous run was painted by Loraine Smith, Esq., who was one of the few who got over the river, and was until very lately in the possession of Robert Haymes, Esq., of Great Glenn, Leicestershire. In this painting, which shows the field in the act of crossing the Soar, we see Mr. Germaine, who has just crossed it, and was

the only one out that day who did so on horseback. Mr.
Musters is in the middle of the stream, and on the point of
throwing himself off his horse, who is too much distressed to
carry him over. The other horsemen in the picture are Jack
Raven the huntsman, Lord Maynard, and his servant, who
are all three coming up towards the stream. Mr. Loraine
Smith, " the Enderby squire," who of course well knows the
locality, is crossing a ford on foot, and leading his horse,
higher up the stream. The hounds are seen ascending the
hill on the opposite side, in full cry, leaving Enderby village
and church to the left. The song was written by the Rev.
Robert Lowth, son of the eminent Bishop of London of that
name. The reverend divine was one of the field, being on
a visit at Melton at that time, and wrote the song at the
request of the Honourable George Germaine, brother of Lord
Sackville, afterwards Duke of Dorset, in consequence of some
incorrect accounts of the run which had been published.

POEM

ON

THE FAMOUS BILLESDEN COPLOW RUN,

BY THE REV. ROBERT LOWTH.

> " Quæque ipse miserrima vidi,
> Et quorum pars magna fui."

With the wind at north-east, forbiddingly keen,
The Coplow of Billesden ne'er witness'd, I ween,
Two hundred such horses and men at a burst,
All determined to ride — each resolved to be first.
But to get a good start over-eager and jealous,
Two thirds, at the least, of these very fine fellows
So crowded, and hustled, and jostled, and cross'd,
That they rode the wrong way, and at starting were lost.

In spite of th' unpromising state of the weather,
Away broke the fox, and the hounds close together:
A burst up to Tilton so brilliantly ran,
Was scarce ever seen in the mem'ry of man.
What hounds guided scent, or which led the way,
Your bard — to their names quite a stranger — can't say;
Though their names had he known, he is free to confess,
His horse could not show him at such a death-pace.
Villiers, Cholmondeley, and Forester made such sharp play,
Not omitting Germaine, never seen till to-day:
Had you judged of these four by the trim of their pace,
At Bibury you'd thought they'd been riding a race.
But these hounds with a scent, how they dash and they fling,
To o'er-ride them is quite the impossible thing;
Disdaining to hang in the wood, through he raced,
And the open for Skeffington gallantly faced;
Where headed and foil'd, his first point he forsook,
And merrily led them a dance o'er the brook.
Pass'd Galby and Norton, Great Stretton and Small,
Right onward still sweeping to old Stretton Hall;
Where two minutes' check served to show at one ken
The extent of the havoc 'mongst horses and men.
Such sighing, such sobbing, such trotting, such walking;
Such reeling, such halting, of fences such baulking;
Such a smoke in the gaps, such comparing of notes;
Such quizzing each other's daub'd breeches and coats:
Here a man walk'd afoot who his horse had half kill'd,
There you met with a steed who his rider had spill'd:
In short, such dilemmas, such scrapes, such distress,
One fox ne'er occasion'd, the knowing confess.
But, alas! the dilemmas had scarcely began,
On for Wigston and Ayleston he resolute ran,

S

Where a few of the stoutest now slacken'd and panted,
And many were seen irretrievably planted.
The high road to Leicester the scoundrel then cross'd,
As Tell-tale * and Beaufremont † found to their cost ;
And Villiers esteem'd it a serious bore,
That no longer could Shuttlecock‡ fly as before ;
Even Joe Miller's § spirit of fun was so broke,
That he ceased to consider the run as a joke.
Then streaming away, o'er the river he splash'd, —
Germaine close at hand, off the bank Melon ‖ dash'd.
Why so stout proved the Dun, in a scamper so wild?
Till now he had only been rode by a Child.⸗
After him plunged Joe Miller with Musters so slim,
Who twice sank, and nearly paid dear for his whim,
Not reflecting that all water Melons must swim.
Well soused by their dip, on they brush'd o'er the bottom,
With liquor on board, enough to besot 'em.
But the villain, no longer at all at a loss,
Stretch'd away like a d—l for Enderby Gorse :
Where meeting with many a brother and cousin,
Who knew how to dance a good hay in the furzen ;
Jack Raven ** at length coming up on a hack,
That a farmer had lent him, whipp'd off the game pack.
Running sulky, old Loadstone †† the stream would not swim,
No longer sport proving a magnet to him.
Of mistakes, and mishaps, and what each man befel,
Would the muse could with justice poetical tell !
Bob Grosvenor on Plush ‡‡ — though determined to ride —
Lost, at first, a good start, and was soon set aside ;

* Mr. Forester's horse.
† Mr. Maddock's horse.
‡ Lord Villiers' horse.
§ Mr. Musters' horse.
‖ Mr. Germaine's horse.

⸗ Formerly Mr. Child's.
** The name of the huntsman.
†† The huntsman's horse.
‡‡ Mr. Robert Grosvenor's horse.

Though he charged hill and dale, not to lose this rare chase,
On velvet, Plush could not get a footing, alas!
To Tilton sail'd bravely Sir Wheeler O'Cuff,
Where neglecting, through hurry, to keep a good luff,
To leeward he drifts — how provoking a case!
And was forced, though reluctant, to give up the chase.
As making his way to the pack's not his forte,
Sir Lawley*, as usual, lost half of the sport.
But then the profess'd philosophical creed,
That "all's for the best,"— of Master Candide,
If not comfort Sir R., reconcile may at least;
For, with *this* supposition, *his* sport is the best.

Orby Hunter, who seem'd to be hunting his fate,
Got falls, to the tune of no fewer than eight.
Basan's king †, upon Glimpse ‡, sadly out of condition,
Pull'd up, to avoid of being tired the suspicion.
Og did right so to yield; for he very soon found,
His worst had he done, he'd have scarce glimpsed a hound.
Charles Meynell, who lay very well with the hounds,
Till of Stretton he nearly arrived at the bounds,
Now discover'd that Waggoner § rather would creep,
Than exert his great prowess in taking a leap;
But when crossing the turnpike, he read ☞ "Put on here,"
'Twas enough to make any one bluster and swear.
The Waggoner feeling familiar the road,
Was resolved not to quit it; so stock still he stood.
Yet prithee, dear Charles! why rash vows will you make,
Thy leave of old Billesden ‖ to finally take?

---

* Sir Robert Lawley, called Sir Lawley in the Melton dialect.
† Mr. Oglander, familiarly called Og.
‡ Mr. Oglander's horse.   § Mr. C. Meynell's horse.
‖ He had threatened never to follow the hounds again from Billesden, on account of his weight.

Since from Legg's Hill *, for instance, or perhaps Melton
    Spinney,
If they go a good pace, you are beat for a guinea!
'Tis money, they say, makes the mare to go kind ;
The proverb has vouch'd for this time out of mind ;
But though of this truth you admit the full force,
It may not hold so good of every horse.
If it did, Ellis Charles need not bustle and hug,
By name, not by nature, his favourite Slug.†
Yet Slug as he is — the whole of this chase
Charles ne'er could have seen, had he gone a snail's pace.
Old Gradus ‡, whose fretting and fuming at first
Disqualify strangely for such a tight burst,
Ere to Tilton arrived, ceased to pull and to crave,
And though fresh*ish* at Stretton, he stepp'd a *pas grave!*
Where, in turning him over a cramp kind of place,
He overturn'd George, whom he threw on his face ;
And on foot to walk home it had sure been his fate,
But that soon he was caught, and tied up to a gate.

    Near Wigston occurr'd a most singular joke,
Captain Miller averr'd that his leg he had broke,—
And bemoan'd, in most piteous expressions, how hard,
By so cruel a fracture, to have his sport marr'd.
In quizzing his friends he felt little remorse,
To finesse the complete doing up of his horse.
Had he told a long story of losing a shoe,
Or of laming his horse, he very well knew
That the Leicestershire creed out this truism worms,
" Lost shoes and dead beat are synonymous terms."
So a horse must here learn, whatever he does,
To die game — as at Tyburn — and " die in his shoes."

---

* A different part of the hunt.   ‡ Mr. George Ellis's horse.
† Mr. Charles Ellis's horse.

Bethel Cox, and Tom Smith, Messieurs Bennett and Hawke,
Their nags all contrived to reduce to a walk.
Maynard's Lord, who detests competition and strife,
As well in the chase as in social life,
Than whom nobody harder has rode in his time,
But to crane here and there now thinks it no crime,
That he beat some crack riders most fairly may crow,
For he lived to the end, though he scarcely knows how.

With snaffle and martingale held in the rear,
His horse's mouth open half up to his ear;
Mr. Wardle, who threaten'd great things over night,*
Beyond Stretton was left in most terrible plight.
Too lean to be press'd, yet egg'd on by compulsion,
No wonder his nag tumbled into convulsion.
Ah! had he but lost a fore shoe, or fell lame,
'Twould only his sport have curtail'd, not his fame.
Loraine†,—than whom no one his game plays more safe,
Who the last to the first prefers seeing by half,—
What with nicking ‡ and keeping a constant look-out,
Every turn of the scent surely turn'd to account.
The wonderful pluck of his horse surprised some,
But he knew they were making point blank for his home.
" Short home " to be brought we all should desire,
Could we manage the trick like the Enderby squire.§

Wild Shelley ‖, at starting all ears and all eyes,
Who to get a good start all experiment tries,
Yet contrived it so ill, as to throw out poor Gipsy,⊥
Whom he rattled along as if he'd been tipsy,

* Said to have threatened that he would beat the whole field.
† Mr. Loraine Smith.
‡ A term of reproach. ‖ Usually very grave.
§ Where Mr. Loraine Smith lives. ⊥ Sir John Shelley's mare.

To catch them again ; but, though famous for speed,
She never could touch * them, much less get a lead.
So disshearten'd, disjointed, and beat, home he swings,
Not much unlike a fiddler hung upon strings.

An H. H.† who in Leicestershire never had been,
So of course such a tickler ne'er could have seen,
Just to see them throw off, on a raw horse was mounted,
Who a hound had ne'er seen, nor a fence had confronted.
But they found in such style, and went off at such score,
That he could not resist the attempt to see more :
So with scrambling, and dashing, and one rattling fall,
He saw all the fun, up to Stretton's white Hall.
There they anchor'd, in plight not a little distressing —
The horse being raw, he of course got a dressing.
That wonderful mare of Vanneck's, who till now
By no chance ever tired, was taken in tow :
And what's worse, she gave Van such a devilish jog
In the face with her head, plunging out of a bog,
That with eye black as ink, or as Edward's famed Prince,
Half blind has he been, and quite deaf ever since.
But let that not mortify thee, Shackaback ; ‡
She only was blown, and came home a rare hack.

There Craven too stopp'd, whose misfortune, not fault,
His mare unaccountably vex'd with string-halt ;
And when she had ceased thus spasmodic to prance,
Her mouth 'gan to twitch with St. Vitus's dance.
But how shall described be the fate of Rose Price,
Whose fav'rite white gelding convey'd him so nice
Through thick and through thin, that he vow'd and protested §
No money should part them, as long as life lasted ?

---

* Melton dialect for "overtake."
† These initials may serve either for Hampshire hog or Hampshire Hunt.
‡ A name taken from Blue Beard, and given to Mr. Vanneck by his Melton
friends.　　　　　§ At the cover side a large sum was offered for it.

But the pace that effected which money could not :
For to part, and in death, was their no distant lot.
In a fatal blind ditch Carlo Khan's * powers fail'd,
Where nor lancet nor laudanum either avail'd.
More care of a horse than he took, could take no man :
He'd more straw than would serve any lying-in woman.
Still he died! — yet just how, as nobody knows,
It may truly be said, he died " under the Rose."
At the death of poor Khan, Melton feels such remorse,
That they've christen'd that ditch, " The Vale of White Horse."

Thus ended a chase, which for distance and speed
It's fellow we never have heard of or read.
Every species of ground ev'ry horse does not suit,
What's a good country hunter may here prove a brute ;
And, unless for all sorts of strange fences prepared,
A man and his horse are sure to be scared.
This variety gives constant life to the chase ;
But as Forester says —" Sir, what KILLS, is the PACE."
In most other countries they boast of their breed,
For carrying, at times, such a beautiful head ;
But these hounds to carry a head cannot fail,
And constantly too, for,—by George,—there's no tail.
Talk of horses, and hounds, and the system of kennel,
Give me Leicestershire nags, and the hounds of Old Meynell !

MR. MEYNELL.

Page 24.

Mr. Meynell was considered the first fox-hunter of his day.
He bought the mansion at Quorndon of Earl Ferrers, and,

* Mr. Price's horse.

after a residence there of nearly fifty years, he disposed of
it to the Earl of Sefton in 1800, upon the death of his eldest
son, which took place May 17th in that year.   Mr. Meynell
died at Bradley, in Derbyshire, December 1808, in his seventy-
fourth year, universally lamented.   He was the first who
established order and discipline in the hunting-field, more by
his good-humoured pleasantry than by the assumption or
exercise of any authority over others.   When two young
and dashing riders had headed the hounds, he remarked,
"the hounds were following the gentlemen, who had very
kindly gone forward to see what the fox was about."   His
grand meet at Quorndon Hall, in 1791, given to the first
nobility and gentry of England, was second only to that
given to Mr. Assheton Smith at Rolleston, in 1840.

THE CRAVEN COUNTRY : BEN FOOT.

Page 25.

"IN a difficult bad-scenting plough, and wet woodland,
country, few men that ever I saw," writes one who often
hunted with the Craven, "could hunt a fox better or ride closer
to his hounds than old Ben Foot, huntsman to the late Mr.
Villebois, who formerly lived with Sir Thomas Mostyn.*   One
day, when we were running a ringing fox with a flashing scent
in Stipe, a well-known covert, just as Foot got his hounds well
settled, a farmer hallooed a fresh fox at the other extremity
of the covert.   Upon this Foot stopped his horse, and fell
a 'moralizing' thus : 'How hignorant, Sir, some folks be !

---

* He has, however, been accused in the preceding pages of " worriting " his
fox.

Now can't he see that we be engaged *to* this fox?'" "Why is our fox like our huntsman?" said an animated citizen on Whit-Monday, just as they had found. "Do you give it up?—Because they are both *a Foot!*"

.

TOM EDGE.

Page 29.

"Mr. Edge and Mr. Smith were an uncommon silent pair. Mr. Edge (who was always styled Mr. Smith's '*better* half,') seldom spoke unless Mr. Smith said something to him. Mr. Smith would never let him have more than a pint of port a day; he said he would get too fat. Mr. Edge used to pound away on that great big horse of his, Gayman: queer-looking creature it was, thin neck, large head, raw hips, and a rat-tail, for all the world like a great seventeen-hand dog horse."*

Gayman used to be styled in the Quorn Hunt, "the skeleton cart-horse;" and his master, "the Ajax" of the heavy weights. Tom Edge's weight, however, did not cause him to do like the heavy farmer in the story, who used to remain a quiet spectator on high ground while the hounds were running hard below. His ideas ran chiefly on the inconvenience of a heavy weight, especially as he was losing the sport in consequence of it; and he used to exclaim, rubbing his hands, "Bless me, how they are a physicking on him!"

* Dick Christian, in Silk and Scarlet, p. 61.

MR. OSBALDESTON.

Page 29.

THERE is an excellent portrait of Mr. Osbaldeston in the Sporting Magazine for January 1836, second series, engraved by Roffe, from a painting by J. J. Woodhouse, M.D., Fellow of Caius College, Cambridge. One of his best horses was Yorkshire Stingo.

THE BURTON COUNTRY.

Page 29.

SIR WILLIAM MILES, the present member for West Somersetshire, hunted with Mr. Assheton Smith in Lincolnshire during the seasons of 1818, 1819, and 1820. Although the latter had at that time a liberal allowance from his father, yet as he hunted six days a week and received no subscription, he was obliged to be as economical as possible. His able management of both stables and kennels, which was even at that period universally known and acknowledged, enabled him to make his income go as far as most men could. He rode at that time, according to Sir William Miles, as hard as he ever did, and many and heavy were the falls he got, as he was "never content unless first;" and the country, then undrained, showed up his horses terribly. Mr. Smith purchased while at Lincoln John Warde's hounds, — good noses, but "no pace," and when mixed with the old pack they tailed terribly; "but nothing," adds Sir William, "with Tom Smith, that was his own, *could* be had, however much the performance might militate against recognised rules." "A good head of hounds" is a common expression; but running very hard one day, and Sir William, who was a bold and resolute rider, being close to him, he exclaimed, "Look, Billy, what a beautiful *stream!*"* Mr. Smith hunted a dog and bitch pack in Lincolnshire; the former showed most sport, the latter were faster, but wilful. He took the hounds away from the Burton kennels, and built stables and kennels in a field which he had purchased at Lincoln, adjoining his dwelling-house. The kennel was abandoned by his successor, Sir Richard Sutton, and the premises were bought by Mr. Charles Chaplin, who afterwards kept his horses there.

Sir William Miles thus sums up his opinion of Mr. Smith: "Nothing ever daunted him, and if hunting had not been his mania, he would, I think, have succeeded in anything he undertook."

JACK SHIRLEY.

Page 32.

"Jack Shirley was one of Mr. Meynell's whips; he was an *owdacious* fellow, big and stout, with a rough voice. He was a great man with Mr. Smith and Sir Richard Sutton in Lincolnshire."† He used to ride young horses for ten shillings the day when he whipped-in for Mr. Smith, and when he asked his master's permission, it was always granted with these words, "Provided they do not kick hounds." The squire was very angry with Jack on one occasion, for riding a young horse with a martingale. Shirley was Mr. Smith's second whip in Leicestershire.

---

* Instead of saying "how they tail," he immediately converted the running into "a beautiful stream."

† Dick Christian, in Silk and Scarlet, p. 20.

TOM WINGFIELD AND JOSEPH HARRISON.

Page 32.

Tom Wingfield was "good in his casts," and a huntsman after Beckford's own heart. His son lived nineteen years with Mr. Drake. Tom had lived with Mr. Meynell as second whip, and he was head whip to Mr. Smith in 1807, when Dick Burton first came to him, then quite a lad. Joseph Harrison had hunted the hounds at Quorn for Lord Foley until Mr. Smith purchased them.

MR. LINDOW.

Page 34.

Lindow always stood up in his stirrups when the pace was most severe. This, Nimrod says, although it has an awkward appearance, tends very much to relieve the rider. "I have seen those two Rawlinsons, from Cheshire (one afterwards took the name of Lindow), ride wonderful in the vale. There was no beating them. It put Goosey (the Duke of Rutland's huntsman) quite out to see them going as they did." *

SIR JAMES MUSGRAVE.

Page 34.

Sir James Musgrave's horse, Baronet, was a mean-looking animal, with only one eye, but so capital a hunter that it was said of him, that if titles could be conferred on the brute creation, this Baronet would have been raised to the Peerage.

* Dick Christian, in Silk and Scarlet, p. 50.

SIR H. GOODRICKE.

Page 34.

SIR HARRY GOODRICKE died 21st September 1833, at Ravens-
dale Park, county of Louth, Ireland, of a cold caught whilst
otter-hunting. He was in his 37th year. He had had the Quorn
for two seasons, and was just entering on his third. He received no subscription, and is said to have spent 18,000*l.* in
his two seasons, inclusive of the new kennels at Thrussington,
on which he expended 6000*l.* He had two famous horses, the
Old and the Young Sheriff. He was painted by Ferneley on the
latter, with the hounds in full cry. Young Sheriff was bought
in at Tattersall's for 400 guineas. Sir Harry was perhaps
the most popular master of hounds ever known in England.
The following are the chorus and one of the stanzas of the song
written at Quorn in 1831, to celebrate his taking the mastership of the hounds:—

" Then round with the bottle and let us not tarry,
  While we hail, while we honour, the man of our choice;
  In a bumper come pledge us—The gallant Sir Harry,
  Whom we love in our hearts, as we hail with our voice.

" Other masters we've had in the days of our glory,
  Osbaldeston and Sefton, TOM SMITH and the Græme (Graham),
  Southampton the last, not the least in the story,
  Giving Melton its mainspring, and Leicestershire fame."

MR. VALENTINE MAHER.

Page 34.

LORD ALVANLEY bet Maher a hundred guineas that the latter
could not jump a brook without disturbing the water; and
Maher made Lord Alvanley the same bet. Maher got over,

but Lord Alvanley's horse threw some dirt back from the bank into the water, and it was given against him. Mr. Valentine Maher died in 1842.

MR. MAXSE.

Page 34.

Mr. Smith always admired the riding of Mr. Maxse, who was one of the most forward of the heavy weights. Maxse had a famous horse, Cognac, whom he hunted for nine successive seasons. His master was over sixteen stone.

AYSTON.

Page 44.

" Ayston tripped on one occasion when he was going to covert, and Mr. Philip Pierrepont, who was alongside of him, said to Mr. Smith, 'If I were you, Tom, I would ride that horse no more.' 'If I were going to ride for my life,' was the answer, 'I would ride him and no other.' *

The village of Ayston in Leicestershire, from which this favourite hunter was called, is in the best hunting part of the country.

BITCH PACK.

Page 51.

Mr. Smith used to say, that, if he hunted only three days a week, he would never take a dog hound into the field.

---

* Silk and Scarlet, p. 282.

MR. ASSHETON SMITH'S FALLS.

Page 57.

" Mr. Smith got a many falls. He always seemed to ride loose, quite by balance, not sticking with his knees very much. He always went slant-ways at his jumps ; it is a capital plan. The horse gets his measure better — he can give himself more room : if you put his head straight, it is measured for him ; if you put him slantish, he measures it for himself; you always see Mr. Greene ride at fences that way. He was first coming out when Mr. Smith was master, and he put him up to many a clever thing in riding. He had another dodge when he rode at timber ; he always went slap at the post ; he said it made the horse fancy he had more to do, and put more power on." *

An instance of one of his diagonal leaps is thus recorded :— The hounds coming in the course of a run to an immensely high and steep bank, with a stile on the top of it, many gentlemen did not like its looks. Mr. Smith, throwing his whip into his left hand, and at the same time taking out his pocket-handkerchief (this was done by way of giving the thing an air of negligence), said, " So you won't have it, gentlemen ? " Then taking the fence diagonally, he, by his peculiarly light hand, made his horse leap in this way, first on the bank, then over the stile and down on the other side. Nobody else could take the fence in the same manner, or would attempt it in any other.

* Silk and Scarlet, p. 57.

JACK O'LANTERN.

Page 57.

" Jack O'Lantern was a particularly gentle and good-tem-pered horse. When Mr. Lindow had broken his collar-bone, and was quite unable to hold the Clipper even with "the clipper-bit," Mr. Smith changed horses with him for the day. The meet was at Scoling's Gorse, near Melton, which has long since fallen under the plough. Mr. Lindow rode Jack with one arm in a sling, and the Clipper was brought out with bit-checks, some eight inches long, and the huge attendant curb chain. Every one thought Mr Smith bewitched, because he would not mount until the curb chain was taken off, and after pledging themselves that he would never be able to pull him up till he reached the sea coast, they heard early in the afternoon, that " Mr. Smith had run away with the Clipper, and that he could never go fast enough for him any one part of the way." *

FIRE-KING.

Page 58.

" Perhaps the most remarkable Irish hunter of the present century was Mr. Assheton Smith's Fire-King—a sixteen-hand, very large-limbed, light-fleshed, and deep-girthed thorough-bred chestnut. He was bought by Mr. William Denham of Kegworth, from Mr. Robert Lucas of Liverpool, in January 1840, for 5l. only, and was just as unmanageable a savage as

* Silk and Scarlet, p. 295.

ever wore a bridle. However, Mr. Denham contrived to
beat all Derbyshire on him, both with fox-hounds and Lord
Chesterfield's stag-hounds; Will Derry, who was riding one
of his Lordship's thorough-bred 300-guinea chestnuts, frankly
acknowledging on one occasion, that he could not live with
him any part of the run. He also distinguished himself in
Leicestershire in two runs, one from Cream Gorse, and the
other from Sir H. Goodricke's Gorse. Next day Mr. Assheton
Smith rode up to Mr. Denham, at Croxton Park races, and
made him an offer of 200l. for him, which his owner declined
unless Mr. Smith would make it guineas. On this the latter
jocularly remarked, that he was the most independent horse-
dealer he had ever met with; and was told that if he had
been independent, he would not have taken 2000 guineas for
the horse, as he was sure that no man could expect to have more
than one such in his life. He was very much blemished at the
time, so much so, in fact, that Mr. Smith could hardly credit
the assurance that he was sound, after having been "repaired
so often." At this juncture Lord Chesterfield rode up, and
Mr. Smith, on hearing his Lordship indorse Mr. Denham's
statement, that he had never in his life seen a horse that
could go better, if so well, to hounds, closed the bargain then
and there for guineas. At first they had rather a weary time
with him at Tedworth. Mr. Smith sent him home on hunting days seven or eight times before he could ride him with
confidence; and there is a legend, that he not only ran clean
away for miles with George Carter, but that the latter assured
his master, when he proposed another mount, that he would
rather run on foot than get on him. His master, however,
charmed the chestnut into a softer mood at last. On 15th
December in the following year (1841), he wrote to Mr.
Denham, to say that he had got him to go "as quiet as any
horse in his stable;" adding, "I have hunted a great number

T

of years, I have kept hounds and hunted them for thirty-eight years, and I am quite sure I never had such a horse as he is before, and fully believe I never saw such a one."*

THE KENNELS AT TEDWORTH.

Page 72.

A WRITER in the Sporting Magazine, speaking of the boiling and feeding-houses at Tedworth, remarks that they are removed from the kennel to avoid effluvia; but this plan, he says, is open to the objection, that the backs of the hounds are exposed to the wet in rainy weather, when coming for their food, and standing to take it.

In Beckford's time the boiling-house and feeding-rooms of kennels for foxhounds were placed in the centre. There were two kennels, the hunting and ordinary kennel. The floor of the lodging-rooms sloped, and was always bricked. There was a hayrick in the grass-yard, for the hounds to rest themselves against. Somerville, in his poem on the Chase, recommends a high situation; but, as Beckford observes, if this be selected, there can be no brook running through the kennels, which is very desirable on many accounts.

* The Post and the Paddock, pp. 260, 261.

HUNTING MORNING.

Page 75.

" THE East looks grey; the early lark
    Mounts upwards to the sky,
And to the rosy-finger'd morn
    Pours forth its minstrelsy.
Right merrily the huntsman winds
    The horn along the vale,
And Echo to the neighbouring hills
    Imparts the gladsome tale."   *Old Song.*

HOLLOW WATER LINES.

Page 105.

MR. NAPIER thus more fully describes in another letter Mr. Smith's determination to adopt his own favourite lines :—

"It is the fact that Mr. Smith, when he ordered the 'Menai' from me in 1829, wanted her built with *hollow water lines,* similar to the lines of his sailing yacht 'Menai.' But there being no such thing then as a steamer having hollow water lines, and Mr. John Wood, who was to build the vessel, being opposed to hollow lines, I advised Mr. Smith, in this his first steam-yacht, which was to cost him a large sum, not to run the risk of any failure, but to adopt Mr. Wood's water lines, he being at that time justly esteemed for his excellent taste, and for building the fastest steamers afloat. Mr. Smith reluctantly consented to allow Mr. Wood to make a model according to his own lines, with the proviso that he should himself make such alterations in them as he might judge best. This was done; the line was modified by Mr. Smith, and the vessel built otherwise wholly to his plans.

"After using this steamer for some years, he wished to encourage building vessels of iron, and ordered the 'Glow-worm' with water lines approaching nearer to his long-cherished plan of hollow lines, than the two 'Menai's' were. This vessel succeeded so well that he determined, cost him what it might, he would have a sea-going vessel built with his favourite hollow water lines. Accordingly, the 'Fire-King' was built strictly in all respects according to his own plans, with hollow lines and a flat bottom. After the 'Fire-King' all his other steamers were built with these lines."

MR. HOLYOAKE, NOW SIR FRANCIS GOODRICKE.

Page 124.

"He was first man at one time for a twenty minutes' thing, was Mr. Holyoake. To see him ride Brilliant, shoving the fox along! This horse was a rich dark chestnut; such a countenance, such an eye; he had him from Newmarket." * Sir Harry Goodricke, Sir Vincent Cotton, and Mr. Holyoake lived together at Quorn, and were called "The Sporting Triumvirate." Mr. Holyoake succeeded by will to the entire property of his brother-sportsman, Sir H. Goodricke, whose name he took, and was afterwards created a baronet. He himself rode Young Sheriff for several seasons. Clinker originally belonged to him, but was subsequently bought by Captain Ross. Sir Francis Goodricke has long since left the

---

* Silk and Scarlet, p. 279.

hunting field under the influence of deep and very sincere religious impressions; the zeal which uniformly displayed itself with such ardour in his case in the pursuit of a favourite diversion, is now directed with even greater strength and intensity into a far higher and nobler channel.

SIR BELLINGHAM GRAHAM.
Page 127.

SIR BELLINGHAM GRAHAM always called a bad seat "a wash-ball seat;" from a round piece of soap, which is always slipping about in a washhand basin. Beeswax, Paul, and Jerry were three of his best horses.

DICK BURTON.
Page 127.

DICK BURTON lived with Mr. Osbaldeston and Lord Southampton after he left Mr. Smith in Leicestershire. He first came to the latter in 1807, when quite a lad. He once met with a severe accident, a gentleman and his horse coming violently in contact with him, just as he was close upon his fox.

VISIT TO BELVOIR, 1840.
Page 128.

" WHEN Mr. Smith was at Belvoir in 1840, with his hounds, he ran a fox through Ingoldsby, Osgodby Coppice, Truham Park Wood and Norwood, right to Grimsthorpe Oaks. Will Goodall, who was then the duke's huntsman, gets into

the wood, and sees the fox in one of the rides. Off he slipped
quietly to Mr. Smith, and told him. He was casting
across the park. When Will brought the hounds, blame me
if the fox was not standing there, still waiting for him. Mr.
Smith came to the spot and saw him too: it would be four
minutes, and he had never stirred. I never had heard of
such a thing, and Dick Burton and Will told me the same." *

MANAGER.

Page 129.

"MANAGER was so fast a hound, that they buckled a shot-
belt round his neck and filled him three parts full of boiled
lights, but he defied them and their handicaps."* Mr. Ferneley
mentions his having in 1815 painted Will Burton, who, he
says, was a wonderful boy at hounds, with Manager, perhaps
"the finest hound he ever painted." Manager was afterwards
drafted and sent to Ireland to the late Lord Lismore, then
Mr. O'Callaghan.

SHANKTON HOLT.

Page 131.

"Mr. Smith was wonderfully fond of Shankton Holt. I
have seen him get away from it with three foxes in one day;
it was a great nursery for them in his time. He liked
Staunton Wood and Langton Caudle uncommonly; he always

* Dick Christian, in Silk and Scarlet, pp. 63, 64.
† Silk and Scarlet, p. 280.

said the wildest foxes lay there — away directly. He used to say that an hour and a half from Widmerpool to Blackberry Hill, near Belvoir, slap across the vale, was one of the best runs he ever had in Leicestershire." *

DICK CHRISTIAN'S HERO-WORSHIP OF MR. ASSHETON SMITH.

Page 147.

" On my last visit," says the Druid, " I found Dick Christian firmer than ever in his hero-worship of Mr. Assheton Smith, Sir James Musgrave, and Captain White." †   " I first knew Mr. Smith in 1798," writes Dick Christian to the writer of the present Memoir ‡, " when he hunted in the Pytchley country. I then lived with Sir Gilbert Heathcote. He certainly was the best man that ever came into Leicestershire. He used to say, ' Dick, what kills is *the pace.*' Yes, and no man put this oftener to the test than himself."

THE DUKE OF WELLINGTON'S OPINION OF FOX-HUNTERS.

Page 171.

" I own," said Sir Hussey, afterwards Lord Vivian, himself a distinguished soldier, upon the order of the day for the third reading of the proposed Game Bill, " I am proud of sporting; and the greatest Commander the world ever had has declared that he found men who followed the hounds brave and valiant soldiers."

---

* Dick Christian, in Silk and Scarlet, p. 58.
† Silk and Scarlet, p. 1.   ‡ In December 1859.

FOX-HUNTERS.

Page 176.

BECKFORD enumerates the five following species of fox-hunters: the "dress" fox-hunter, the "mahogany" fox-hunter, the "health-hunting" fox-hunter, the "coffee-housing" fox-hunter, and the "genuine" fox-hunter. As the name so well describes each, analysis of their respective merits is unnecessary.

NIMROD.

Page 177.

NIMROD'S popularity as a writer on sporting topics was never equalled. When a ship once arrived at Calcutta from England, Colonel Nesbitt, who then hunted the Calcutta hounds, hastened down to the beach and asked, "What news?" "There are new Ministers in," was the reply. "Hang the new Ministry," said the colonel; "is Nimrod's Yorkshire Tour arrived?" "A man," says Nimrod, relating the anecdote himself, "must be dead to fame to be insensible to such a compliment as this." Charles Apperley was the son of a clergyman in Shropshire.

PLUCK.

Page 179.

"IT was a great speech of Mr. Smith's, if ever he saw a horse refuse with his Whips, 'Throw your heart over, and your horse will follow.' He never rode fast at his fences. I have heard him say scores of times, 'When a man rides at fences a hundred miles an hour, depend upon it he funks.'" *

Sir William Miles confirms this statement. "Mr. Smith," he remarks, " always said, ' Go slow at all fences except water. It makes a horse know the use of his legs, and by so riding he can put down a leg wherever it is wanted.'"

GOOD HUNTSMAN.

Page 180.

" If he is active, and presses them on while the scent is good, always aiming to keep them as near the fox as he can; if, when his hounds are at fault, he makes his cast with judgment, not casting the wrong way first and blundering on the right at last, as many do; if, added to this, he is patient and persevering, never giving up a fox while there is a chance of killing him, he then is a perfect huntsman." †

It is for the reader to compare the above description with the subject of the present Memoir.

RIDING OVER HOUNDS.

Page 182.

" Do you think *you* can catch him?" said a master of hounds to a young aspiring sportsman. " No," was the reply. " Then let my hounds catch him if they can." ‡

* Dick Christian, in Silk and Scarlet, p. 57.
† Beckford, p. 254.   ‡ Ibid., p. 175.

SIZE OF HOUNDS.

Page 183.

"WHEN Mr. Smith bought Lord Foley's hounds, he liked them small, and he used to call the 'Pytchley,' when John Warde had them, 'the great calves.' There was hardly a dog hound in Mr. Smith's first pack much above twenty-three inches. Afterwards he thought that the small hounds could not jump over the long green briars which were too thick to admit of their creeping through, and he did not rest till he had raised his bitch standard to as much over twenty-three as he could get it, and his dogs to as near twenty-five as possible." *

BRITISH HOUNDS.

Page 183.

" IN thee alone, fair Land of Liberty,
  Is bred the perfect hound; in scent and speed
  As yet unrivall'd.   .   .   .   .
  His glossy skin, or yellow-pied, or blue,
  In lights or shades by nature's pencil drawn,
  Reflects the various tints; his ears and legs
  Fleck't here and there, in gay enamell'd pride
  Rival the speckled pard. His rush-grown tail
  O'er his broad back bends in an ample arch;
  On shoulders clean, upright and firm he stands;
  His round cat foot, straight hams, and wide-spread thighs,

* Silk and Scarlet, p. 281.

And his low-drooping chest, confess his speed,
His strength, his wind, or on the steepy hill
Or far-extended plain.   .   .   .   .
Observe with care, his shape, sort, colour, size;
Nor will sagacious huntsmen less regard
His inward habits."*

MUSIC OF HOUNDS.

Page 184.

The sportsman will remember the story of the Londoner. "There, there's music for you," said an enthusiastic farmer to a cockney; "what splendid melody! Don't you hear it?" "No," replied the other, "I can hear nothing for those *confounded dogs.*" Sir Roger de Coverley having received a valuable hound from a friend returned it with many expressions of civility, saying that it was an "excellent bass, but at present he only wanted a counter-tenor."†

BOLDNESS.

Page 185.

"First attribute of a good huntsman is courage; next, hands and seat."‡

FIRST QUALIFICATION OF A HUNTSMAN.

Page 187.

"The first thing and *sine quâ non* of a huntsman, is to ride up to his head hounds."§

---

* Somerville.   † Spectator, No. 116.   ‡ Beckford.   § Ibid., p. 177.

CICERO.

Page 193.

A SPORTSMAN so keen, that he rides miles to covert,
To look at a fence, he dares not ride over.

BULLFINCH, OR BULLFINCHER, AND OX-FENCE.

Page 198.

AN Ox-fence consists of a wide ditch, a blackthorn hedge, and a flight of rails. A Thorn-fence is one composed of a ditch and a thick, bushy, or blackbird hedge, leaning over to the grass; it is called a Bullfinch, or Bullfincher. "Doubles" are the most difficult and dangerous jumps of all. Here there is a ditch and rail, then another ditch and another rail. Dick Christian calls the "bullfinch" a "regular stitcher." They are thickest between Ashby Pastures and Barkby Holt.

SECOND WIND.

Page 199.

HORSES sometimes get second wind. Mr. Robert Canning's Conqueror once showed symptoms of distress, and began to kick his belly with his hind legs. "You are not going to stop, are you?" said his master. The animal rallied at the well-known voice, and took a large fence out of the very field where this circumstance occurred.

SPEED.

Page 200.

" Each seems to say, Come let us try our speed ;
    Away they scour, impetuous, ardent, strong,
    The green turf trembling, as they bound along."*

Mr. Assheton Smith found a formidable rival in Mr. Adamson, who hunted the Vine hounds. On one occasion, when Smith was out, these two had shaken off every other man in the field. At last Adamson's horse declined, and Tom Smith played solo to his pack.

STRATAGEM IN DISTRESS. — THE FIFTH SHOE.

Page 200.

Sometimes fox-hunters will resort to an ingenious device to conceal the fact that their horses are beaten. Not long ago, in Leicestershire, during a run in which the pace had been very severe, a rider was observed walking very leisurely towards a stiff fence, but without any intention of taking it, with a horse's shoe in his hand. " What is the matter ? " said a friend, " why don't you screw him at it ? " " Can't you see," was the reply, " that he has cast a shoe ? " " Why," observed a third, who had just come up, " my good fellow, your horse has got *four shoes on*."

* Bloomfield.

THE RIGHT SCENT.

Page 201.

" SEE how they range,
Dispersed, how busily this way and that
They cross, examining with curious nose
Each likely haunt."*

One of the first characteristics of a good huntsman is to distinguish between different scents. Dick Burton was always famous for his acute discernment in this respect.

FIELD LECTURES.

Page 201.

A LUDICROUS circumstance once occurred at Chute Gorse, illustrative of the discipline Mr. Smith always maintained in the field, and of the especial care he took to keep all persons back from heading a fox when he was drawing a gorse. All were as usual in their right places, when he espied a *white smock frock* in a gap, just at the spot where he expected the fox to break, and at this intruder he hallooed, and waved his hat, using at the same time rather *unparliamentary language*. "Do ride up," said he to a friend at his side, " and make that scoundrel come back." "He will not attend to anything I can say," was the reply. " Then, by Jove, if he does not walk off I will horsewhip him," said the now furious squire. Up accordingly he rode, and just as he was raising his whip he discovered, amid the laughter of the field, in which he heartily joined, that the object of his indignation was a mauk or scarecrow to frighten away the rooks.

* Somerville.

RUNAWAY HORSE.

Page 201.

A HORSE once ran away, during the chase, with a bold and determined sportsman; he placed his hands over the eyes of the animal and thus stopped him.

GRAFTON HOUNDS.

Page 206.

"GEORGE CARTER brought up sixty couples of the Grafton hounds. Among these were Sensitive, Saffron, Goneril, and Watchman; Nigel, Collier, and Bertram, were also great favourites. Rifleman and Reginald were two of Mr. Smith's most famous hounds. They were by Sir R. Sutton's Trimmer." *

"Champion and Chorister, by Ranter, were also two noble hounds belonging to Mr. Smith. Saffron was father of some of his best stock. He was sold to Mr. Morrell for the Old Berkshire." †

PRICE OF HOUNDS.

Page 206.

FOR good hounds Mr. Assheton Smith would give any price. He offered 400 guineas to Lord Forester for his bitch Careful,

---

* Silk and Scarlet, p. 284. † Ibid., p. 305.

also 100 guineas to Mr. Conyers for Bashful, but in both cases their owners refused to part with them. Mr. Conyers was almost a match for Mr. Assheton Smith in enduring fatigue, and sometimes would ride more than sixty miles inclusive to and from covert. He was no great hand at taking a fence, but when on his grey horse Canvass, whom he rode for seventeen seasons, he was seldom behind. Canvass was purchased of Lord Chetwynde for 150 guineas, and Mr. Assheton Smith afterwards offered Mr. Conyers 300 guineas for him without success.

Mr. Mytton's hounds did not fetch a high price; their master had played such tricks with them, that it was said they could hunt anything, " from an elephant to an earwig." Lord Middleton, in 1812, gave 1200 guineas for the pack he purchased. Mr. Horlock gave Mr. Warde 2000 guineas for his when he gave up the Craven country. Lord Suffield gave Mr. Lambton 3000 guineas for his hounds without seeing them. These prices present a striking contrast to the story told by Beckford of an auctioneer, who, having sold off all a country gentleman's property, came at length to his hounds. " What shall I say, gentlemen ? " said the knight of the hammer, " one shilling a piece ? " On sportsmen present making an exclamation of horror, " Why," he remarked, " that is more than I would give for them."

OLD JACK O'LANTERN.—LEAP NEAR THE COPLOW.

Page 211.

" Nothing ever turned Mr. Smith. If we had come near the Coplow I would have shown you that big ravine he jumped; twelve feet perpendicular, blame me, if it isn't, and twenty-one across; it has been nearly the same these forty years. They had brought their fox nearly a mile and a half from the Coplow, and he went to ground in the very next field. He was riding Guildford, a very hard puller, and go he would. The biggest fence he ever jumped in Leicestershire, was a bullock fence and hedge with ditch and back rails, near Rolleston; he was on Jack o' Lantern." *

FAVOURITE HOUNDS.

Page 213.

GEORGE CARTER mentions Royalist, Conqueror, Purity, and Charity as being especial favourites. These hounds are around Mr. Smith, who is on Rob Roy, in the picture by Saxby, presented to Mrs. Assheton Smith by the county of Hants. The squire's likeness in this picture is not however so good as in that by Cooper, which forms the frontispiece to these Reminiscences.

GEORGE CARTER.

Page 213.

Quæ cura nitentes
Pascere equos, eadem sequitur tellure repôstos.
VIRG. Æn. VI.

CARTER'S religious Faith, and fidelity to his old master, were strongly but very quaintly exemplified in the following manner :—

After Mr. Smith's death, when it was generally expected

* Dick Christian, in Silk and Scarlet, p. 57.

at Tedworth that he would be buried in the Mausoleum, George sought an interview with an old friend of the family, and with much earnestness made the following proposition :— "I hope, sir, when I and Jack Fricker and Will Bryce (the Whips) die, we may be laid alongside master in the Mausoleum, with Ham Ashley and Paul Potter *, and three or four couple of his favourite hounds, in order that we may be all ready to start again together in the next world !"

CHORISTER.

Page 215.

CHORISTER was one of Mr. Smith's most valuable hounds, and was painted by Mr. Ferneley in one of his hunting pictures. The squire had been absent, relates the artist, from Quorn for a short time, and on his return was looking through his stables, when the appearance of some of his horses did not please him. He began to find fault with his groom, Tom Jones, when the old man, to divert his master's attention and avoid further reprimand, said in his odd way, "Did Wingfield tell you Chorister's dead?" "Chorister dead ! Chorister dead !" exclaimed Mr. Smith ; and away he rushed at once to inquire about the hound, a very beautiful yellow-pied. "He was wonderfully fond," Mr. Ferneley adds, " of his hounds."

LORD PLYMOUTH'S QUORN PICTURE.

Page 216.

" IN Lord Plymouth's celebrated picture by Ferneley, Mr. Smith is standing by the side of Gift, a light chestnut (he

* Two excellent hunters.

had him from Sir R. Sutton), with Dick Burton holding the
rein; and he is talking to Mr. Mills on his iron-grey. Barkly
Holt, in the spring of 1815, is the meet; and the eye, passing the church at Hungerton and Quenby Hall, rests upon
the fir-clad Billesden Coplow. Dick Burton and Mr. Ferneley alone survive of that memorable party. Tom Edge is on
the back of Gayman. Jack Shirley is looking at his favourite
hounds from the back of Young Jack-o'-Lantern. Young
Will Burton is lingering on the outside to see the throw off,
before he takes his master's hack home." * He was then
only fourteen years old, and died a few months afterwards.

SIR R. SUTTON.

Page 217.

SIR RICHARD SUTTON'S and Mr. Assheton Smith's were the
only hounds belonging to private gentlemen ever known to
hunt six days a week.

TEDWORTH HUNT.†

Page 223.

THE following anecdotes of some runs with the Tedworth
Hunt, have been furnished by an old member of it. The
descriptive powers of the writer do ample justice to his

---

* Silk and Scarlet.
† Hampshire was always famous for its breed of dogs. In the time of the
Romans, an officer always resided at Venta or Winchester, in order to purchase
hounds for the Imperial kennel.

theme, but his manuscript unfortunately arrived too late for
admission into the Memoir.

A fox stole away from Lower Conholt Hanger, and waited
for us at Mexcombe Wood. *I* viewed him going away, and
it was one of those splendid hunting days when hounds
can run as if tied to a fox. Up and down the perpe-
tually undulating hills we rode, pointing first for Wilster
Wood, through that, and straight for Netherton Hanger,
down the steep pitch, through the churchyard, and up to
Faccombe Wood, leaving the village to the left, and Privet
to the right, through a corner of Charldown to Brick Hanger,
and into the vale below towards East Woodhay, and on to a
farm in the meadows. Up to this point there was neither
check, stop, nor turn. It was in 1826, the first year
that Mr. Smith hunted from Penton, before he had bought a
regular pack from Sir R. Sutton : the hounds were drafts
from fifteen different packs, and most of them *skirters*. This,
however, was just the day for them, so glorious was the scent,
that if one flashed over it, another took up the parable, and

> " a cry more tuneable
> Was never holla'd to, nor cheer'd with horn."

At this farm, then, up went their heads, and they stood
looking about as hounds do when they know the fox is somewhere near, but cannot tell exactly *where*. The squire (on
Anderson, a famous little thorough-bred dark-brown nag)
made a rapid cast around the buildings to make sure our
fox was not forward. He then jumped off his horse and seized
a great country fellow by the collar, and swore he would
horsewhip him if he did not tell him what they had done
with the fox. The fellow blubbered out, " It was not *I*, it
was Charley Dickman as had him." " Show him to me, if
you value your bones," said the squire ; and while they went to

look for him, I and the late Mr. Henry Pierrepont kept the hounds back in the farm-yard. All at once they began baying at the stable door, which I opened, and they rushed at the corn bin, and in it was the fox in a sack, out of which he was turned, and so the tragedy ended.

"Now, sir," said the squire to Mr. Dickman, "give an account of yourself, or you or I shall have as good a licking as one man can give another."

"Please sir," said Dickman, "I zee'd a fox come into the yard, and thinking that Parson Lance's hounds were 'worriting' the poor crittur, I cotches him up, and was agoing to take him over to Squire Smith, of Penton."

This pacified the squire, who putting his hand in his pocket and turning *down his cuffs again*, said, "Your excuse is a good one, and here is half a crown for it, although I do not believe a word of what you say."

This was about the best hour and twenty minutes with hounds I ever saw, and the best scent—downward all the way.

Another famous run I must record, also in the *first* year of Mr. Smith's reign in Hants and Wilts. We found a fox late in the day (when they always run *best*, being *lighter*), in Collingbourne Woods. After one turn there, he broke by Honey Bottom, up by Dean Farm, to Scott Poor's, then across the hills as if pointing for Fosbury Wood. However, leaving this to the right, he bore for Oxenwood and Botley Clump, and we caught a view of him going down into the vale from the plantation on Shalbourne Hill. Down this hill, nearly as steep as the Falls of Niagara, Mr. Smith rode at the head of the field as if he was winning the Derby, with his hat off, screaming to his hounds; and I shall not forget the gallant way "little Anderson" flew over a gate bushed up in the corner of a paddock, just before we killed, as the fox faced the open, pointing for Stype; time forty-three minutes, without a single check. Here too, we had like to have had a row. A sheep-dog pitched into one of the hounds while breaking up the fox, for which the squire kicked him heels over head.

"What do you kick my dog for?" said a great burly shepherd, with a pig eye and a fighting phiz. "Because he did not know how to behave himself," was the squire's reply; "and take care what you do, or I will serve you the same," added he, buttoning up his coat, and taking off his gloves.

The shepherd looked him over from head to foot, and then seemed to conclude he had better leave things as they were, which perhaps was better for *both*, as the squire was in his last half hundred, and youth, weight, and *wind* were on the debit side of the balance-sheet.

The best run I ever witnessed, when the gallant Dick Burton hunted the hounds, was the following. The squire, Mrs. A. Smith, and Lord G. Bentinck, had ridden to Stockbridge to see his Lordship's stud, then in training at Day's. We met at Collingbourne Wood, found by the keeper's house, went away at once by Biddesden Farm, over Luggershall Common, leaving Predenham to the left, to and by Shoddesden, across the large fields to Thruxton Copse. Here for the first time was a check in a piece of turnips, out of which our fox jumped up in view, and we ran him, as a farmer not unhappily said, *sword in hand*, across to Quarley, skirting the park there (where, by the by, poor Will Cowley the whip, and a famous one he was, got a roll over the rails), and up to and through Quarley Wood, out again in view up to the Roman Camp, then across the flat to Cholderton Clumps; and, going down that steep pitch, the hounds positively seemed to *plough him up* as they rolled him over, such a head did they carry, and such a rush did they make. Nothing could be more perfect than this fine run, both in result and adjuncts. Every hound up, but not every horseman.

"Excepto, quod non simul essent, cætera læti." Hor.

During the hunting season Andover was filled with sportsmen, all of whom were welcomed to Tedworth hospitality *after an introduction*. This was always insisted on in consequence of the following misadventure.

A certain lord of considerable notoriety, who then resided at Penton, was invited, and begged permission to bring as a friend a "*Captain Montagu*," which of course was acceded to.

It so happened, that the late Lord George Bentinck was staying at Tedworth, and it was observed, that when Lord H. introduced his friend, the latter rather kept in the background when Lord G. Bentinck appeared. Soon after dinner was announced, and the Captain sat opposite to Lord G. Bentinck. During a pause in the second course, the eyes and attention of all were riveted, by his Lordship saying in his slow, full, soft voice, "Allow me the pleasure of taking a glass of wine with you, *Captain Montagu*" (great stress on the last words). A low bow from the Captain in reply, and nothing more then passed. As soon, however, as the guests were departed, Lord George Bentinck said, "Perhaps, Smith, you may not be aware of the honour, but you have to-day entertained one of the greatest blackguards, and the biggest scamp and black-leg that even the 'Ring' can produce."

Measures were being devised next morning, when an ample apology arrived from the Penton Lord, who had been also imposed on, and had just turned "the *Captain*"* out of doors, and thus this affair ended. One of the most constant attend-

* His real name was Cauty ; he was afterwards transported.

ants in the field, and an always welcome guest at Tedworth,
for many years, was the worthy General Shubrick, whose
fine stud of horses, and princely entertainments to all
his friends and neighbours, will not soon be forgotten at the
Star Hotel, Andover. " Who is your best customer?" inquired
I of the ostler. " Oh, sir," was the reply, " the General is
worth the whole lot put together. He is an Emperor." We
had also another worthy military friend, rather inclined to
corpulency, and *not* a teetotaller, who rejoiced in the name of
Bacchus. Two farmers were one day disputing about his
weight, and not agreeing, referred the point to one Osmond,
a sporting butcher. The knight of the cleaver, running his
eye over him, and remarking how good he was about the
biling (boiling) *points* and brisket, inquired with a knowing
leer, " Do you sink the offal ? "

Although the country around Tedworth was mostly so
open, that an old woman on a broom might ride across it,
still there were times and parts of it that showed off good
riding, particularly in the Pewsey vale. On such occasions
as these, when fine horsemanship was required, there was no
man who rode better or straighter than Mr. John Rowden,
of Durrington, a wealthy yeoman, with a hand as light as a
lady's, a heart as bold as a lion, and a frame fit to contend for
the championship.

He was invariably selected by Mr. Smith to purchase his
horses, generally at that time bought of Mr. Smart of Swin-
don ; or in case any horse was heard of at a distance, Mr.
Rowden was requested to pass his judgment on it, and many
hundred miles has he ridden for that purpose. Nor did his
labours end here ; for if ever there happened, as was often
the case, to be a violent *fractious* animal that required *hand*
and temper, he was also requested to be the private tutor ;
and so highly did Mr. Smith think of his riding and judg-

ment, that I have often heard him say, he would rather trust
a young horse to Rowden than any man he knew. I shall
never forget his coming down a steep plantation on a violent
bay horse who had broken away with him, crying, "*Take
ca-are, ge-entlemen, take ca-are, I don't know whe-ere I'm
coming*" (he had a little hitch in his speech, like Dick Burton), as his horse bounded through and over the young trees.
"No," said a farmer, "I don't much think you do, for it
appears to me you be out *a bird's nesting.*" On another
occasion when his horse reared up bolt on end, and there
stood, he coolly remarked, "*I suppose he will come down
again once to-day.*" He was our *Dick Christian.*

TEDWORTH HUNT AFTER MR. SMITH'S DEATH.

Page 223.

THE finest run I ever witnessed last season, 1858–1859,
(writes a member of the Tedworth Hunt,) was from Collingbourne Woods on the last day of March. "The wind in the
east forbiddingly keen," and the sun scalding hot, promised
anything but such an event. Jack Fricker the first whip,
who has as many eyes as Argus, viewed "*him*" stealing
away, but inclined to hug the woods. A crack of his whip,
and one blast with the horn, however, made him turn his head
straight away from his old haunts, and when once down wind,
he never turned it again. We first ran between Ludgershall
and Medenham to Shoddesden Gate, through the little covert
there, and then for New Down Copse, leaving this to the
right, and Kempton Lodge close to the left, through the fields
to Thruxton Farm. Up the opposite hill we viewed him
pointing for Lord Winchester's new lodge. And here, by

way of episode, a kid grazing on the slope was so capti-
vated with the appearance of a reverend gentleman, mistaking
him either for father or mother (*sub judice lis est*), that it
fairly pursued him for two miles, notwithstanding the mild
rebukes uttered by the said Divine, which formed a pleasing
duet with the bleating of the kid. The hounds, in the meantime, carried a tremendous head into and through the New
Gorse at Newport, across the Park, straight through Sarson
Wood, and over the railway; thence through the broad hedgerows to the cross road. Here was the first stop; but we were
soon righted, and away for Abbots Anne great woods. Disdaining to enter these, and likewise declining to hide his head
in any of the Redrice coverts, our gallant fox pointed straight
for the smaller oak cuts. A sheep-dog in some high turnips
(who apparently had given him a rally) caused some slight
confusion; but George Carter making up his mind that ours
was a travelled fox, returning home from a midnight frolic,
held his hounds on, and hit the scent beautifully going into the
oak cuts. Out of these Jack Fricker caught a view of him making for Danebury Hill, where was an earth open, big enough to
hold the worthy proprietor of the soil. Another crack with the
whip made him decline the Hill for Mr. Day's racing pad-
docks, and in the fir belt around these, this glorious run terminated: time, one hour and forty-five minutes; distance
from find to finish, at least fourteen miles. Every hound
was up, and George Carter, with the fox raised high over his
head with both hands, fairly pirouetted as if he was setting
his partner in a quadrille.

"I will have that fox's head, and I will keep it as a trophy
of this day," said a distinguished foreign Baron, "and I will
drink to his memory and to all your healths;" and without
doubt he kept his word.

MR. HORLOCK.

Page 224.

MR. HORLOCK hunted that part of Wilts which adjoins the Duke of Beaufort's country, and also part of Somerset.

OBJECTION TO FOX-HUNTING.

Page 224.

EVEN in Beckford's time, as he observes, the intemperance, clownishness, and ignorance of the old fox-hunters were quite worn out, and fox-hunting had become the amusement of gentlemen. The "Thoughts on Hunting" were written in 1779, in a series of familiar letters, but the work was not published until several years afterwards. One of the best works on the "Noble Science" is that written by Mr. Robert Vyner, once a very forward rider with the Warwickshire hounds, who learnt his first lessons in sporting when a boy at Rugby School.

JOYS OF HUNTING.

Page 224.

" FOR myself I cannot fancy a more happy frame of mind,
 Than his who rides well up to hounds, while ' care sits on
  behind.'
There is nothing to allure him in the vanities of life ;
Ambition, scandal, politics, hatred, emulation, strife,
And all those dire diseases men really good discard,
Are merged in forgetfulness when hounds are running
  hard."   *Old Song.*

"Now where are all your sorrows when the fox is found, and your cares, ye gloomy souls? or where your pains and aches, ye complaining ones? one halloo has dispersed them all." *

OPINIONS OF ADDISON AND CERVANTES ON HUNTING.

Page 224.

ADDISON, who was a Secretary of State as well as a celebrated essayist and a perfect master of the English language, during his visit to Sir Roger de Coverley, writes thus: "For my own part, I intend to hunt twice a week during my stay with Sir Roger; and shall prescribe the moderate use of this exercise to all my country friends as the best kind of physic for mending a bad constitution, and preserving a good one." †

The physician Galen, in his works, recommends hunting as one of the healthiest of diversions.

"You are mistaken," said the Duke to Sancho Panza, who asked what pleasure there could be in killing a poor beast that had not committed any fault; "Hunting is an image of war; in it there are stratagems, artifices, and ambuscades, to overcome your enemy, without hazard to your person" (he is speaking of hunting a more dangerous animal than Reynard); "in it you endure the extremities of heat and cold; idleness and sleep are despised; the natural vigour is confirmed, and the bodily frame rendered active and supple,

'Toil strings the nerves and purifies the blood;'

in short, it is an exercise which may be enjoyed without pre-

* Beckford, p. 159.   † Spectator, No. 116.

judice to anybody, and with pleasure to many. Therefore, Sancho, change your opinion, and when you, are a Governor exercise yourself in hunting, for assuredly you will find your account in it." *

WANT OF ENTHUSIASM.

Page 227.

THE want of enthusiasm produces the want of originality which is very manifest at the present day. The *genus homo* is stereotyped. As a man's neighbour talks, thinks, and acts, so he talks, thinks, and acts. We cut our political creed out of our newspaper, and take our social opinions down from the pegs at our club. It is like Canning's story of the Red Lion over every chimneypiece in the tavern, variations in size and posture, but still always the same animal.

VAENOL.

Page 228.

MR. ASSHETON SMITH's Welsh property amounted in all to 47,000 acres; but by far the greater proportion of these consisted of mountain land.

* Don Quixote, pt. ii. bk. iii. ch. ii.

THE END.

LONDON
PRINTED BY SPOTTISWOODE AND CO.
NEW-STREET SQUARE

2